TO THE DEATH

Also by Andrea Tang

Rebelwing

Renegade Flight

These Deadly Prophecies

Kingdom of Without

TO THE DEATH

ANDREA TANG

G. P. PUTNAM'S SONS

G. P. PUTNAM'S SONS
An imprint of Penguin Random House LLC
1745 Broadway, New York, NY 10019
penguinrandomhouse.com

Edited by Gretchen Durning
Design by Claire Young
Text set in Fairfield

Library of Congress Cataloging-in-Publication Data

Names: Tang, Andrea author
Title: To the death / Andrea Tang.
Description: New York : G.P. Putnam's Sons, 2026. | Audience: Ages 14 years and up | Summary: "Two teens are pitted against each other in a magical duel for revenge, but they will have to fight their growing attraction first"— Provided by publisher.
Identifiers: LCCN 2025027110 (print) | LCCN 2025027111 (ebook) | ISBN 9780593858219 hardcover | ISBN 9780593858226 epub
Subjects: CYAC: Revenge—Fiction | Dueling—Fiction | Lesbians—Fiction | Fantasy | Romance stories | LCGFT: Fantasy fiction | Thrillers (Fiction) | Romance fiction | Lesbian fiction | Novels
Classification: LCC PZ7.1.T3757 To 2026 (print) | LCC PZ7.1.T3757 (ebook) | DDC [Fic]—dc23/eng/20250320
LC record available at https://lccn.loc.gov/2025027110
LC ebook record available at https://lccn.loc.gov/2025027111

First published in the United States of America by G. P. Putnam's Sons, 2026

Manufactured in the United States of America
BVG

ISBN 9780593858219 (hardcover)
ISBN 9798217238507 (international edition)
1st Printing

For the ladies of District Martial Arts, plus everyone I've sparred with at the DMV women's open mats over at Kogaion Academy. Thanks for inspiring me to write an entire book about absolutely savage girls who love fighting each other. Please never change.

TO THE DEATH

1

TAMSIN

I'M ABOUT TO MOP the floor with one of the best magicians in the state, and all I can think about is what Dad will say backstage.

Maybe he'll be pleased—because the nasty little chain of curses I cast actually worked.

Or maybe—and this would suck, but it's realistically more probable, knowing Dad—he'll be pissed off because I didn't use any of the spells he actually wanted me to cast. Which means I'll need to come up with a plan to deal with a potential foul mood from Dad.

Fantastic.

A crackle of pure arcane energy whizzes right toward my nose. The audience gasps—they're so collectively stunned that I can hear them even over the pulse of blood thrumming in my ears.

I barely dodge the curse in time. Sloppy.

Right. First things first: I need to win, here in this arena. The last thing I need right now is to preemptively tire myself out figuring out how to manage Dad before I actually beat the man in front of me.

With considerable effort, I return to studying my opponent. We circle each other like two dogs on the hunt—but by the end of this duel, only one of us will prove itself the prey, the other its predator.

My opponent, Dallas McCullough, is thoroughly stuck on his back foot. Less than eight minutes ago, he entered this arena brimming with confidence, the all-American golden boy with the pretty, pearly-toothed smile, famous for casting close-quarters curses that cut his last three opponents up something awful.

Curses of that nature skirt the bounds of legality—it's part of what separates legitimate arcane duels from the underground magicians' circuit, after all. We have rules in place to keep truly dangerous illegal spells out of our arenas. But that doesn't mean our fights don't get bloody or vicious.

Some members of the magical community frown on curses that cut opponents up as bad as McCullough's do. I don't have a problem with it, personally. His favored curses aren't technically illegal—not yet, anyway—and he's always honored an opponent's decision to yield before further blood is shed. I respect McCullough and his willingness to do what's necessary to secure victory even when it gets nasty.

To that end, I can't fault my opponent for his confidence. You don't get to be one of the top five magicians in the state by accident. McCullough earned his place in this arena tonight with blood and sweat and a hunger to win.

Unfortunately for McCullough, he's sharing that arena with me.

Eight minutes have taken their toll on my opponent. Right now, McCullough's pretty, square-jawed face is beet red with exertion, his golden curls dark with sweat. A bruise blooms purple over one of McCullough's sea-blue eyes, and his pearly whites have gone pink with his own blood.

My handiwork isn't half bad. I should know; I planned every curse I cast, every counter I threw at McCullough's increasingly desperate spell-casting attempts. We've got less than two minutes left of allotted time in this arena before the judges call a stop to our little war—and it's clear which of us will emerge the victor, unless McCullough does something drastic.

But I refuse to get cocky. Not when McCullough's still got fight left in him—and, knowing him, a couple fail-safe curses hidden up his sleeve.

As if he's heard my thoughts, McCullough grins at me with those bloodstained teeth. Wordlessly, he beckons me forward with one hand. I'd almost buy the bravado, if not for the fear lurking in my opponent's gaze.

Oh, he's ready to do something drastic, all right.

Quietly, I shake my head at McCullough, as I offer him a close-mouthed smile. Magicians lose duels all the time because they assume they've already won before their opponent actually yields. Better magicians than me have eaten nasty curses that knocked them out cold in the last thirty seconds of allotted duel time. Undefeated phenoms suddenly rendered mortal. Beatable. Laughable, even.

That's not going to be me. I refuse to be the duelist who loses because she assumes she can't.

I sprawl flat to the floor, as another desperate Hail Mary curse from McCullough whizzes over my head. Good. He's already tired. If I can bait him into depleting his energy on do-nothing magic, I can wear him down for the final seconds of our duel.

I might not even have to cast anything else myself.

"Come on, Blackwood!" roars McCullough from the other end of the arena. "Quit stalling and fight me for real!"

I smile at him. "I appreciate the sentiment," I call back, "but I'd rather just win."

As I speak, I crook the fingers of both hands and plant my feet. It's such a simple spell. It barely counts as casting. But as any decent magician could tell you, the complexity of a spell is nothing compared to how well we time the casting.

McCullough's final Hail Mary roars toward me. He's not stupid. This curse has wider range than the sparklers he threw at me earlier—way wider. I have nowhere to run. McCullough knows the clock's ticking. He knows he's almost out of time. So he's chosen this moment to empty his last reserves of arcane energy into a spell that I can't just dodge.

Which makes my timing perfect.

I close my eyes, right as the curse envelops me—and the spell I've prepared. I hear another crescendo of gasps and screams from the crowd, but I don't open my eyes. I need to focus.

Even without the aid of eyesight, I know what's happening. Magic at this level is more about what you sense than what you see. Everything happens precisely as I planned it: My little shield springs to life. A bubble of bright, arcane energy closes around me, creating a spherical mirror. And McCullough's curse crashes right into it.

Mind you, mine isn't an especially powerful spell. Most magicians learn to cast their first mirror shield within the first three or four months of study. No one thinks mirror shields are sexy. Practical, obviously, and an important fundamental skill. But a basic mirror shield is not going to make anyone's highlight reel, not if they're trying to show off how fancy and advanced their magical repertoire is.

A basic, well-timed mirror shield, though, is also exactly what I need to finish McCullough off.

His curse ricochets off the surface of my mirror. I open my eyes just in time to see McCullough pancake himself flat to the arena floor. He's too late. The fragments of his failed curse roar right back toward their maker. Flattening himself out allows McCullough to avoid the worst of my counter—but not all of it.

The remnants of McCullough's curse—glittering, sharp-edged pieces of arcane energy—bury themselves in his exposed back. He cries out, trying to rise to his feet, then falls.

Forty seconds remain on the clock.

Slowly, I walk toward him. "It's over," I tell him as kindly as I can.

He shakes his head, gritting those bloodstained teeth, as he tries to rise again. I wince as he yelps and falls again, shuddering.

"You can yield," I tell him. I pitch my voice low so the audience won't hear. These words are for my opponent, and my opponent alone. "You know I've already won the judges' favor. Yield, and you won't hurt yourself worse. There's no shame in that."

McCullough stares up at me with bright, bruise-blackened eyes. "You're a real piece of work, you know that, Blackwood?"

I offer him another tiny, toothless smile. "I get that a lot." I bow my head. "You're a great magician. It means a lot, coming from you."

McCullough's answering laugh rattles inside his chest before it turns into a nasty cough that fades into a whimper.

Twenty-five seconds remain on the clock.

"Please," I whisper. "Please, just yield. I don't want to keep hurting you."

Twelve seconds.

McCullough finally slaps his palm against the arena floor. "Yield!" he screams. "I yield, I yield!"

I close my eyes against the delighted roar of the audience. Now it's time to prepare for my real battle: facing Dad.

I don't get to see Dad immediately, of course. First, the arena promoters need to run me through the usual pageantry that accompanies the aftermath of a magicians' duel.

Which means that—while medics drag poor Dallas McCullough backstage—I get to stand beneath a blinding spotlight with this arena's master of ceremonies and answer his questions about how, exactly, I beat their golden boy into a bloody pulp.

"Tamsin Blackwood, what a performance you just delivered!" booms the MC. He's an enormous, barrel-chested man with a voice to match. I'm surprised he hasn't exploded out of his suit jacket. "That was your senior debut, was it not?"

I bow my head, all respect and deference. "Yes, sir. I just turned eighteen last week." Humility and good manners can go a long way in the magical world, especially coming from girls like me. "I'm honored that your arena allowed me the opportunity to show this audience what I can do."

More roars of approval from the audience.

The MC chuckles. "We already had some idea though, didn't we? Tell us, Tamsin, what was your record on the junior magicians' circuit, and just how long did you duel there with your fellow teen magicians?"

"I've been dueling in the juniors since I was fourteen," I answer dutifully. "My father got me into it young." I hesitate before offering, "In the juniors, I had sixteen wins and zero losses."

The MC whistles. "Quite impressive."

I shake my head. "It's the juniors," I say. "Plenty of teenagers go undefeated while we're competing against other youth magicians, but I know the senior circuit is on a different level. I never assume I'm unbeatable."

"Well, you sure looked it tonight!" The MC chuckles, clapping me hard on the shoulder. "We'll look forward to seeing more of you in this arena and beyond, if I do say so myself. Ladies and gentlemen, give it up for your victor tonight, Tamsin Blackwood—making her senior debut here at Raven Queen Arena, and still undefeated!"

I take my bow, trying to ignore the cold creeping into my veins. I'll be ushered backstage now—which means my time is up.

Dad's waiting.

My dressing room backstage is dark. Dad rarely bothers with more than a couple lights—he claims they hurt his eyes after he got knocked around a magicians' arena one too many times in his youth. As I slip inside, I catch a glimpse of him silhouetted against a window, backlit by the moon's glow, as shadows flood the space between us.

I bow my head without budging from the entrance. "Hi, Dad."

Dad stirs, very slowly, without answering. I can tell even before he says a word that it's going to be bad. Silence rarely ever means anything good coming from Dad, especially after one of my duels.

"Shut the door behind you, Tamsin," he says at last. His voice is flat.

I obey. There's not much else I can do, in moments like these, but obey.

"I beat Dallas McCullough," I venture cautiously.

"I saw." Slowly, Dad turns around. The edges of his glasses glint in the scant moonlight. "Maybe my vision is going. But I don't believe I saw you use any of the spells we agreed you would cast."

"With respect, we never agreed on any specific spells for me to cast." Not that that's going to make a difference, but I might as well point it out.

"Oh?" Dad's voice goes low and amused. Dangerously amused. "Then I must be misremembering all the spells I trained you on specifically for this duel."

"We practiced your spells in training, yeah. But what we agreed was that I'd cast whatever was necessary to win the duel."

"I see." Dad's voice is silky soft. He hasn't budged an inch from his spot by the window. "So you, my daughter, determined all by yourself, in the heat of the moment, that you didn't need any of my spells to win your duel."

I didn't, but I'm also not stupid enough to take Dad's bait. "I'm sorry, but that's not what I said," I tell him instead. I keep my tone measured so he can't accuse me of raising my voice to him. "I didn't know what spells I would need to cast to beat McCullough. I never know what I'll need to cast to win. Every magician is different. Every duel is different. So I practiced your spells in training because, as you have taught me"—I'm careful to emphasize the credit there— "it's better to know a spell and not need it than to need a spell and not know it.

"So, no, I didn't use your spells to win this duel," I continue. "Not directly, at least. But because I knew them, I had the confidence to win. I knew I could answer whatever McCullough threw at me." I shrug, trying to look offhand and not like my heart's racing a mile a minute. "He just . . . didn't throw anything at me that called for the spells we practiced. Just my simple old tricks. We should be grateful for that, shouldn't we?" I smile. "Just like I'm grateful that you took the time to teach them to me."

Dad doesn't answer me immediately. He's quiet for a while, in fact, turning over my words in his head. Probably trying to figure out how he can twist what I've said into something awful.

"So you're grateful then," he says at last.

"Yes."

He laughs bitterly. "Then why didn't you say so in your interview?"

I wince. I didn't anticipate him pivoting to a new topic of accusation. Clumsy of me. "I did," I stammer in protest, but I'm unprepared, and Dad can tell. Clumsy, clumsy Tamsin. "I said—"

"You had every opportunity," Dad continues, his voice growing slowly in volume. "You could have said to that interviewer that I was the reason you were victorious in your senior debut. You could have expressed your gratitude for everything I've done for you. But you didn't say a word."

"That's not true!" The volume of my voice climbs as well, despite my best efforts. "I told him—I told him that you were the one who got me into practicing magic." I rein myself in. It's a weak effort, and I know it, but it's all I've got. A flimsy defense, weaker by far than any beginner magician's mirror shield. "I told him that you started me young."

"Oh, you did, didn't you?" My father's voice is rich with mockery. "That's right, I remember now. 'My dad got me into it young.'" He imitates my voice, pitched high, as he bats his eyelashes at me from behind those glinting glasses. "That's all I did, is that right? Just paid for your magic lessons and sat back like every other parent at their kid's first class? You've been doing the rest of this on your own now, have you?"

I force myself to take a deep breath. "That's not what I said at all."

"Could've fooled me!"

"Well, what do you want from me?" I demand at last. "All I can control is what I say. I can't control what you hear. Or what you think you hear."

I regret the last of those words as soon as they leave my mouth. Even before Dad's eyes narrow at me, I know I've taken it a step too far.

"What I think I hear, huh?" His voice has softened again, in that silky, dangerous way I hate. It's worse than yelling. Slowly, he makes his way across the room as he speaks. "Right, then. Maybe I hear things wrong when my old promotion connections offer us duels for you, practically fawning over the Blackwood name. Maybe I hear them wrong when they tell me that you deserve opportunities to show off your craft, to prove yourself a magician worthy of my legacy."

He stops in front of me. "Maybe I should stop paying your way through these silly little duels and call it a day."

"No!" I can't help but cry out. It's stupid. I know Dad's bluffing. The great magician of our era, Master Mateus Blackwood, has no other kids. He doesn't even have other magic students, not serious ones. He's invested everything into me since his retirement from the dueling circuit. He wouldn't give me up, not when I'm his best shot at reliving his glory days in the magicians' arena.

But this one threat from Dad—empty as it is right now—still scares me. Because one day, he might decide to stop caring. He might decide that punishing me, keeping me in my proper place—which for the record, is in his shadow—is more important than living vicariously through me.

It's a hell of a choice.

"I'm sorry," I tell him, cowed, just the way he wants me. "I didn't mean any of it. You're right. You're the reason I've won all my duels. I owe you everything. I should say so next time. I promise I'll say so next time, all right? Just . . . I need you, Dad."

I hate that it's true. I do need him. His connections, his purse strings, and most of all, that damnable, door-opening Blackwood name. The name that convinces all the promoters I'm a wunderkind before I so much as step into the arena.

Never mind my own accomplishments, or painstaking magical study, or long, grueling hours practicing my curses and counter-spells. It's my father's name that makes me desirable. Talented teen magicians are a dime a dozen—but everyone wants the great Mateus Blackwood's only daughter on their magic show.

"I need you," I repeat. I'm pathetic. But I'd rather be pathetic than forgotten. And every magic promoter in town will forget me—if my father tells them to.

Dad sighs. "I know, Tam," he says. He's all fatherly kindness now. "I know you just need reminding sometimes."

"I do. Thank you."

He chuckles. "You're quite welcome." He checks his watch. "I need to run to a meeting. You good to wrap up here on your own?"

I close my eyes. "Sure. I'll see you at home."

"Good girl." He kisses my forehead. "It's good that you won tonight, Tam. But you played things too safe. No promoter will keep inviting you to duel on their magic shows if all you do is stall and counter your opponent's curses. We'll work on it in training tomorrow."

I wait until the dressing room door shuts behind him—until I hear the retreat of his footsteps. Then I grab a cushion off the nearest chair, press it against my face, and sob.

I give myself a little over five minutes to cry before I force myself back into business mode. I'm already compiling a mental list of crap that needs to get done: I need a hot shower, I need to post on my social media channels, I need to answer the messages currently blowing up my phone, and at some point, I need to review tape from tonight so I can consider what to work on in training this week.

I start with the easiest task, which is opening my phone, while I wait for the dressing room shower to heat up. I pause on the first message.

Dear Tamsin Blackwood,

I'm writing to you to congratulate you on your victory over Dallas McCullough tonight and to invite you to consider taking a duel against my champion, Lysander Rook. As Rook's second, I'm partly responsible for proposing appropriate opponents to magic show promoters, and as you're probably aware, we haven't been able to secure a suitable magician to share an arena with Rook in quite some time. We believe, however, that you would make an excellent match for him.

I know that your father and second, Master Mateus Blackwood, has yet to secure a duel for you with a cash prize on the line.

Given your impressive record as a magician, Rook and I, along with the rest of our team, agree that you are long overdue for a potential payday.

With that in mind, should you accept our proposal, I have convinced Rook's promoter to offer a generous purse to the victor of this duel. I have attached the proposed amount below.

Please provide your answer by the end of the week.

Yours sincerely,
Samantha Chan

My hands shake as I open the attachment. I practically drop my phone over the side of the shower stall when I see the figure Samantha Chan's people are offering. It's what Dad would call "screw-you money." It's money that would set me up independently for years to come.

It's money that could support me even if Dad cut me off.

I can't decide if I want to laugh, or scream, or throw up. Everyone knows who Lysander Rook is. He's almost as famous as Dad. Another teen magician—also undefeated, like me.

The difference between us is that, unlike me, Lysander Rook isn't new to the senior circuit. He left the juniors at fifteen—and he's been destroying full-grown adult magicians in their prime ever since. So far, five grown magicians have retired after dueling him, their spirits crushed by whatever they experienced in that arena.

People call me a chip off the old block. My father's daughter. A credit to the Blackwood name.

People don't call Lysander Rook any of those things. Instead, they call him a genius. A prodigy. They also call him l'enfant terrible, the bad boy of the magical world, the young terror of the dueling circuits. They call him a monster. They call him invincible.

If I can beat Rook, I'll have enough money to buy my freedom from Dad and enough clout to attract promoters without Dad's help.

On the other hand, if I can't beat Rook, it might end my career. He's broken five grown, established magicians in the arena. Five brilliant duelists at the height of their careers, so traumatized by whatever Rook did to them that they'll never practice magic again.

No wonder Samantha Chan's people are offering such insane money. Talk about high risk, high reward. This duel is a gambler's dream and nightmare, all wrapped up in one.

And it's my choice to make, for once. Mine, not Dad's. Samantha Chan came to me, not him. Which means I get to call the shots on this one.

I close my eyes, and with trembling fingers, set my phone aside. I inhale and exhale as carefully as I can. Shower steam fogs the mirrors in my dressing room, filling the atmosphere, condensing on my skin. I breathe through the moisture clogging the air. I breathe and breathe, even though I feel like I'm swimming deep underwater.

When I open my eyes, I pick my phone back up and send my answer to Samantha Chan.

Then I take the longest shower of my life.

2

SAM

LYSANDER ROOK IS THE perfect magician.

For the hundredth time, I review my champion's profile, flicking through the talking points I've compiled in the notes on my phone. The obvious high-ticket sellers are all there, of course. Lysander Rook, the belle of the ball and l'enfant terrible, seamlessly combined in one pretty package. Entered the senior circuits at the tender age of fifteen. Undefeated on both junior and senior circuits. Virtually flawless magical technique, even in the pressure cooker of the dueling arena.

It's been great for branding.

Talent alone might have turned promoters' heads anywhere across the country—but Rook's not just talented. He's pretty. A pretty face always helps with these things, and a pretty white boy's face? Better still. I took all that into account when I picked him. That was important. Hopefully, the Blackwoods will see it that way, too.

I tap my foot. I'm trying not to display obvious impatience, but Mateus Blackwood makes it hard. He's already more than five minutes late.

God, I hate when these guys are late.

I set my phone aside, settle back into my seat, and try to make myself comfortable. Mateus Blackwood agreed to meet me at an upscale coffeehouse in the city, which at least means I'm not stuck slipping a fake ID to some self-important bouncer at a dive bar. Thank god for small blessings. Half the champions' seconds I've dealt with seem to think dueling contracts can only be finalized in the sleaziest twenty-one-and-over-style venues. As if signing dueling agreements while leering at exhausted cocktail waitresses in skimpy outfits is the only way to prove you're a hardcore negotiator.

Still, I would have been happy to seal the deal over a video chat or a phone call, like a normal human being living in the twenty-first century, but these old-school magicians are always a little, well, old-school. And Master Mateus Blackwood is as old-school as they come.

I should know. I've been watching him for long enough.

"Samantha Chan?"

Well, it's about time.

I turn and greet the man at my table with the best smile I can muster. I may not have Rook's camera-melting star power, but I can manage an old man. Even Mateus Blackwood.

"Sam is just fine," I tell Blackwood, offering him a hand to shake.

For a few seconds, Blackwood just squints at me through those glasses. My heart thunders against my ribcage. He has no reason to recognize me. We've never seen each other in person. And Chan is a common enough surname. There are thousands of families just like mine across the country. For all I know, Blackwood broke more than a few of those families too, just like he broke mine.

To Blackwood, I'm just another teen magician with a forgettable name.

I hope. Otherwise I'm screwed.

After what feels like an eternity, Blackwood chuckles and takes my hand. His grip is firm and callused. I breathe again. "You sure you're old enough to be a magician's second on the senior circuit?"

I keep smiling. "You're not the first person to ask, Master Blackwood. Don't worry, I'm eighteen. Want to see my ID?"

"That won't be necessary, my dear. Though if my information's correct, you and your champion entered the senior circuit as children, still."

I shrug, deliberately nonchalant. "We wouldn't be the first. Rook's parents don't care. And my parents signed off on it because I was with Rook."

"How understanding of them."

My smile widens, sweet as pie. "I have a supportive family."

I'm offering Blackwood little nuggets of truth. The truth is useful in a negotiation, up to a point. I need Blackwood to trust me. I've worked too hard, for too long, to blow my plan up in an overpriced cafe.

But if I want the plan to work—if I want Blackwood to agree to my terms—I can't give him any reason to suspect I want anything other than a perfectly ordinary duel between two promising young magicians. A mutually beneficial arrangement, favorable to both his champion and mine.

"A supportive family is a wonderful thing." Blackwood's answering smile is surprisingly genuine. "Your parents must be proud of you. Are you their only child?"

My heart skips a beat. I need to tread carefully here. If Blackwood figures out who I really am—if he deigns to remember what happened four years ago—then I'm cooked.

I spread my hands like I'm presenting myself to a crowd. "The one and only child under the Chan family roof," I tell Blackwood, breezy-voiced.

Also technically true, if we're talking in present-day terms.

"Ah, an only child," says Blackwood, which is exactly the assumption I was hoping he'd make. "The apple of your parents' eye, no doubt."

"It's a lot of pressure to succeed," I agree without correcting him. "My parents aren't magicians, but they know how good Rook is. They think it's an honor that he chose me as his second."

"I'm sure they do—it's true." Blackwood's got a distant look in his eye. "Only children are so precious. I've given my Tamsin everything."

Ah, and at last, we've arrived at the main battleground for this meeting. "Your daughter."

Blackwood's gaze flicks back toward me, dagger sharp. "My champion," he corrects me, then relents after a moment. "But yes, also my daughter."

Well. That tells me everything I need to know about this father-daughter pair. Or, more accurately, confirms what I've already guessed from the years I've spent researching these two.

"Is it ever difficult?" I wonder. "Being both a parent and a second to her?"

Blackwood looks amused by my question. "I don't believe there's a difference."

"Isn't there?"

"Like I said, I've given my Tamsin everything. You'll understand one day, if you ever have children." He laughs at the look of distaste I've probably failed to mask. "Or not. But I'll tell you this much: I've been called one of the most accomplished magicians in the history of modern dueling—that's not bravado or ego, my dear, that's a direct quote from a profile piece in the *New Yorker*. I was named to the Magicians' Hall of Fame before I turned forty. I have, on an objective and measurable level, accomplished more in the art of magic than most accomplish in any field in a lifetime. But my Tamsin?"

I lean slightly forward. "What about her?"

The look on Blackwood's face softens. He's a naturally hard-edged man, the sharp-cut planes of his face better suited to tossing shit-eating smirks to a camera than fawning over anyone or anything. The softness of his expression now looks so at odds with the way his face naturally moves that the effect is actually kind of jarring.

"Of everything I have accomplished in the course of my life," says Blackwood, "my daughter—my champion—will be the greatest of them all. I swore that much on the day she was born. She's going to do great things."

My heart swells. Blackwood is a brutal and brilliant showman—famously so. But in this moment, he's not lying or embellishing. He's as honest as I've ever seen a man. Raw. Vulnerable. He can't cover up how he feels about his kid.

This is perfect. Tamsin Blackwood is everything I need for my plan.

"I'm sure she'll be a real credit to your legacy." My voice is smooth. Businesslike. I don't let the triumph I'm feeling show. I can't give myself away this close to the finish line. "Which brings us to my proposal."

"Ah yes, the duel between my Tamsin and your young Lysander

Rook." Blackwood cuts me an appraising glance. "I'll say, I was surprised that you approached my champion directly instead of talking to me first."

"I'm sorry if you felt that I overstepped. But before talking to her father—her second—I needed to know that your champion is game." I meet Blackwood's flinty dark gaze without blinking. I'm not quite staring him down, but I'm not looking away either. "You get what I'm saying, right? You must. You were a duelist yourself once."

"I was." Blackwood folds his arms with a thin smile. "But do enlighten me, my dear."

"It doesn't matter what the second says, if the magician themself isn't all in—and I really do mean all in. A duel with stakes like these only works if both champions are completely committed to putting on a show. And the only way I could ensure that I got an honest answer out of Tamsin is if I asked her directly."

"And you were satisfied with her answer, I take it?"

"Very." I grin at him. "Like father, like daughter, right?"

This, at least, seems to please Blackwood. The thin smile grows into a grin that matches mine. "I'd expect nothing less of my girl. You have the contract terms on hand?"

Check and mate. I produce the paperwork from my messenger bag. "Naturally."

All in all, it's one of my shorter negotiations.

We debate the usual terms: location (the New York Magicians' Arena, naturally), dates (we choose October, right before Halloween weekend), and ruleset (ten minutes of allotted time, all curses permitted, winner decided by either loser's voluntary yield, physical inability to continue, or, if neither of the first two options come to pass, a judge's decision).

It won't go to a judge's decision. It never does when Rook stands in the arena.

By the time we shake and finalize the contract on behalf of our champions, the legendary Master Mateus Blackwood is practically salivating. Some magicians don't know when to quit the dueling circuit. They duel into their midforties, even their fifties, unable to leave the arena behind, even when the hungry young twentysomethings are beating them to a pulp on a regular basis.

Once upon a time, Mateus Blackwood was almost one of those magicians. He hadn't quite stumbled onto a losing streak, but he was close to it. Commentators and analysts on the dueling circuits clucked their tongues and spoke wistfully of Blackwood in his prime: the beautiful, terrible boy he'd once been. But he couldn't quit. Like so many other champions, he couldn't give up the picture he carried around inside his head of the magician he'd once been. The magician he'd never be again. The magical world had been half convinced he'd be carried to his grave on a stretcher after one too many duels gone bad.

Then Blackwood's daughter began winning duels. And everything changed. Blackwood finally retired. And everyone who'd worshipped at Mateus Blackwood's feet began calling Tamsin Blackwood the second coming of Master Mateus.

It was all hype, of course: a good story and a nice marketing spin to sell another pretty young face to an audience eager to consume violence and beauty in equal measure.

But pretty soon, Master Mateus himself started believing the hype, too. He became his daughter's magic teacher, then her second. Eventually, you couldn't book Tamsin Blackwood on a magic show without her father following in her wake like the world's most obsessive stage mom.

So, when I offer Mateus Blackwood the opportunity for his daughter to duel the youngest, most popular magician of our generation in the biggest magicians' arena on the East Coast, for an astronomical amount of prize money, he doesn't see Tamsin.

He sees himself. All that glory, all those accolades, they're all for him. They're all within his reach. That makes him hungry. Greedy.

And that greed is all I need to destroy him.

Rook calls me as soon as I leave the coffeehouse. "How did it go?"

He sounds artfully disinterested. I can picture him lying on his back in the middle of the training arena at Master Silverstein's, a towel tossed over his dark curls. He's got the whole act of the troubled genius—the too-smart bad boy above it all—down to an art.

"You've got yourself a duel," I tell him. "Tamsin Blackwood, just like we talked about."

Rook whistles low. "You roped in daddy's little girl, huh?"

"It wasn't a hard sell. Your promoters are offering a king's ransom to anyone willing to risk life and limb in the arena with you."

"And Tamsin's daddy is willing to take it?" He makes a mocking sound of disapproval, like an old auntie clucking at a misbehaving toddler. "I didn't realize the great Master Mateus was so hard up."

"Correction: Tamsin's the one who wants to take it. And as for her father, I don't think he's in it for the money."

"No? What else is there?"

I hesitate. I know Lysander Rook better than anyone in the whole world. But I've never let him know me the same way. Not all of me. I can't risk that. Not when he could get in the way of what I really want.

"He just wants to live vicariously through his daughter," I say at last, which is true. "He wants a taste of glory. You know how these old timers on the dueling circuit get—they miss who they used to be, and their kids are the closest they'll get to having their youth back."

Rook makes a derisive sound on the other end of the line. "Pathetic."

"Maybe. But it's getting you a duel with a willing opponent. One who actually cares about winning and isn't just terrified of you. That's what you wanted."

"Oh, my," drawls my champion. "Are you saying that Tamsin Blackwood isn't terrified of me? Maybe I'm losing my touch, Sammy."

"I think Tamsin Blackwood is smart enough to know she should be scared of you." I glance back over my shoulder at the coffeehouse. Mateus Blackwood has long since departed the premises, but there's something of his aura that hangs over the place, dark and proud and viciously hungry. "But I've got a hunch that there's something else that she finds even scarier than you."

"And what's that?" Rook chuckles. "Maybe you can book a duel for me with them."

"I don't know yet," I confide. "But I'll find out."

It's a promise, even if it's not for the reasons Rook probably assumes. For all he knows, I'm the loyal second, dutiful to a fault. Everything I do, I do for him, to make him better. And for what it's worth, he's not entirely wrong.

I need Rook to perform at his best if he's going to beat Tamsin Blackwood—not just beat her but break her completely, the same way he broke those five magicians whose careers ended in his arena. I need her utterly destroyed, in body and soul.

It's only fair, you know. Her father destroyed my family once. And come October, beneath the bright lights of the New York Magicians' Arena, I'll finally see that debt repaid.

3
TAMSIN

"THIS DUEL WILL CEMENT our legacy as a family."

I sprawl flat to the floor. "I know." The telltale heat of arcane energy whooshes over the top of my head, barely missing my ponytail. "Which is why I intend to win."

My father advances on me. His gaze bores into me while he tosses flickers of casually conjured sparks of magical energy between long white fingers. Dad's got eyes black as coal, and they give nothing away. I've always hated the way he stares at me unblinkingly while we train. Like I'm a clock he'd like to take apart, to see how I tick, without a care in the world for whether he could put me back together again.

"Intend?" The side of his mouth twitches—with derision or amusement, I'm not sure. I'm never sure, with him. "That sounds like you think you might lose."

I drag my knees into my chest. With a grunt, I hop into a squat, my stance low. Strong base, strong magic—or so the saying goes. Exhaling, I shove a tendril of arcane energy right back at my second. "Overconfidence never did any duelist any favors."

"There's overconfidence, and then there's a lack of confidence entirely."

"I'm confident," I don't quite snap.

Dad catches my attack one-handed, chuckling, as the little orb of silver energy douses the sparks of power between his fingers. "Not bad, not bad."

I hate the way two words of praise immediately mollify me. Even now, even after years of dealing with Dad's ego, his mood swings, his narcissism, I'm still hungry for his praise.

And I hate that about myself.

"Even if you lose," muses Dad, "you could still do wonders for our name. So long as you put on a show."

I bite my lip. Our name. Like I'm not the one entering the arena to risk my neck against one of the most violent magicians of my generation. Like I'm not the only remaining Blackwood who actually takes the duels that keep my father's name relevant in magical circles.

He's still Master Mateus Blackwood, one of the greatest magicians ever to enter an arena. People still get starstruck when they see him, ask for autographs, beg for selfies. None of the other old masters from his generation get that kind of reception from a modern-day crowd—respect, sure, and name recognition. But Dad is the only retired duelist of his age who still receives the same kind of adulation he did in the prime of his career. And that's because I'm still here, doing what he can't anymore. Keeping the Blackwood name alive. Keeping us both in the spotlight.

Of course, I've only had the chance to do what I do because of Dad's old connections. So until I earn a major purse of my own, the two of us need each other. Father and daughter, a pair of codependent parasites. And the worst part is, we both know exactly what we are.

I dust off my knees without looking at my father. "You say that like you don't believe I can win."

"Oh, Tam. My sweet, hardworking girl. Of course I believe you can win. I just don't want you to be disappointed. It's Lysander Rook, after all." Dad's voice, artificially gentle and thick with sympathy, is poisoned honey. "And you said it yourself: even you're not entirely confident you can beat him."

"That's not what I said."

Dad snorts. "You might as well have."

"Then I misspoke."

"I've found you an opportunity here, Tam," says Dad. "Do you really think Lysander Rook's second, Sally or Sarah or whatever her name is—"

"Samantha. Sam Chan."

"Sure, Samantha. Do you really think that girl would have approached you if it hadn't been for all the time I've spent building your brand? Advocating for your worth to every promoter I ever dueled for? Don't squander that for the sake of pride."

"I don't intend to." I keep my voice as steady as I can. "I accepted the duel, didn't I?"

"Before you even cleared it with me, yes, how could I forget? Lucky thing that this Samantha girl was still smart enough to meet with me to finalize terms. There's a reason every champion needs her second. You show poor judgment when you ignore yours. You're better than that, Tamsin. I raised you better than that."

I flinch but ignore my father's rebuke. Instead, I opt for flattery. "You raised a winner," I tell him. "I'm not in the habit of accepting duels I don't think I can win."

"And maybe you could." Dad's voice is breezy, like he's already dismissed the possibility. "All I'm saying is, we could build an entire career off holding our own against a boy like that."

I reach for my water bottle. My movements are jerky with frustration. "Right."

"You're angry."

"I'm not," I lie.

"You think I don't believe in you?"

"I think you're my father—and more importantly, my second." I take a long gulp of water, wishing it were wine. "So I think I should listen to your wisdom."

"But you'd rather listen to your own, is that right?" He chuckles bitterly. "After all, what do I have on young up-and-coming star Tamsin Blackwood, aside from twenty years more experience in the arena?"

"Dad—"

"Aside from the fact that I raised you? Taught you? Trained you? Aside from the fact that you owe what you are to me?"

"Dad!" I don't quite shout. Dad doesn't abide shouting, but I come dangerously close to it. "I already told you, I'm here to listen. I . . . I need your guidance."

Dad doesn't look entirely convinced, but at least he quits ranting. "Have you looked at the betting odds on this duel?"

I bite back a sigh. "The matchup was just announced two days ago. I didn't think oddsmakers would work this quickly."

"Oh, oddsmakers work quickly all right, especially when a name like Blackwood is thrown in the mix against a boy like Lysander Rook." A shadow of hesitation crosses my father's face. "I don't know that I should tell you this, but if I don't, I know you'll just look it up yourself. But Rook is, for the first time in his career since his debut, listed as the underdog."

My heart drops into the pit of my belly. "That's impossible. That means that—"

"You are popularly favored to win the duel, yes." Dad doesn't look especially pleased, but I don't have time to overanalyze that right now.

"That doesn't make any sense," I insist. "We're both undefeated, but I'm a rookie on the senior circuit. Rook's already destroyed five grown magicians in the prime of their careers."

"But you're my daughter." A tiny, toothless smile plays across my father's mouth. "That typically works in our favor. It opens doors. It gets promoters to take chances on you that they wouldn't on another rookie. But it also gives you a certain . . . aura, shall we say. A mystique. Magicians have always been a superstitious lot. And no one wants to bet against a Blackwood. Even if it means betting against Lysander Rook."

I close my eyes. "People think I can win. They think I can beat him."

"Yes." My father's voice is silk soft. "Which is why we need you to lose."

My eyes snap open. "Excuse me?"

"We need you to lose," Dad repeats. I search his face for some sign of irony, some hint of a joke, but he's dead serious. "Don't worry, Tamsin. You won't suffer the same fate as those five fools who let a child get into their heads and wreck their bodies. You're going to make it look good."

The world tilts before me. "You're asking me to throw the duel."

"I'm not asking you. I'm telling you."

"The prize money—" I begin faintly.

"Oh, the prize money is spectacular," Dad acknowledges in dismissive tones. "It would set you—us—up for life if you win it. But that's quite the if."

The world keeps tilting. "You don't actually think I can win." To my horror, heat pricks at the corners of my eyes. I haven't cried in front of my father in years.

"Maybe you can." Dad's still speaking in that dismissive, singsong tone that means he doesn't actually care one way or the other. "But it's not exactly a sure thing, is it? You've never faced a magician of Lysander Rook's caliber before. You'd be taking quite the risk."

"Every duel is a risk."

"But you want to take a smart risk, Tam. That's what I've trained you to do, don't you understand?" He sighs. "Think of it this way. What sounds better to you? The possibility of losing this duel and possibly your career and health, hell, maybe even your life, with no cash prize to show for it? Or the guarantee of finishing this duel on your own terms with a respectable loss that preserves your body and spirit, leaves you healthy enough to fight another day, and still nets a financial reward?"

I go cold. "You're going to rig the betting, aren't you." It's not a question. For years, I've ignored the shadier side of Dad's career. I'm not stupid. Dad threw around too much cash after his retirement for all of it to have come from legitimate, saved-up duelist's prize money. All you need to do is spend about five minutes on the average magicians fan forum to find all the old rumors about Master Mateus Blackwood's alleged hand in unregistered underground duels.

Respectable magicians don't talk about the underground scene. The underground existed long before the modern—and, importantly, legal—dueling circuit existed. Legislators seemed convinced that legalizing magic would stamp the underground out, which tells me that ordinary lawmakers don't know human nature terribly well.

There will always be some magicians who want more: to cast the illegal curses forbidden to respectable duelists; to disallow their opponent the option to yield; to draw a fight far beyond the clean, contained confines of an arena. Even after magic shows were fully legitimized as public entertainment for the masses, the underground continued thriving, simply because some magicians will never be satisfied without the real possibility of a death in the arena. So far as they're concerned, duels to the death are the only duels that prove anything real about a magician's skill—about the terrible, beautiful things magic can accomplish.

The underground thrived, in other words, because of men like my father. Allegedly, of course.

There's never been quite enough evidence to make a real fuss, but Dad's under-the-table income has always been our family's dirty open secret, the elephant in every room he enters.

I shouldn't be surprised that, in addition to financing underground clubs, Dad also rigs dueling bets. And I guess I'm not. I just never expected him to make me participate. In all his years of back-alley business dealings—from the illegal magic clubs he ran to the bribes he bartered in to keep them open—he's never once involved me. He's always kept my hands clean. I thought that meant something.

Apparently not.

"All betting is rigged," says Dad. He doesn't even sound ashamed. "Why shouldn't we turn a profit off it?"

"I could get banned from dueling ever again," I protest. "If we're found out, we'd both be pariahs."

"And who's going to find out?" Dad barks a laugh. "I didn't get this far without a decent sense of subtlety. No one would know except you and me."

"If someone even suspects—"

"They'd need hard evidence. And we'd leave none." Dad snorts. "Face the facts, kid. You're a damn good magician. I wouldn't accept anything less. But the odds of anyone finding out about our little secret are so low, they're practically negligible. The odds of you walking out of an arena with Lysander Rook as anything other than a bloody, half-mad carcass, on the other hand? Well, I like those odds a lot less." He shrugs. "Unless we do things my way. The choice is yours."

Dad's never once hit me. Not in my childhood, not in the training arena, not even a spanking when I was a little girl.

But the way I'm feeling now, he may as well have slapped me full across the face.

"So you want me to take a dive and risk my career—and yours, for that matter—for . . . what, exactly?" I laugh bitterly. "An easy payday?"

"Pay is one thing. My daughter's safety is another."

"Right. You want me to lose the biggest duel of my career on purpose for my *health*."

Dad's hands grasp my shoulders before I even register the movement. I inhale sharply as his fingers dig into tender flesh. I forget how quick he is sometimes, even now, a master duelist's reflexes built into his muscle memory through years in the arena.

"Don't you understand?" he hisses. His eyes bore into me. "If Lysander Rook defeats you, he doesn't simply defeat you. He destroys you. Breaks you down into parts, body and mind both. You'd never be the same magician again. You might never even be a magician at all again."

He closes his eyes for a long moment. When he opens them again, something weary lurks in his gaze. Suddenly, he seems years older, and so very tired. "So yes, Tamsin. I'm asking you to take a dive for your own health. At least that way, you control the circumstances, and we earn a little cash for our trouble. It's the best strategy for making the most of a bad situation."

I hate that I actually find myself wavering a little. I try to remind myself that this is exactly the sort of game Dad plays: he always makes his way sound so reasonable. When I was younger and stupider, Dad's explanations and excuses worked like a charm. But I'm not a little girl anymore. And I no longer believe everything my father says just because he's my father.

I won't fall for Dad's tricks again. Not even when he looks at me with such seemingly genuine, weary resignation in his eyes.

"Why would you even let me duel Rook at all?" I demand at last. "If you're so worried about me losing to him, why did you agree to his second's proposal in the first place? Why not refuse her terms?"

Dad lets go of me abruptly. His answering smile is thin-lipped, his gaze distant. "Because you already said yes. Who am I, as your second, to prevent my champion from doing what she wants?"

I close my eyes. That tells me everything I need to know. I remember exactly how Dad reacted when I first told him I'd agreed to take Samantha Chan's offer. He never tried to get me to back down. He never tried to turn my yes into a no. Instead, he stayed silent for a very long time, chewing my words over.

Then he smiled and told me not to squander the opportunity.

The thing is, the way he sees things, these opportunities are never really for me. They're for him. And if I'd said no to Samantha Chan, Dad would earn no profit. Just like he'll earn no profit if I beat Rook. If I win that prize money for myself.

His only chance at squeezing any kind of profit out of me is by playing the betting odds. Dad just doesn't want to lose his cash cow.

"You won't order me to reject a dueling challenge," I say softly. "But you'll order me to lose."

"I'm not ordering you to do anything, my girl. I'm just an old man, remember?" Dad chuckles. It's a bitter sound—and the bitterness, I'm pretty sure, is real, at least. "I can't force you to do anything. All I can do is tell you the facts and let you make your own decisions."

When I open my eyes, reluctantly, to meet his, he's watching me softly. If I didn't know better—if I gave in to the fantasy I want to believe—I'd say that he's watching me with love. The kind of love that every parent has for their child.

It's a beautiful fantasy.

"I put everything I had into raising you," my father whispers. "All I can do now, as a parent, is hope that it was enough to help you choose the right path."

He lets go. "Practice is over."

I watch him walk out the door of the training arena. He doesn't demand a final answer from me. He doesn't make me promise obedience. And he doesn't look back.

He just leaves me there, thinking about Lysander Rook and those five magicians, their blood spattered across the floors of those arenas. And I can't help it: as soon as I'm alone, I start thinking about whether I'll end up one of them.

If any of this is really worth it.

4

SAM

PEACE LASTS ALMOST A week before a girl at school asks me to slip her number to Rook. This is, for what it's worth, a new record. Blythe Davison corners me in the girls' bathroom on the third floor as I'm escaping from study hall. She makes it look innocuous at first, peering at her reflection in one of the mirrors as she touches up her lipstick. It's a gorgeous coral shade that brings out the gold in the movie star blond waves that billow over her shoulders.

I know what I'm in for when she smiles wide at my reflection over the sink. Smiles like those are never really meant for me—not when the giver knows who I spend most of my waking hours with. "Hey, Sammy. Long practice the other night?"

I smile back. It's actually mostly genuine. I'm very well versed in the steps of this particular dance these days, but even if I wasn't, it would be hard not to smile back at Blythe. Girls like Blythe have this weird, effervescent magnetism. They're probably the reason men used to make up stories about sirens and succubi and beautiful women who gave up feathers or wings or seal skins to marry their mortal husbands.

"It's always a long practice, Blythe," I tell her, shrugging. "That's practicing magic in a nutshell. Long and hard and thankless." I laugh a bit to take the sting out of the complaint. "But hey, when it's spectacular, it's spectacular, am I right?"

"When you're Lysander Rook's second?" Blythe whistles, long and low. Her china-blue eyes go low-lashed as she purses her lips at her reflection. "I can't imagine magic being anything else."

I shut down the familiar pang of annoyance at yet another fan fawning over Rook. I get it: He's the most talented magician our age, he's classically hot, and he has this whole tortured, brooding Byronic soul vibe to him. All the ingredients for lady bait. Also, incidentally, all the ingredients that make him my perfect weapon against Mateus Blackwood.

Still, that doesn't mean playing bouncer for his endless parade of fan club members doesn't get old for me. Instead of snapping at Blythe, I just shrug again—hopefully with the air of nonchalance I'm aiming for. "It's a lot of work."

"He must get lonely," muses Blythe, pouting at herself. "Rook, I mean."

"I don't think he notices."

"Are you sure? Maybe he just needs more . . . friends. Besides you, I mean." She studies our reflections. I wonder what she must see, looking at our faces side by side. Blythe, all pretty-blond-white-girl features and kind smile and expertly chosen makeup palette. Me, the Chinese girl with resting bitch face, looking vaguely sweaty and rumpled with baby hairs sticking out of my too-tight chignon, which is probably going to give me a receding hairline one day. Also, I'm pretty sure there's a zit coming in on the tip of my nose. Goddammit.

My brother, Jamie, was the pretty one, the chiseled, striking firstborn son that all our aunties used to coo over. Despite spending most of his time sweating in worn-out dueling robes, Jamie always had these well-coifed Asian-boy-band looks and dimpled smiles. Blythe probably would have loved him. They would have been one of those infuriatingly stunning couples, Blythe and Jamie, smiling side by side, pearly-toothed in social media reels, going viral for their blinding combined charisma.

Too bad Jamie's four years dead.

"I'm damn well sure," I tell Blythe, then wince at how harsh I sound. It's not Blythe's fault that my brother is dead, or that she's beautiful and charming, or that she's the fifteenth person this year who's tried to get into Rook's pants.

Sure enough, I immediately clock the surprised hurt in her eyes. I sigh, relenting. "Look, I know what you're getting at. Rook's a great magician, but all great magicians are goddamn weirdos. The younger they get good, the weirder they are. You'd do better trying to date some normie guy who's good at like, the guitar, or soccer, or something. Trust."

She laughs nervously. "Nah, it's not like that," she backpedals. "I'm just . . . Well, if he ever wants to hang out. If either of you do! We can trade numbers." She makes a big show of checking her phone and tosses in an, "Oh crap, late for AP Chem already. I'll see you later, Sammy."

I sigh again. "I'm sure you will." I don't look away from the mirror, even as Blythe's reflection scurries off, practically letting the bathroom door slam on her back. I'm left behind with nothing but myself and my own cranky face staring back at me in that mirror.

"Oh, don't look at me like that," I tell my reflection. "You can't afford distractions. Which means that neither can Rook."

I can't blame poor, gorgeous Blythe for acting or feeling how she does about me and Rook. She's in good company. My friendship with Rook—if you can really even call it a friendship—confuses a lot of people. Granted, those people rarely say so to my face directly, but I see hints of it all the time. They make all these carefully veiled comments:

"No offense, but you're not what I picture when I imagine Lysander Rook's second."

"You two are quite the odd couple, but I guess it's working for you both!"

"Hey, I bet no one expects a guy like Rook to take advice from you, am I right?"

I know what they're all really saying, behind the awkward jokes and hasty "no offense"–laden observations and backhanded compliments. Every one of those comments is just a euphemism for "Rook is too good for you. So why does he bother with you instead of picking someone cooler, hotter, better?"

I get it, optics-wise. Rook could have had anyone for his second: a grizzled veteran magician turned master instructor, known for creating champion duelists, or another famous young prodigy, or hell, even a girl that he'd actually look at twice in the hallways at school.

But Lysander Rook picked me. I made sure he would, just like I picked him.

He was a local boy, lucky for me. We even practiced magic in the same training arenas. His dueling partners rarely lasted longer than a week. The ones who lasted more than a month were practically legendary. We all talked about it. Some of the other trainees even started a betting pool.

Lysander Rook was, in other words, perfect for me.

I've never been naive, not even before my world fell apart four years ago. If you want to ensure access to the glittering world of the magical elite, you can't simply be good at magic, like I am. You need talent, sure, but you also need charisma, looks, the building blocks of a sellable brand. You need to be a guy like Rook.

If I played my cards right, I could ride Lysander Rook's coattails right into the most exclusive arcane circles—the same circles where the Blackwood family resided. But I didn't just need someone who'd be my entry ticket. I needed someone who'd be my weapon. Someone nasty and violent enough to carry out my plan in the arena.

When I saw Rook putting away dueling partner after dueling partner, I knew I'd found my boy.

The riddle for me was this: How the hell do you get one of the biggest young stars on the magicians' dueling circuit to look twice at you when you are, comparatively speaking, nobody?

The answer, naturally, is completely unhinged.

"You don't want this job," said Master Silverstein immediately, as soon as I broached it with him. "Have you lost your mind, Chan? No one wants this job. It's not even a job." He snorted. "Not like we're paying the poor suckers."

I smiled sweetly at him. Master Noah Silverstein's a classic old timer magician: a retired duelist with a reasonably respectable record and impressively little permanent physical or emotional damage. He's owned the local magicians' training arena for as long as anyone in town can remember, and he's produced his fair share of champions for mid-sized magic shows peppered throughout the East Coast. Jamie probably would have wound up as one of those champions, if he'd lived—old Silverstein was my brother's first real instructor. Silverstein is a veteran magic teacher, a learned master of the arcane arts, and a steady-minded businessman. Nothing fazes him.

Or, at least, nothing fazed him until Lysander Rook's existence made itself known.

"You can pay us in experience. Isn't that the party line you trot out whenever some poor wide-eyed kid with great big dreams gets suckered into a star magician's training camp?"

Silverstein didn't smile. "You can't tell me you seriously want to spend your training hours here playing glorified punching bag to our savage little prima donna?"

I felt my lips twitch. "Is that really what you call Lysander Rook?"

"It's what he is." Silverstein was utterly unrepentant. "The kid's got talent. A rare talent. I won't deny that. That doesn't mean he's not also a little shit. I'd even venture to say that talent has made him more of a shit than he'd otherwise get away with."

I hummed noncommittally. "Probably. He sounds like a real princess."

"So why do you want to step into an arena with him?"

"Because our princess needs someone like me." I looked Silverstein right in the eye. To his credit, he stared me back down with aplomb. Then again, I guess you don't get to be an old master at a magicians' dueling center without being tough to rattle. "Think about it, Master Silverstein. You've been throwing cannon fodder at Rook. Clueless, wide-eyed baby magicians who think they're hot shit and want to have a go at the champion for some delusional shot at glory."

"Yes."

I sighed. "They're a poor match for each other. It's not fair to Rook any more than it is to those poor idiot kids. The idiot kids need a gentler hand that can dole out tough love instead of no holds barred beat-downs, and Rook needs—"

"You?" Silverstein's gray eyebrows sat just below his thinning hair-line, arched as high as I'd ever seen them.

I forced myself not to scowl even though my ego was stung. I knew what the old master was probably thinking. When I first joined Jamie at Silverstein's training arena, the cranky old bat insisted on calling me Kid Sister long after he'd learned my actual name. Even now, when Silverstein sized me up as a magician, it was hard for him not to compare me unfavorably to my tragically talented—and very much deceased—brother.

I was about to change that.

"Rook needs someone," I stressed, "who can bully him back a little. And before you say anything, yes, I'm well aware that I can't beat him fair and square in a true magicians' duel, not with the level he's at."

I took a deep breath. Here was the risky bit of my proposition. "But I can hang with him. I know I can. You know I can. Better, at any rate, than your rookies. At the very least, I'll be able to handle some sparring with him without leaving the arena in tears and threatening to sue the teaching staff."

Silverstein snorted. "You really need to work on selling yourself."

I smiled. "That wasn't a no."

"I still think you've lost your mind, Chan."

"Maybe I have." Cheerfully, I winked at him. "But what have you got to lose?"

Silverstein grimaced. “I wish I’d thought to record this conversation,” he groused. “Then you wouldn’t be able to accuse me of failing to warn you.”

“Hey now,” I protested. “I signed a waiver, didn’t I? Should be insurance enough for you.”

He shook his head, sighing. “Well, I won’t stop you, if you’re this determined to get wrecked.” He jerked his head toward the hallway. “The prima donna will be running warmups over in Arena C. Go ahead and introduce yourself. Just try not to incur a hospital bill.”

“What are you thinking about?”

I brace my palms against my knees, trying not to hurl my guts out. “How we met.”

That’s only partially true. One piece of my brain is thinking about how we met, because it’s impossible not to remember how terrible my self-preservation instincts were at the time. In fairness, not much has changed, because another piece of my brain is replaying the last forty minutes: I told Rook that we needed to work on cardio and endurance for his duel against Tamsin.

As it turns out, Rook’s cardio remains excellent. Mine, on the other hand, needs work.

Which brings me to the remaining third piece of my brain, which is focused on, in the following order: how much my joints ache, how tired I am, wondering if I’ve bruised my ribs (again, second time this month), and generally feeling quite sorry for myself.

Rook’s big, callused hand appears in my line of sight. Grumbling, I clasp it and let him pull me upright. “You going sentimental on me, Chan?”

"Never." I try not to wheeze. I don't entirely succeed. "Just reflecting on poor life choices."

That at least earns me a snort of amusement. "I thought you were insane for wanting to join my training camp all those years ago."

"So did Master Silverstein." I spread my hands magnanimously. "And look at us now, princess."

Rook casts an unimpressed eye around our practice arena. Arena A is the smallest in the facility, which makes it a pain for group practices, but it's perfect when you're working one-on-one. "Look at us now," he echoes, his voice a little sour. "Preparing for yet another spectacle as a performing monkey."

I bite back a sigh. Rook gets like this sometimes. Half the time, magic seems like his whole world. Every time he wins another duel, he's jubilant. Ecstatic. His celebrations in the moment of victory are so expressive, they're practically grotesque. Some have complained that it's crass, that he's over the top, smug in his superiority, unsportsmanlike. Some folks want a humble champion, even while his fan base basks in the fantasy that an eighteen-year-old boy could be so utterly confident in his own worth—and back it up every time.

But then there's the other half of the time. When Rook decides that he's sick of the adulation, the press obligations, the nitpicking from Master Silverstein. When he falls a little out of love with magic—and by extension, out of love with himself.

"You're a lot more interesting than a monkey," I tell Rook. "Not to mention prettier." I wince as I crack my neck. "Not that it takes any power out of your left-side Rising Crescent Moon. I hate that spell."

He almost cracks a smile, but that flash of an upturn vanishes from his mouth within seconds. "You'll get better at countering it." I've always found it incredible how easily Rook makes things that would otherwise be compliments sound like condemnations. "What if I don't keep this up, Sammy?"

"Keep what up? Your ability to cast a Rising Crescent Moon off your southpaw side?"

"Any of it." His voice has gone small. The merciless enfant terrible of the magical world sounds like a child. The actual child that, I suppose, he never really got to be. "The duels. The hype. The interviews where everyone wants to know, behind all those polite reporter questions, whether I'm finally gonna crack."

"You're not."

When he catches my gaze, Rook's eyes are slits of blue practically buried beneath the jet-black fringe of his lashes. "Is that what you actually think? Or just what you want to think?"

I rub aching temples with my forefingers as I consider my response. It's bad enough that Rook has to beat up my limbs with his magical thrashings on a regular basis. Now he's slowly working his way into my skull. "You're not going to crack," I repeat. "I forbid it."

Rook finally laughs, wagging a finger at me. "Now that, Sammy, I believe. Once you set your mind to something, heaven forfend anyone gets in your way." He sits back on his haunches right there in the middle of Arena A and pats the space beside him.

With a sigh, I plop down next to him. He really is like a child sometimes. Right now, crouched like a gargoyle on the floor with his stupidly flexible hips, he looks years younger than eighteen. Curious. Innocent.

What a crafty illusion.

Rook looks at me. "That girl Bertha asked me out today."

"We don't know a Bertha."

"She's in some of your classes," Rook insists. "Blond. Nice lipstick. Pretty," he adds, practically as an afterthought. "Like, really pretty."

A beat. "Do you mean Blythe?" I venture. My heart rate speeds up. "Blythe Davison."

Rook shrugs, which tells me everything I need to know. "You know I'm no good with names."

Privately, I'm pretty sure he just doesn't like expending effort on anything that isn't magic. "What did you tell her?"

"That she doesn't want to date me because I'm nuts."

I breathe a little easier, which immediately makes me feel stupid. "Did she agree?"

"She let it go after that. Didn't seem too happy, though."

"Uh-huh." Against my better judgment, I press further: "Why didn't you tell her yes?"

Rook blinks rapidly at me. It's a remarkable effect, the blue of his eyes and the black of his lashes flickering at me like that. Small wonder Blythe tried to shoot her shot, despite my warning in the bathroom. "Why on earth would I want to go out with Bertha?"

"Blythe. You just said she was pretty!"

"So?" He shrugs. "What do I care about that? Dating a pretty girl isn't going to make me better at magic." His eyes narrow again. "And it certainly isn't going to win me that prize money they're putting up for the Tamsin Blackwood duel."

"Life is more than just being good at magic."

Rook actually laughs. Full belly laughs out loud at me. "Wow. That's—Truly, the irony of hearing that coming from you, Sammy, that's something." He swipes an elbow across his streaming eyes. "I remember how we first met, clear as day."

My heart starts pounding again. "You do, do you?"

"Absolutely." He chuckles, still wiping at his eyes. "You joined the cannon fodder brigade. Another disposable sparring partner. I thought you'd throw a few cheap shots, get embarrassed, and be done working with me inside the week. And then, instead, you fought me like an animal. Like the devil itself. I must have forced you to yield ten, twenty times that first day, and you kept coming back for more. And then you did the same thing day after day, week after week."

"I know," I tell him sourly. "I was there, remember?"

He doesn't pay me any mind. "I'd never met anyone like you before," he continues. "You were the first person I ever met, a kid my age, that I thought might get it."

"Get it?"

"Magic," whispers Rook. His gaze snaps toward mine abruptly. He waggles his eyebrows at me as he leans forward. "Hey, want a smoke?"

"You can't smoke," I tell him automatically. "It'll destroy your cardio."

"Bah, humbug," Rook shoots back. He pulls out a long white cigarette, seemingly from nowhere, then a lighter. "I'll be just fine."

"Rook—"

"Come on, Sammy." He's practically whining now as he flicks the lighter on. "Tell me something, and tell me true: When have you ever actually seen me gas out during a real duel?"

I haven't. I scowl at him. "It's the principle of the thing."

"Aha!" he crows. "See? 'The principle of the thing' is what people say when they've run out of actual useful arguments to make."

"That is not—"

"Anyway, what was I saying?" He takes a long drag on the cigarette. "Right, magic. You get it. You get that nothing else really matters, not after you've tasted real magic." He blows smoke at the ceiling of the arena. "Our classmates can act like we're crazy, but we know what's up. They're the ones who have lost touch with what really matters."

"Magic doesn't matter to everyone." At least, not in the modern era.

"Magic used to be all that mattered to anyone. Before we declawed it and confined the same stale old repertoire of permissible spells to some sanitized arena." He closes his eyes, sucking on the cigarette. "Can you imagine what the world was like?" Another cloud of smoke, even bigger than the first, fills the air between us, fog-like. "Back when magic was everywhere. Back in the old days."

"The old days," I echo, my voice dry, "before regulations were set in place to keep magicians from blowing the whole world to hell. Yeah, I can imagine those old days all right. The good old days, before the rest of the world woke up and figured out that maybe being good at casting a spell shouldn't mean that you get to play god with everyone else."

Rook takes another puff on the cigarette. Discontentment continues to drape over him like a cloak. "Say what you like, Sammy. But you and I were born in the wrong era. After I saw the way you fight, I knew you were just like me. Once you tasted magic, you knew nothing else would ever matter the same way again. Once you tasted magic, it meant everything to you. In the old days, we'd have been generals, royalty, gods even. Hell, we could have run this whole sorry world if we wanted to."

"Well, I don't want to run the world. And neither do you—you'd hate running the world. You'd chafe under the sheer weight of responsibility."

"Would not!"

"Would so. You'd throw a tantrum the first time you had to actually sit through a meeting with your world domination cabinet of ministers, or whatever, and that would be the end of that. So, no, princess, you don't want to run the world." I pluck the cigarette from Rook's fingers before he can take another drag. I pitch my voice to speak over his undignified squawk of protest: "Also, not for nothing, it's pretty hard to run a world with magic when nuclear warfare and machine guns and all that crap exist. Can you imagine how much energy a few puny human magicians would have to expend to match the power of even, like, the cheapest automatic rifle? When most magicians are gassed after trading blows with each other in the arena after five minutes?"

Rook doesn't look convinced. "Maybe if we were allowed to develop more advanced curses, we could adapt—"

"But that's not what you want," I interrupt. "What you do want—what I know you always want—is to beat your next opponent. And you're not going to get there by speculating on kooky ideas about out-magicking the global arms race or giving yourself lung cancer."

My champion glowers at me as I grind his cigarette beneath my heel. "Ah, Sammy. You're no fun. No fun at all."

"It's not my job to be fun. It's my job to be your second. And a second's job is to secure victory for their champion." I clap a hand on Rook's elbow and drag him back to his feet so I can look him properly in the eye. "So like it or not, you're going to duel Tamsin Blackwood. And you're going to win."

Of course, now that I've promised my champion a victory against Tamsin, I need to make sure I deliver.

Rook could almost certainly take Tamsin without my help. The oddsmakers currently favor her, but that's largely because of who her father is. Rook's the one with real skill—a freakish combination of natural-born talent with an obsession he's used to hone that talent into a weapon that started turning promoters' heads before his fifteenth birthday. And he didn't need a famous surname to do it.

You can't exactly sleep on Tamsin Blackwood either, though. I'm not so consumed by hatred of the Blackwood family that I can't see Master Mateus's darling daughter for the threat she is. Being the magical world's nepo baby to end all nepo babies, little Tamsin's been trained in the arcane arts since she was old enough to toddle. The Blackwood name may be the reason promoters salivate over her, and dueling fans hype her up so hard—but that's not the reason I'm wary of her.

Unfortunately for me and Rook both, Tamsin is, in fact, good at what she does. Which means that I can't take any chances. Not even with Rook in the arena with her. I need to find her weakness—her Achilles' heel. Every duelist has one, even Rook.

I just need to find Tamsin's before she can figure out his.

So when I get home, the first thing I do after my post-training shower is hop online. At this point, my laptop looks like a serial killer's, and I know it. I've got my main account on all the magicians' forums, but like any decent amateur stalker, I also use sock-puppet accounts: fake online identities that I always log on to from scrambled IP addresses so I can gain access to Internet discourse that the public persona of Samantha Chan, designated second to Lysander Rook, can't afford to dirty herself up with.

Lucky for me, so far as targets go, Mateus Blackwood's darling daughter slash protégé is a pretty easy mark. Like most kids in our generation—and teen magicians especially—when she's not practicing magic, she's terminally online, which gives me a wealth of material to work with. I don't take that for granted. I attack the tome of Tamsin Blackwood's online persona with all the scholarly, detail-obsessed gusto I've used to study actual magic. I examine her online footprint—her social media feeds, her forum posts, even semi-private group chats when I can snag an invite under a sock-puppet account—until I know the online version of Tamsin almost as well as I know my own champion.

I know that she publicly credits her dad with her success in the dueling arena but never smiles with her teeth in photos with him. I know she was homeschooled her entire life, no doubt so she could focus on studying magic. I know that—unless you count a few training partners here and there—she doesn't have many real friends her own age. And I know that she talks openly about her famous father's messy split from her mom, who didn't give a crap about magic, gave less than a crap about her kid, and took off before the ink on the divorce papers was dry—leaving an infant Tamsin in the sole care of one Master Mateus Blackwood.

While I scroll carefully through all my Tamsin-stalking tabs tonight, I scribble absently on a Post-it note. *Potential Tamsin Blackwood weaknesses: Daddy issues galore? More likely than we'd think.*

It's a start, at least.

Now, unlike Rook—who has an absurd number of followers on all his platforms, despite his stubborn refusal to put a modicum of effort into his online presence—Tamsin Blackwood curates her appearance carefully on social media, no doubt under instructions from her father. While she isn't the head-turning beauty that Rook is, she's got nice features to work with; she's undeniably a pretty girl, albeit in an unconventional kind of way. She was born Chinese like me, thanks to the estranged former Mrs. Blackwood's genetics, but her face is a paler shade of peach-gold than mine and freckled across the tops of her high cheekbones. She wears her curly auburn hair in a variety of styles, sometimes twisting it into a severe chignon at the nape of her neck like a ballerina's, other times letting the curls flow wildly in colorful-scrunchie-adorned half ponytail styles.

For a while, I flip through her photos, which isn't especially productive. She looks good in all of them, obviously, because that's what happens when you're an eighteen-year-old nepo baby who's either good at photo editing or pays someone else to be. Still, it's hard to pin down her vibe. I play a game with myself as I flick through one picture after another. Which version of Tamsin Blackwood will I see next on my browser? The cool, composed ballerina type with her sleek updos and collection of no-nonsense, neutral-toned athleisure-style uniforms? Or the carefree, bright-grinned girl with the free-flowing, wild red hair, dressed in fit-and-flare sundresses and strappy platform sandals?

I wonder if either of those girls are even the real her. Probably not. It's social media, after all.

But, as with most things you observe for long enough, eventually, a pattern emerges.

At first, I think I might be imagining things. I pause on the picture I'm currently staring listlessly at: a high-effort (and therefore effortless-looking) selfie of Tamsin looking contemplative against the backdrop of an old-school, mid-twentieth-century-style jukebox diner. I squint at the booths, the chairs, the décor. She hasn't tagged a location, but something's pinged the back of my mind.

Frowning, I flip back through her pictures. I speed-scroll through a few months, then a year, then another. I take a few screenshots. I zoom in. I stare some more. I squint and compare.

And then I start to smile.

Do any of you guys have a place that's just yours? writes a fifteen-year-old Tamsin in one of her old captions. *That's what this diner is to me. I go every time I'm in New York, just me. I never feel more peaceful than when I'm sitting in my favorite booth alone, with a milkshake flavor of the week and a new sandwich off the specials menu.*

Innocuous enough. Tamsin doesn't tag the name or location of the diner she's waxing poetic about, but I see the same pattern on the booth seats appear over and over again in the background of her photos throughout the years.

Call it luck or providence if you want to. But Tamsin Blackwood and I have, apparently, been haunting the same diner on and off for the past three years. Agatha's, a hole-in-the-wall joint nestled in the heart of Arcane New York, the intersection of streets where all the magic shops are. Tamsin's right about one thing: Agatha's does serve up a damn good milkshake.

According to the last three years of Tamsin's social media trail, she has stopped at Agatha's for a solo lunch on her first day in New York on every visit she's ever made to the Big Apple. She's got a favorite go-to booth and everything. She's turned her little pilgrimage to Agatha's into tradition. Ritual, even.

I pull up the itinerary of events leading up to Rook's duel against Tamsin. Both duelists are expected to arrive in New York about three weeks early for press obligations. I check Tamsin's feeds again, just to be thorough. I do some quick mental math on logistics.

In a week, Tamsin Blackwood's going to arrive in New York City.

She'll sneak out from under her father's watchful eye that Monday—my guess would be sometime between eleven a.m. and one p.m., ish. And she'll spend at least an hour in the far-left corner booth at Agatha's, cheating on her very strict pre-duel diet with her one indulgence for the month before returning to her usual prescription meals of unsalted chicken and broccoli: a diner milkshake and a greasy, delicious sandwich.

It just so happens that this time, she won't be alone.

5

TAMSIN

AGATHA'S, MY FAVORITE RESTAURANT in the entire world, opens her doors to me like a mother's embrace. Which, given my relationship—or lack thereof—with my own mother, maybe isn't the best metaphor I could use. Still, it's the one that comes to mind as I sneak through the familiar, winding alleyways of Arcane New York.

I breathe in deep as I step through the creaky circular doors of the diner. The festive gold-gilded trim over the entrance has begun to peel with age, but that somehow seems right for this place. Agatha's never pretends to be anything it isn't.

Inside, my diner is all cozy, old-fashioned cheer. The air smells like Agatha's fresh-baked apple pie, which is one of my favorite dessert options—with or without a milkshake to really indulge a sweet tooth. The fire engine–red jukebox in the corner of the waiting area—which I'm pretty sure is an actual relic from the sixties—hasn't worked in years, but no one's bothered getting rid of it. But the music that actually wafts through the restaurant, no doubt curated via someone's Bluetooth, is exactly what you'd expect to play on that jukebox, if it worked: classics from the seventies, the sixties, the fifties. God forbid Agatha's plays anything that hits a Top 40 chart in this decade.

I love it here.

I make a beeline for my usual booth, and I'm only a little disappointed to see it already occupied. I've been usurped by a mystery guest who's currently engrossed in the giant oversized plastic menu, their face hidden behind its multiple pages.

I sigh. This isn't the first time someone's beaten me to my favorite seat in the house—Agatha's has never exactly been super popular, but for a hole-in-the-wall in Arcane New York, my diner does well enough during the lunchtime rush to have stayed afloat all these years. It's not the end of the world for me to take another booth or a stool over at the bar-top counter.

I'm about to do just that when a voice from behind the menu calls, "Oh, dude, don't pick another table on my account, please."

I freeze. Nothing locks me more effectively or awkwardly in place than a social interaction with a stranger that I didn't anticipate or plan for.

The menu lowers to reveal the face of a girl who must be around my age. East Asian features, aggressively practical ponytail, and a black hoodie so nondescript, it's got to be deliberate. She's smiling at me, though she looks about as awkward as I feel.

This makes me like her immediately, despite her intrusion on my favorite Agatha's booth.

"You were going to sit here, right?" The girl sounds sheepish. "It's a big booth. I don't mind sharing. Uh, unless you want to eat alone, I guess. Or unless you're waiting on more people. Don't want to assume."

She speaks in a low voice, practically a monotone, but there's something earnest about the way she almost trips over her words.

"I usually eat alone here," I admit. "But I don't mind sharing, either."

The girl brightens immediately. "Oh, perfect! I haven't been here in, like, a year, and the menu keeps changing. I could use recommendations."

I laugh as I slide into the booth across from her. "Definitely whatever the milkshake flavor of the week is. And a Reuben or a cheeseburger, maybe. Something off the sandwiches section of the menu. They're all really good."

"Mmm, good to know. You a regular here?"

"Not exactly." I slide my plastic menu back and forth across the fresh-wiped tabletop, pretending to be absorbed in the soda selections. "I'm in New York for, um, for a duel, actually. A magic show. I'm a magician." God, do I always sound this awkward? Everyone tells me I'm charming in interviews. Where did that version of Tamsin go?

"No way!" The girl's eyes go huge. "I love magic."

"I'm glad you do." I laugh again, but it's more uncomfortable now. I never know how to talk about magic with people who romanticize it. They're always my biggest supporters, the reason magicians can get paid at all to do what we do, but the chasm between their idea of a magician and my actual day-to-day life, well. Let's just say that it's a pretty wide gap.

I glance sidelong at the girl. If she's really such a big magic fan, there's always the off chance that she'll put two and two together and recognize Tamsin Blackwood in the flesh. I've got enough social media followers that it's not an unreasonable possibility. Do I want her to recognize me? It's the wannabe celebrity dream, sure, but I don't come to Agatha's to feel like a celebrity.

The girl blinks at me and smiles again, looking slightly confused, probably because of the longer-than-normal pause in our conversation. I breathe a little easier despite the awkwardness of the silence. So she doesn't follow me on any of my platforms. Or at least, she's awful enough with faces not to recognize me in real life. I can't blame her, what with all the edits and filters and curation my pictures go through.

Good. It means that I can just be me.

"It's good to meet someone else who likes magic—magicians are always grateful to have an audience," I tell her at last. There. Not even a lie.

Maybe she's better at reading between the lines than I assumed, because the girl's expression softens immediately. "Sure. But magic probably feels pretty different for you than it does for the fans, though, right? You being a duelist and all. A champion." She shrugs. "I assume it's a different kind of relationship with all things arcane, when it's like, your whole life and not just entertainment."

I scratch the back of my neck. I wish I'd put my hair up this morning. It's warmer than I'd expected here, and my curls are starting to frizz. Right in front of this surprisingly observant stranger. "I don't know that magic itself feels different, necessarily," I say slowly. "But you're right that it's a different kind of relationship. I owe a lot to the promoters and the people who buy tickets." I snort. "I owe a lot to my dad, probably most of all. At least that's what he'd say if he were here."

Hell, why did I have to say the quiet part aloud?

My new friend catches on to my slip immediately, because of course that's the kind of luck I have. "Your dad?" she repeats softly.

"He's my second," I explain. I hesitate, then add, "He was a magician before I was born, a good one. He's the one who trained me. So it kind of just worked out that way, that he'd end up being my second once I started dueling."

"Sure, that makes sense," the girl agrees. "Is that ever weird, though? Having your dad around so much? I mean, my dad's a history teacher. He teaches all the Honors and AP classes at my high school, so like, during my sophomore year, when I signed up for AP Euro, I was always scared that I'd end up in his class instead of the other teacher's." She shudders. "Having to take the horrible exams he invents. Do the homework he assigns. Get caught at home for procrastinating on the homework he assigns."

"Did you end up in his class?" I ask, curious despite myself.

"No, thank god; I ended up in Mrs. Bakshi's AP Euro section. She's a way easier grader. Phew!" My friend feigns relief, wiping imaginary sweat from her brow. "The point is, I feel like being a magician and having your dad be your second is maybe a little like that? But possibly worse?"

"It's absolutely worse," I blurt out. I should stop talking, but she just looks at me, soft eyed, silently inviting me to continue.

So the venom emerges, bleeding out of me. "It's like my dad's trying to relive his glory days through me. He wants me to be this great magician, which sure, great, I want to be a great magician, too, obviously, otherwise what's the point? And yeah, I wouldn't have gotten as far as I have without him. He retired so he could focus on training me, and it paid off, obviously.

"But it's exhausting, feeling like I owe him this giant debt I'm never fully going to repay, you know? And any time I want to go my own way, or disagree with him, or do anything other than exactly what he says, he trots out that debt I owe him. And, like, the only real collateral I have is myself. The things I want. The goals I have. The life I want to live."

I only pause in my tirade when a smiling waitress arrives to take our orders. We both ask for mango milkshakes and sandwich lunch specials—a BLT for me, a Reuben for my new friend—which offers me a moment to breathe.

"Do you find yourself disagreeing with your dad a lot?" asks my friend, once the waitress departs. There's no judgment in her voice, only a gentle sort of curiosity.

"More than usual, lately," I admit. The waitress has taken our menus, so I've lost my fidget toy. Instead, I drum my fingers on the table. If this bothers my companion, she's nice enough not to say so. "There are some lines he wants to cross, or I guess boundaries he wants to push—and I get why, but I don't know if I can do it."

The waitress returns with our food, which saves me from explaining further.

My companion takes an enormous bite out of her Reuben, moaning with delight. "Agatha's does it again."

I take a more cautious bite out of my own sandwich. It is, admittedly, delicious. "She's reliable, all right." I chew and swallow, then add, a little sheepishly, "Also, um, thanks for listening. I know that was a lot."

My new friend laughs at me before slurping up an enormous swallow of her milkshake to chase the Reuben. "Not really. I think everyone's got angst of some kind about their parents at our age. Do you think your dad's going too far? With the boundaries thing you mentioned."

I hesitate.

The other girl probably sees it in my face because she adds, a little awkwardly but kindly, "Obviously, you don't have to tell me more if you don't want to. I just thought, you seem like you need to get some stuff off your chest, and—"

"My dad wants me to throw my next duel," I interrupt. I feel remarkably calm when I say it, but the world tilts around me as soon as the words leave my mouth. "The one I'm here in New York for."

The Reuben pauses on the way to my friend's mouth. Delicately, she puts it back down, expressionless, save a little lift in her eyebrows. "Oh. That's . . . oh."

I bury my face in my hands. My sandwich and milkshake sit forgotten on the table. "I'm sorry. I know we literally just met. You didn't ask to hear about all my family drama, and you shouldn't have to. I just . . ."

I just what, exactly? I just have no real friends of my own to talk to? I just feel more comfortable confiding in a kind-eyed stranger than I do talking to my own father about the way he treats me?

"He's just worried that I'm going to lose, I think," I finally say. "He's worried about me. So he wants me to go out on my own terms, I guess." I laugh bitterly. "At least, that's the way he spun it for me. Never mind that it's technically against the rules. Never mind the scandal it would cause if someone got wind of it."

My companion is silent for so long, I actually have time to consider what I've just done. It's one thing to tell a friendly, sympathetic stranger at my favorite diner about my day-to-day family troubles and the normal stressors of a magician's life. It's entirely another thing to admit to her that my own father just asked me to risk my career and reputation.

When I finally peel my fingers away from my face, the other girl is still watching me with that unreadable expression. She seemed so free of judgment earlier, but now I'm not so sure.

My heart rate picks up as I clear my throat. I don't remember the last time I felt so tense, every muscle in my body strung painfully tight. Part of me desperately wants to walk back everything I just said. But the other part of me—the same part of me apparently so starved for catharsis that I just dumped all my problems on a total stranger in less than thirty minutes—lets my words hang stubbornly in the air.

"I'm not actually going to do it," I continue. I don't realize until I say so aloud that I mean it—really mean it. "Maybe Dad doesn't think I can win. But I still do. So I'm going to deliver a good duel. A real duel. Not some half-staged charlatan's magic show." I swallow. "I wouldn't be here, I think, if I didn't really believe I could win."

A small smile curves my friend's lips up at the corners. "And that's what's important."

"Thanks." I go warm inside as my body relaxes, just a little. "Also, um, I'm Tamsin, by the way." I shake my head, laughing, as I cover my face with my hands again. "God, I can't believe I told you all that without introducing myself. I'm so sorry."

The other girl's mouth forms a little O of surprise. "Wait. You're not Tamsin *Blackwood*, are you?"

"The one and only." I laugh ruefully. "Let me guess. You've heard of my dad." I try to keep the bitterness out of my voice. I'm not sure I succeed.

My new friend looks mortified, which doesn't help. "I can't believe I didn't recognize you in person," she groans. "I've definitely seen you on social media and stuff, but I'm awful at connecting people's real-life faces with their photos."

"Hey, no worries. I've totally been there." I smile encouragingly at her. "Also, a million apologies, but I don't think I ever caught your name."

"Oh." The girl smiles again, looking more sheepish than ever. "I was trying to think of a good moment to slide this smoothly into the conversation, but uh, I couldn't really find a decent segue that didn't seem incredibly awkward." She shakes her head with a groan, closing her eyes. "And now it's, well, probably more awkward than ever. I'm sorry."

I frown. "Don't be sorry." What on earth does she have to be sorry for? I'm the one who just ran my mouth at her for half an hour. "Better late than never."

"I guess." She ducks her head, sucking in a breath. "I'm Samantha Chan." Peering up at me through the fringe falling loose from her ponytail, she sticks a hand out across the table, between our long ignored milkshakes. "It's nice to finally meet you in the flesh. I'm the second to Lysander Rook. Your opponent."

6

SAM

THE SLACK-JAWED EXPRESSION SITTING on Tamsin Blackwood's face is the most beautiful thing I've seen all week. I give myself a few seconds to drink it in.

I really didn't think the daughter of Mateus Blackwood would be such an easy mark. Tamsin walked into Agatha's looking so perfect, so effortlessly put together. Even now, with horror slowly filling her eyes, she still looks like an off-duty ballerina—but the fun kind. She's wearing one of those sleek little mesh shrugs and a deep blue crop with princess seams that that hug all her generous curves, but she's paired the elegant top ensemble with a pair of high-waisted, very comfy-looking gray joggers. A cheery petal-pink scrunchie sits in her hair, pulling half her curls out of her face but leaving the rest loose, cascading over her royal-blue shoulders.

Meanwhile, I'm sitting across from her in one of Rook's old hoodies, sporting a pair of leggings with a hole in one knee. Yet Tamsin Blackwood is the one of us who looks like she might fall apart at any moment. I've got to savor this, just a little.

When she finally speaks, I'm braced for her fury. Instead, she says in a very small voice, "I'm the one who owes you an apology. I should have recognized you, too."

I blink a few times. I thought Blackwood's daughter might shout at me or accuse me of tricking her (which I guess I technically did, but whose fault is that?), or beg me not to go public with her many, many daddy issues—particularly the juicy little tidbit that might get her disqualified from dueling in the New York Magicians' Arena entirely.

I did not expect, of all things, an apology.

"Uh, it's okay," I say, and god help me, in my moment of triumph, I still just sound so awkward. "I don't really have a super active social media presence."

Not under my own name, anyway.

I consider what comes next. I was right on the money with the daddy issues, sure, but Tamsin's given me far, far more than garden variety family trouble. If I want her disqualified and dishonored before she even enters the dueling arena, I can make it happen. For a moment, I'll admit, I do savor the possibility: cutting Tamsin's legs out from under her before my champion even touches Mateus Blackwood's darling daughter. I could keep her talking, record this conversation, and send it to Master Silverstein, who'd send it to the New York City Magicians' Arena commissioner. I might be able to end Tamsin's career right here, at Agatha's.

But would it be enough?

I already know my own answer before the question crosses my mind. No. As tempting as the easy route is, the Blackwoods have taken too much from my family for me to pay them back in anything other than bloodshed. None of this ends before Tamsin gets at least a taste of what happened to my brother on the night he died.

For her part, Tamsin just stares at me in miserable silence while I silently contemplate her destruction. I guess that's fair enough. I probably wouldn't know what to say to me right now, either.

I finally take pity on her. I've decided that I can afford to be magnanimous right now. "Look, this is really no big deal. We've never actually met in person before. How could we be expected to know each other on sight?"

"Well, it's not like I gave you the chance to introduce yourself." Tamsin's voice is bitter, laced with humiliation. "I was too absorbed in regaling you with my sob story. This is what I get for turning a friendly stranger into a free therapist without consent."

"Hey now, that's a little harsh." Impulsively, I reach across the table to pat her hand. She never shook mine when I offered it—which again, totally fair—but her fingers are outstretched halfway between our plates, still frozen in place. They're warm when I touch them. "I told you I was willing to listen. I meant it."

The way Tamsin's gaze locks on mine—wary, yet desperate with hope—makes my insides twist for reasons I don't fully understand. "About my dad's . . . suggestion," she begins gingerly, "about how I should handle the match with your champion—"

"Don't worry about it," I tell her immediately. I've earned the upper hand here. I get to play the gracious sportsman now. "I'm not going to tell anyone about what your dad asked you to do. I promise."

Tamsin continues to look suspicious, so I add, "Anyway, it's not like you would actually go through with throwing the duel against Rook." I hold her gaze. "Right?"

Because now that my decision is made, I do actually need Tamsin to stay in this duel. I need to deliver my sheep to the slaughter. It simply won't do for her to bow out before then.

Blood needs to be repaid in blood.

Tamsin averts her eyes for a moment. "Why did you pick me?"

I blink a few times, surprised by the subject change. "What do you mean?"

"You're Lysander Rook's second. You help him choose his challengers. You invited me to duel him. I remember your name, signed off on the message. Not his." She meets my gaze at last, steady eyed. "So I just want to know. Why did you pick me?"

Well. I guess Blackwood's daughter has some of her old man's steel in her after all. I'm oddly pleased by this.

So I grace her with the truth. At least, a partial truth. I've decided she deserves that much.

"Everyone is afraid of my champion," I tell Tamsin. My tone is blunt, so she can't mistake my meaning. "Facing Lysander Rook in the arena means both certain fame and near-certain ruin. He's cleaned out prospective up-and-comers in the arcane world so thoroughly, it would be funny if it wasn't also such a massive headache for his go-to promoters.

"I needed to find someone who'd be willing to challenge Lysander who wasn't also completely insane. I could find plenty of one but not both—anyone good enough to give Rook a run for his money in a duel is too sane to risk both their career and their bodily longevity, and anyone insane enough to take the risk is a desperate try-hard with little to no real skill." I chuckle as my gaze flicks up to meet my mark's. "Except, it seems, for you."

Tamsin Blackwood's face makes an interesting series of minor contortions. If I had to guess, I'd say the expressions go in roughly this order: surprise, pleasure, and finally, interestingly, fear. "You don't think I'm an insane try-hard just coasting into the New York Magicians' Arena on my father's name?"

There's so much that I could say to that if I were willing to show my full hand.

I think you're a great magician, but an easy mark.

I think you seem like a nice enough girl, but alas, destroying you is the only way to destroy Mateus Blackwood, so it's a lucky thing you turned out to be a half-decent duelist, too.

I think that you're your father's daughter—and your father's a bloodthirsty monster, just like Rook, so let's let a monster duel a monster, why don't we?

I settle, at last, on "Being a nepo kid doesn't mean you lack for talent. Your dueling record speaks for itself." I smile. "And, as it turns out, you're not a coward."

I'm getting better and better at telling the truth without revealing the whole of it.

"I don't know about that." Tamsin looks down at the remnants of the sandwich on her plate. "I might be a coward."

"A coward wouldn't have said yes to my invitation. Not against Lysander Rook. Not during a marquee event at the New York Magicians' Arena."

To her credit, Tamsin doesn't blink. Instead, her gaze narrows, going cold, and for a moment—just a moment—the pretty little off-duty ballerina with the cute pink silk scrunchie is gone. For a moment, all I see sitting across from me is Master Mateus Blackwood reborn.

Excellent.

"Did you mean it when you said yes to me?" I ask Blackwood's daughter.

Tamsin stares me down. "I did."

"Why?"

"Because I believe I can win."

I smile at her. "Then let's shake on it."

Uncertainty creeps back into her eyes. "Shake on what?"

"A promise." I offer her my hand once more. "Promise me that you won't throw this duel. Promise me that no matter the outcome, when you stand across from Lysander Rook in that arena three weeks from now, you're going to give it your all. Promise me that you're going to show me some beautiful, terrifying magic."

Tamsin's gaze flickers toward my outstretched hand then back up to my eyes. That coldness—the coldness she shares with her father—holds steady behind her stare when her fingers close around mine, her hand still incongruously warm.

"I promise," she tells me. "You're going to have the duel of your life on your hands."

7

TAMSIN

I'M A PERFECT GODDAMN fool.

After Sam says her goodbyes—because of course it's Samantha Chan, second to Lysander goddamn Rook, that I've been spilling my guts to this whole time—I sit alone in that booth for a long time.

This was my favorite booth at Agatha's. Now I don't know if I'll ever see it as anything other than the place where I made a complete and total fool of myself. The exact spot where I nearly imploded my own career before Lysander Rook ever had his chance at breaking me, body and soul.

The only thing saving me is, it seems, the pity of Samantha Chan, if you can call it that.

Promise me that you're going to show me some beautiful, terrifying magic.

Isn't that exactly what I promised myself I'd do when I accepted her invitation?

I look down at my hands. They're shaking. Remarkable. My skill with magic is as deft as ever. I've never worked harder or felt more dominant in the training arena during practices. So why does the idea of delivering on that promise scare me now?

My phone buzzes. The preview of my father's perfunctory text slides across my screen, accusatory in its brevity: Where are you?

I breathe out slowly and count to ten. Then I type back, On a walk. Grabbed a bite to eat. Heading back to the hotel now.

I don't bother sticking around long enough to read his response.

"That was a long walk," Dad observes.

I sigh into my hamstring stretch and put on a faintly exasperated face. Maybe a performance of nonchalance will disguise the volume of my racing heart. "Didn't you tell me I was neglecting steady state cardio days? Besides, I told you, I needed to eat."

"Where?"

"Some hole in the wall in Arcane New York."

Dad pauses. "You went for a walk through Arcane New York?"

"For cardio. And food. Yes."

My father sighs. "Tam. Do you know why I plan out your schedule so meticulously?"

"I imagine that whatever my answer is, you'll have a better one."

Dad actually chuckles at that one. I breathe a little easier as I stretch out my other leg. Making my father laugh—genuinely laugh—is good. Laughter usually indicates approval. Laughter rarely indicates that his ego has been bruised.

Dad is most dangerous when his ego is bruised.

"Before your mother left, I thought my job as a parent would be simple." Dad paces the length of the Pilates studio he's rented out.

"She was supposed to be your primary caretaker. All I had to do was wait for you to grow up, keep you in reasonably good shape, and make sure you weren't a complete idiot when it came to the technical knowledge of magic."

It's a speech Dad's given before, but I can't help but flinch hearing it this time. Condescension always smarts more when you've actually done something to merit being talked down to. When you've actually been objectively stupid. And Samantha Chan made me stupid today.

No, that's not fair. I can't blame Sam. She never agreed to become my personal confessional. I made her into that all on my own. All she did was listen.

It's been so long since anyone has ever listened to me.

"I know you didn't plan on having to do the job of two parents," I tell Dad, which he's also heard before, but acknowledgment of his labor usually mollifies him. "I can't imagine how hard it probably was."

"Parenting is always hard," agrees Dad. "But it's harder still to be parent and teacher and second all at once. I don't mind the work—I relish it, in fact—but I can only do all three well when I know where you are and what you're doing. You understand, yes?"

I sigh again. "I understand."

"I don't want you to overextend yourself."

"I won't." Dad has a point. Today is a rest day—or, excuse me, an active rest day. Long walks are nominally acceptable, but there will be no work on spell-casting (so that I can outdo my opponent when we face off in the magicians' dueling arena), or laboring under a barbell to slap more muscle onto my frame (to better withstand my opponent's attacks in that same dueling arena), or sweating through hill sprints meant to lengthen my endurance (so that I don't tire before my opponent).

Instead, I'm meant to be quietly working on my mobility and checking in with my body, and probably practicing mindfulness or learning to meditate, or whatever it is that they've recommended on the trendiest new magicians' podcasts for a duelist's physical recovery.

But naturally, instead of mindfully meditating and learning to unite my spirit with my body, I'm tensing up as I gird myself for another soliloquy from my father.

"You meet anyone for lunch?" My dad's tone is casual, but I tense up even tighter. "A lot of our friends live near Arcane New York." By our friends, he means his friends—or really, his business associates. I'm not sure that Dad has real friends, so much as he has pleasantly transactional partnerships. "You'd give my regards if you ran into Master Oliver or Master Theodore, right?"

"I would. But I didn't."

"Lunch all by yourself."

I shrug. "I find it peaceful." I've gotten good at lying by omission to my father.

Now my dad's the one sighing. "Next time, see if you can invite Oliver or Theodore along. It would be good to catch up with them. Maintaining the right connections, well, that's just as important as spell-casting if you want to make it as a magician in the big leagues."

"I'll keep that in mind."

"I could come along with you next time, if you feel awkward inviting an old master on your own. I'd make proper introductions. Make sure they see you the right way."

"I'm sure you would." I smile at Dad. "And if I invite Masters Oliver or Theodore to lunch the next time I'm in Arcane New York, I'll be sure to text you so you can join us."

I will absolutely never invite Masters Oliver or Theodore out to lunch. The last time Dad made me eat with them, Master Oliver—a man three times my age—spent the whole time staring openly at my boobs, and Master Theodore interrupted me every other sentence to sneak in snide comments about how clever and industrious it was for me to get my duels in "while I can," before I inevitably develop more of an interest in marriage and babies.

Dad doesn't quite smile back. "I do all of this for you, Tamsin. A father may be a mentor—a guide, even—for a young magician, but to be a second? That's something more. A second is an extension of the magician themselves. That's why so many of us are our magicians' primary sparring partners in the training arena. We know our champions' magic most intimately, inside and out, from receiving every attack without complaint. Absorbing the suffering to better the skill of the champion."

Dad stands behind me, gazing at our joint reflection in the giant studio mirror. There are a million stories you could tell about us, each more cliché than the last, based on the look of us, side by side. The older yet meticulously well-kept white man with his dark hair and eyes, his expressive brows and dimpled smirk. His young ingenue, not necessarily a classic beauty, but appropriately striking, as suits her role in these stories: the long dark eyes and high cheekbones of her Asian mother, the curl and reddish tint to her hair courtesy of an Irish grandmother alongside a splash of freckles across her winter-pale skin. Both of us well-formed, our bodies corded through with muscle, pared down by hours sweating in the arena.

Dress us up the right way, set up some good lighting, and we look precisely the way modern-day magicians ought to look: hungry and athletic but tempered with a certain stereotypically witchy vibe. The romance of magic wielders past rebooted for contemporary eyes. All packaged in a heartwarming father-daughter story.

"A second shares in their champion's triumphs and despairs in their losses," Dad continues. He stares unblinking at our shared reflection. "Your victories are mine, but so are your failures. So is your pain. And so is your power. A second is the champion's true confidante. It's a relationship imbued by trust that cannot be replicated by any mere garden-variety parent. We are one force, one mind, sharing two bodies."

Never let it be said that Dad doesn't have a creative take on pep talks.

I twist my head to look at him directly. "That's a lot, Dad. A lot of expectation. A lot of pressure."

My father tips two fingers under my chin. A smile flashes across his features as he tilts my face this way and that. No doubt assessing my marketing value for sponsors. "Don't let the pressure get under your skin, Tamsin. Remember, you're a Blackwood. And I've already given you all the tools you need to make this duel a success."

A success. Not a win. Because for all his flowery, put-upon speeches about doing everything he does for my sake, and my sake alone, Dad doesn't actually believe I can beat Lysander Rook.

And even if I can, why would he want that? If I win, I set myself up for independent success, financially and reputationally.

If I lose, I remain dependent on Dad. And he takes home the payday that should be mine.

"Maybe we should practice." I straighten abruptly, struck by reckless inspiration. My heart pounds. Fear or excitement? Maybe both. I always tell myself it's both, when my nerves start buzzing before a duel.

And talking to my father gets my nerves going better than any duel I've ever fought. "It's been a while since we've sparred. And, as you've pointed out, you're not just my dad—you're my second."

Dad blinks at me. "It's your rest day."

"Active rest day."

"Active rest days are for mobility and walks. They are not for hard sparring."

"Tomorrow, then." I stare my father down. "Don't you want my duel to be a success?"

Dad shakes his head. "You don't need hard sparring for that."

"Right, I just need to practice conceding the duel I'm favored to win, right?" My heart rate picks up as I speak, but I press forward anyway. "What's your brilliant strategy for that, Dad? I mean, yielding voluntarily isn't exactly something we've spent a ton of time practicing in the training arena."

Immediately, my father's features harden. "Careful, Tamsin."

"No, I mean it." I rise to my feet and face my father head-on. "You're my second. This is the strategy you've advised me to use. So advise me: How do I implement it? How do I set it up?" I spread my hands. "How should I go about practicing my planned surrender to the opponent I'd give anything to beat? What's the optimal timing mid-duel for that?"

Dad narrows his eyes. A muscle jumps in his jaw. The tension strung between us right now would rival that between most duelists on some of the biggest stages in the world. His hand flexes. If it curls just the right way, and he focuses his energy, with a flick of those fingers, he'll summon magic that will blast an opponent back ten paces. I see the temptation in him, clear as day. Some part of him wants to teach me a real lesson the old-fashioned way, magician to magician. Some part of him misses the arena and wants to show his upstart little girl that her old man can still hang. Master Mateus Blackwood, the one-time terror of the magical world.

"Before Lysander Rook tears my daughter limb from limb," says Dad at last. His voice is blunt, thick with an emotion I can't quite identify. "That's the optimal timing, you hear? You yield before you allow that . . . that monster of a boy to do something to you that can't be undone."

There have been moments in my life when time itself seems to hit its own pause button. This is one of them. Dad's breathing hard, nostrils flared. Usually, that's a sign of mounting anger, but anger is nothing new to me, coming from my father.

This emotion, on the other hand, is new.

I don't answer Dad's outburst. I don't make any promises. I don't, in fact, say anything at all for a while. Instead, I just stare back at my father. And sure enough, the longer I stare, the more certain I am that I'm seeing something I've never truly before witnessed behind the cold black eyes of Master Mateus Blackwood.

Fear.

8

SAM

ON SOME DAYS, LYSANDER Rook truly, genuinely strikes awe into my heart. When he's in top form, the magic he casts is beautiful and terrifying to witness. He's like a magician of old, a god on earth, his wrath a tangible work of art and destruction in equal measure.

And then, on some days, I don't see so much as a whiff of that. All I see, when I look at my champion, is a pain in the ass that I was nuts enough to shackle all my hopes and dreams and dark, dark desires to.

Today is one of the latter days.

"I can't believe you're making me watch grainy videos of some girl's old duels all afternoon," grouses Rook. "This is such a waste of time."

"I'm very sorry to interrupt your regularly scheduled itinerary of preening in the lobby, bumming cigarettes from strangers, and lying on the carpet feeling sorry for yourself," I tell him dryly, "but studying tape on your opponent is, in fact, important."

Rook heaves his best drama-queen sigh. "Isn't that what I have you around for, though? A champion's second is meant to handle all that bullshit."

"If by 'all that bullshit,' you mean understanding your opponent's habits and strategy so that you don't eat a nasty surprise in the arena, yes, I can help you to a point, but you need to see it for yourself to really understand what to look for." I sigh. "You know all this, Rook. Why are you being deliberately difficult?"

Rook's full mouth tugs itself into a mulish line. He's sprawled out on the floor of our shared quarters, looking like nothing so much as an overgrown toddler in the aftermath of a particularly exhausting tantrum. Master Silverstein got us a hotel suite on the promoter's dime, conveniently located right next door to the New York Magicians' Arena. Rook's bedroom and mine are adjoined by an unusually spacious common area—no doubt so we'd have extra training space, in case the local magicians' sparring arenas were all taken up.

Instead, so far, that space has mostly gone toward my champion's insistence on lying in the middle of the floor and complaining at the ceiling any time I try to convince him to do anything productive with his time.

"They're going to hate me," Rook says. His voice is curiously empty of emotion, those striking blue eyes of his poised on the clean white ceiling of our suite. He's fascinated by something I can't see, or pretending to be, at any rate.

I sigh. "No one hates you." A blatant lie. I, for one, kind of hate him right now, at least a little. So does a small but outspoken corner of the Internet—a minority within the magicians' community, compared to the hordes who worship the ground he walks on, but one that bothers him more than he lets on.

"But they will," Rook insists. He continues to stare up at the ceiling, the back of his head pillowed on his arms. "If I lose, I mean. Everyone will hate me if I lose."

Stifling another sigh, I plop down beside him on the carpet. I could lie to him again. I could feed him sweet consolations. I could tell him that he's going to win no matter what, so why does it matter?

"To hell with them," I say instead. "To hell with the lot of them."

Rook's head twists, blue eyes swiveling to find me. "To hell with the lot of them? That doesn't sound much like the dedicated, discipline- and duty-driven second I know." He pauses, then waggles his eyebrows at me before snickering to himself. "Give me another minute or two, and I'll give you even more *D* words that describe you, none of them a synonym for 'fun-loving.' Shocker, I know."

I roll my eyes. "To hell with the lot of them," I repeat, insistent. "It doesn't matter who hates you or who loves you. What matters is what you do in the arena."

"Winning, you mean."

"Magic, I mean," I counter. "You're the one who whines and moans about the pageantry and parades around magicians' duels, right? Well, you can hate all the pomp and circumstance as much as you'd like, but you know why all this frippery exists."

I reach over and tap Lysander Rook right on the nose. "Magic," I tell him. "That's why. That's what it's all about. Because people will pay through the nose to witness real magic, and it's worth it, every time."

"Every time," repeats Rook, skeptical, scrunching up his nose. He swats at my finger.

I retract the offending finger deftly. "Every time."

I lean a little closer toward him without meaning to. I'm telling my champion the truth now. Full stop, no lies of omission, no uncertainty, no obfuscation. I don't think I could be more truthful if I tried. "It's worth it, every time, for the chance to experience—just for a little while—something extraordinary." I smile, though not without bitterness. "Something terrifying and beautiful."

My brother used to say that the best of magic was the best of beauty and terror entwined. That in a magicians' arena, neither could be distinguished from the other.

I wonder if Jamie saw beauty or terror the night he died in the arena.

Slowly, Rook sits up on his elbows. He makes a great show of yawning at me. "And is that what you're going to show me on these dusty old YouTube videos of yours?" he asks. "Something beautiful and terrifying?"

"It's Mateus Blackwood's daughter." I smile wider at him. "You tell me."

Rook harrumphs as he pulls himself into a fully seated position, but at least he doesn't complain or try to stop me as I pull up one of Tamsin's old duels on my laptop screen.

It's a well-fought duel. There's less one-sided dominance than her victory against poor, doomed Dallas McCullough. Chianne Nichols is made of sterner stuff than the McCullough boy, and she lands several nasty unconventional hexes against Tamsin before a cut-up, bloody-faced Tamsin grimly finishes Chianne with a well-timed curse that knocks the other girl out cold.

Rook's silent for the entire duration of the duel. As the master of ceremonies raises Tamsin's hand to declare her the victor, he whistles low. "So that's her."

I hit pause on the video footage. "That's her."

He shakes his head with a bitter chuckle. His eyes haven't left the screen. I can see Tamsin's jubilant, bloodstained face reflected in those bright blue irises. "You know, the betting odds currently favor her."

"You can't think about the betting odds. You're barely an underdog; the numbers might as well be fifty-fifty, they're so close. Besides, you know it's only because of who her father is. That doesn't matter."

Rook's head whips around toward mine. "Doesn't it? A lot of guys say Mateus Blackwood was the best to ever do it, back in his heyday—and that his daughter's better now than he was at her age."

"It doesn't matter," I repeat firmly. The last thing I need right now is for Rook to doubt himself.

Rook's eyes narrow thoughtfully at me. "Does it matter to you?" His hand goes to his heart. "Methinks the lady doth protest too much."

"What's that supposed to mean?"

"Oh, come on, Sammy." Rook huffs impatiently as he gesticulates toward my laptop. "This is one of, like, fifteen different Tamsin Blackwood videos you've got lined up for me to watch. Half the magicians on the senior circuit haven't even *had* fifteen duels to their name. There's studying tape, and then there's obsession. What are you, in love with her?"

My blood runs cold. "Watch it, Rook."

"Wait, are you?" Rook looks just short of delighted. "I wouldn't blame you, you know. She's really pretty. Like, maybe not as pretty as that Blanche chick—"

"Blythe."

"Whatever. Anyway, she's still really pretty. And unlike Blythe, the Blackwood chick is one hell of a magician, and it's hard not to find that attractive." Rook laughs, wagging a finger in my face. "Though I gotta say, Sammy, I'm gonna be pissed if I find you sleeping with the enemy." A dark expression flickers through his eyes, despite the laughter dimpling his handsome face. "You do still want me to destroy her, don't you? Because that's what we came here to do."

"Of course I want you to destroy her!" I snap. "You think I spend hours dealing with your asshole behavior for fun?"

"Whoa, whoa." Surprise flashes across Rook's features. Surprise that almost looks like hurt. "I'm just playing, Sammy."

"Well, don't," I practically snarl at him. "You want to destroy Tamsin Blackwood? You want to beat the betting odds on this duel?" I tap the screen of my laptop, an aggressive clack clack clack of my finger against the plastic. "Study the tape," I spit. "I want you to watch her curses, her hexes, her physical combative skills. I want you to watch her mistakes and her triumphs. I want you to become, yes, obsessed with her, because unless you're obsessed with her, she's going to have the upper hand on you."

"Why?" Rook lifts his chin stubbornly. "Because of Mateus Blackwood?"

Yes. Because she's a Blackwood. Because she's her father's most precious possession. Because Mateus Blackwood will stop at nothing to ensure her safety. To ensure that I leave this duel empty-handed, my fingers damnably clean of the blood I've craved for the last four years.

I can't say any of that to Rook. Rook wouldn't understand. Rook wouldn't care. So instead, I speak to Rook—my awful, brilliant, violently ambitious champion—in the only language he understands.

"Because," I tell him softly, "right now, Tamsin Blackwood wants to beat you more than you want to beat her." I pat his cheek gently. "Never underestimate how much that matters. Now watch the tape."

I leave him to it and get the hell out of that suite before I reveal more than I can afford.

Because luck apparently has no desire to favor me today, I run into Master Silverstein almost immediately. And I literally do mean run into. I'm rounding the corner from the suite and practically bark my nose on his chest.

"Augh!" I backpedal awkwardly, my balance thrown off.

Silverstein grabs one of my windmilling arms before I can make a bigger fool of myself than I already have. "Samantha? What the hell's the matter with you?"

"I'm fine!" At the rise of his eyebrows, I sigh and force myself to relax my limbs. At eighteen, we don't technically need an adult guardian to accompany us on Rook's duels, but Silverstein's presence in New York lends more credibility to our side of the show. At the end of the day, an arcane master is still an arcane master. And if nothing else, I respect the hierarchy of the magical world.

I amend my tone, and repeat, "I'm fine. You just startled me is all, Master Silverstein. I wasn't expecting to see you." Dryly, I throw in, "Please don't take my clumsiness as a reflection on my abilities as a training partner to your active duelists."

"Relax, kid." Silverstein doesn't even look offended. "And don't be so jumpy about running afoul of an old man. Remember, I'm just down the corridor from you and Rook."

I sigh. "I told you before we left. I don't need help babysitting my champion. I can handle him, I promise."

"It's not just Rook I'm babysitting." Silverstein peers at me. An odd pensive look sits behind his usually gruff-eyed gaze. "I worry about you, kid."

Mortifying heat pinches me behind my nose and eyes. I don't remember the last time an actual adult—a real adult, the kind with a job and tax obligations and stuff, not just an overgrown kid who can vote legally—expressed worry for me. My parents mostly just tell me how nice it is for me to have a "good head on your shoulders for your age" and trust me to do as I please. I think they gave up on worrying about their kids when it failed to save my brother.

I can't decide whether to be embarrassed or oddly touched that of all the grown-ass people in my life, my master instructor—scarred-up veteran of decades of magicians' duels and all-around certified curmudgeon—is the one getting on my case now.

I say none of this aloud, of course. Instead, I force a smile as I hug my elbows. "I'm fine."

The aforementioned curmudgeon snorts. "The hell you are. You look like crap, Samantha. When was the last time you slept?"

"Last night!"

"For longer than five hours?

"At least . . . six."

"Jesus. You're worse than your champion in some ways."

I can't help pulling a face. "Literally no one on the planet is worse than Rook."

Silverstein chuckles. "I did warn you years ago that you wouldn't want to be his second." That odd look creeps back into his gaze. "Everything okay with you two? For a given value of 'okay' where Lysander is concerned, at least?"

I hug my elbows a little harder. "We're fine."

"You're not a good liar."

I'm a better liar than Silverstein thinks I am, actually. Which is probably part of the problem. I've never talked to my revered master instructor about what really happened to my brother or who was responsible. I've never shared the real reason why I fought so hard to become Rook's second. And I've definitely never revealed what I plan to make Rook do to Tamsin Blackwood in that beautiful New York City arena her father helped me book.

Maybe Silverstein would get it. More likely, he wouldn't. I don't think anyone can truly understand why I'm doing what I'm doing unless they've been in my shoes. Silverstein hasn't. No one I know has. And I can't risk Silverstein—however gruffly well-intentioned he may be—disrupting my plans.

Which means I walk this road alone.

"Maybe we're not fine—not entirely," I tell my master instructor. "Rook and me, I mean. The pressure of the New York Magicians' Arena is a lot for anyone to handle. It would be weird if it didn't get under his skin—or mine." I shrug. "But we've been through rough patches before. We'll get through this one, too."

Silverstein sighs. "You're a good second, Chan. Sometimes, I wonder if that's a bad thing in some ways."

I laugh. "How do you figure?"

"You're eighteen. It's an age for growth. For figuring your own crap out." He shakes his head. "It's no time to tether yourself to another magician so entirely. And that's what you have to do, as a second."

I smile wide at Silverstein. "And I've been happy to do it for the past three years. No call to stop now." I try to ignore the fact that Silverstein doesn't smile back. "Rook and I will be fine, I promise. I'll be at the hotel gym if you need me."

I end up at one of the magicians' training arenas attached to the hotel fitness center. This time of day, it's mercifully, blessedly empty. As the door shuts behind me, I close my eyes and breathe in the familiar scent of sweat and rubber, mixed with that faint burning smell I've always associated with the aftermath of a spell being cast, like the remnants of a previous night's campfire.

The scent of magic, still alive and well, even in this modern age of ours.

I set up my targets first. Whoever staffs the training arenas has had the good grace to provide their patrons with no shortage of stout canvas dummies. The plain rubbery material covering the canvas surface has been cracked and torn at the seams—the obvious product of years and years of use without replacement or repair—but these tried-and-true dummy targets will do just fine for my purposes. I set up four dummies, spaced evenly against the farthest wall of the room.

Then I retreat to the opposite end of the arena. I shake out my hands as I walk. The energy coiled inside my body stirs, like a sleepy snake waking at last from a well-deserved slumber. Muscle memory crooks my fingertips, itching to turn that energy into arcane power, to shape the spells I used to memorize every night, laughing at Jamie's side.

Here, alone in a dusty old training arena—with no Rook, no Silverstein, no other magicians to disturb my peace—I can pretend, for a little while, that my brother's still alive.

Jamie and I didn't have much in common back when he was alive, truth be told. He fit in everywhere he went, naturally gregarious, effortlessly handsome, and full of natural warmth. As a shy, awkward kid, I thought my brother's brand of charm might be its own kind of magic, with the way it bewitched people. I tried to figure out how he did what he did, the way he could read a room and instantly know how to make every person in it smile. I could never quite replicate Jamie's magnetism, though. It was this innate, unquantifiable social intelligence that I think—much like a certain degree of magical talent—you're born with, or you're not. Whenever I tried to act like my brother, my words always got stuck in my throat, and I felt more awkward than ever. So I watched my brother charm the world and gave up on having anything useful to say to him.

Until he fell in love with magic.

When Jamie fell in love, he fell hard. And I'd never seen my brother fall for anything the way he fell for magic.

It was the first time I really understood him. I couldn't charm a whole room the way my brother could, but I could do magic and do it well. And the more I did it, the more I loved it, too. Magic became the language Jamie and I spoke to one another during late nights up past curfew, trading grimoires back and forth under a blanket fort with a flashlight or watching grainy footage of duels between our favorite magicians before dinner while spoiling our appetites with the stash of chips and candy Jamie snuck out from under our parents' noses.

Jamie, older than me by four years, knew more than I did, of course, but he was an eager teacher, and had an even more eager student in me. "Beauty and terror," he'd crow at me with a wink as he showed off some new spell. "All great magic is beauty and terror. And we're gonna master it all, you and me, together. Promise me, sis."

I promised him, my heart full, over and over again. I didn't expect him to renege on his end of the deal by dying three days after his eighteenth birthday.

I open my eyes and stare into the empty space of the training arena I've picked. "Beauty and terror," I whisper to no one in particular. I bounce on the balls of my feet for a few seconds, shifting my weight around experimentally as I loosen my joints. And then I begin my sequence of spells.

I start with the Four Elements. It was the first real sequence of spellcraft—the kind that legitimate duelists use in the arena—that Jamie and I ever mastered together. The Four Elements may be basic, the kind of spells that even beginner magicians can pull off, but they work at the highest levels.

Fundamentals, Jamie called them. The kind of thing accessible to the most elementary of students but elevated into their finest and purest form by the great masters of the dueling arena. The kind of thing you might learn in a day but spend a decade perfecting. Rook turns his nose up at the Four Elements—they're too routine, too elementary, too predictable, he insists—but what I've never told my own champion is that they're my favorite magical sequence. Not everything has to be flashy or complicated to be beautiful, after all.

I begin with the Spell of Water. Arcane energy coils down the length of my arms, wrapping lazily around my fingertips as I trace the familiar sequence. A wave of magic rises like an ocean's high tide behind me, pure liquid power, higher and higher, until I can barely contain it.

I twist my hand, and the wave of magic crests, glittering white and blue, and breaks with a roar. I move with it, squatting low as I chase the wave toward its target, all the way at the opposite end of the room.

My wave crashes against the first dummy with a satisfying crack. The dummy buckles and falls. Magicians' dummies are specially crafted for relative durability—a durability that's enhanced by no shortage of arcane energy, to withstand the abuse we dole out—but I'm satisfied to see a new tear appear in the plain black material.

I cast the Spell of Air next. Artificial wind roars through my ears as arcane energy spins with the twirl of my fingers. I circle the space in front of my second dummy as I sight the target. As I move, a tornado of arcane energy whips itself to life, covering the space between my body and my target. I hold it in place for just a moment, letting it spin and spin. Sweat beads my temples. My spell buckles against the constraint of my willpower. It wants so badly to attack, to destroy, to do exactly what I crafted it to do.

I hold it for just five more seconds, to prove to myself that I can. And then I let it go.

The tornado is one of my more neatly cast arcane creations. I've historically struggled with keeping the Spell of Air contained within its traditional vortex, but this one remains on point, twirling with deadly precision toward my second dummy. When it makes contact, the target goes flying, spinning off the wall. It hits the opposite wall with a slam that vibrates through my bones. Beauty and terror indeed.

The Spell of Earth comes readily enough to my body when I cast it. The floor rumbles beneath my feet as I step heavily from side to side, knees bent as low to the ground as I can manage. I draw power up from below, arcane energy rooting me in place as a ripple of magic coasts along the arena floor toward my third target. It explodes upward at the last moment, dragging the dummy off the wall and down to the ground.

I pause to catch my breath before I prepare for the Spell of Fire. Fire was always Jamie's favorite in this sequence. Fire called to something nestled deep within my brother's spirit: light and warmth, but also an appetite for aggression, a blazing hunger that drove him far from home to places where his kid sister couldn't keep up.

The Spell of Fire has always come hardest to me.

Still, I try. Sparks of magic lick their way down my fingertips. With painstaking care, I gather the arcane energy threaded through my muscle. I need to turn it into kindling that will take down my target without making a mess of the whole arena. The Spell of Fire is the wildest of the Four Elements, the hardest to control, but that's the challenge of it. The beauty and terror of it.

It's why Jamie loved the Spell of Fire best of all.

Sweat drips down my forehead and stings my eyes, blurring my eyesight as I try to marshal my focus. I blink stubbornly, refusing to be deterred. "Come on," I whisper. Heat builds inside me. I can do this. Jamie could always do this so beautifully. And right now, I just want to feel Jamie close to me, if only for a moment.

"God, you're incredible."

My focus breaks at the stranger's voice. I let go of the spell and, with it, my focus on controlling arcane energy. The sparks of magic at my fingertips wink out as if they never existed at all. Heat vanishes from beneath my skin, leaving me cold.

Carefully, I turn around.

Tamsin Blackwood stands at my back, on the training arena's threshold, as the door swings ajar. "Um, the lock didn't stick properly," she says by way of explanation. "So I thought this arena was empty. I was about to help myself, but this one is clearly . . . occupied." She ducks her head. "I'm sorry."

I look Blackwood's daughter up and down. She's dressed for training, which is to say, she's got a designer-branded dueling robe thrown over her usual athleisure uniform. It makes her look a bit more chilled out than usual. Her auburn curls, however, have been pulled aggressively upward into a tightly coiled bun that would make the most stringent of ballet mistresses proud.

"Nothing to be sorry for," I say at last, my tone a bit more curt than intended. "My fault for not checking the lock."

"I didn't mean to snoop." Tamsin's looking past me at the three dummies I demolished with a strange light in her eyes. "I just . . . I didn't know you could cast magic like that. You know, the Four Elements are—"

"Basic."

"Fundamental," says Tamsin. "But it's rare to see them cast at such a high level. You're really polished. And just . . . well, really good." She laughs nervously. "But I guess I shouldn't be surprised, right? Lysander Rook wouldn't pick a crappy magician to be his second."

"Thank you." The beginnings of a headache stir in my temples. Tamsin's being perfectly pleasant, but I didn't expect to deal with her here and now. At this point, I've practically got her training schedule memorized, thanks to all my deep dive Internet stalking, and her appearing here right now is a deviation.

I don't like deviations. I'm thrown off my stride, and I know it.

"Anyway, I love the way you cast magic." Tamsin's still rambling, but I'm only half listening. "I'd love to pick your brain on that, actually.

Maybe we could go for a walk? I haven't really seen much of Arcane New York—I only ever stop through Agatha's when I'm in town, really—and it would be cool to check out more of the shops and stuff. Want to come with?"

"Tamsin. With respect." I massage my temples. "I'm not sure that you should be 'picking my brain,' as you call it, a few weeks out from facing my champion in one of the most hotly anticipated magician duels of the year. Conflict of interest and all."

"Oh." Blackwood's daughter visibly deflates. I don't know why my heart twinges a little at the way her face falls. Get a grip, Sam. "No, you're right, that makes sense. I'm sorry."

"It's fine. Really."

"And I'm also sorry to have interrupted your training."

I sigh. "You really need to quit apologizing so much."

"I will. Sorry. I mean, uh—yeah." Tamsin gives me an awkward little wave. "Anyway, I'll be seeing you around, then?"

"I don't think it can be helped," I say dryly then wince at how dismissive that sounds. Not that I should care about sounding dismissive around Blackwood's daughter. "Hey, why don't you take this training space? I'm going back to my room, anyway."

"Oh, that's all right, I don't—"

"Don't worry, I'll clean up the dummies." I roll up my sleeves and set about doing just that. "Just make sure you check the lock behind you before you start your practice session." I throw her a sidelong smile.

"Are you sure?" Tamsin looks dubious, eyeing my remaining unscathed dummy. "You didn't finish your Four Elements sequence."

"And I don't have to." I finish placing the targets back upright. They look a little worse for wear, but presumably, they'll do for Tamsin

Blackwood's purposes. "I'm not the one dueling you in a matter of weeks."

I let the door shut behind me without bothering to say goodbye. Maybe that makes me a coward. If I had bigger balls on me, I'd stick around longer and find a way to spy on Tamsin's practice. I'd even record her on my phone, maybe, and take my findings back to Rook so I could make him pick apart all her weaknesses. I'd hand my champion every weapon I could, even the smallest of knives, just to hurt Blackwood's daughter worse.

It's the least of what I owe Jamie.

Instead, I retreat to the suite. Rook's fast asleep over my laptop, while some clip of Tamsin trouncing a man whose name I've forgotten plays in the background. Quietly, I hit pause and close the lid of the computer. Rook doesn't even stir.

I consider my champion for a moment. Then I fetch a pillow and blanket and proceed to tuck him in, right there in the middle of the common room floor. Carefully, I fold the corners of the blanket around him, and upon some consideration, fetch an extra quilt to toss over him. He gets cold easily, especially in his sleep.

"Sweet dreams," I whisper.

Rook just keeps snoring, blissfully oblivious.

My handiwork complete, I retreat to my own room. I don't think about beauty, or terror, or Tamsin Blackwood. I throw myself into bed, still in my sweaty clothes, close my eyes, and for once, I don't think about anything at all for a while.

9

TAMSIN

LET ME JUST OPEN by saying I think I deserve a decent amount of credit for the sheer amount of effort I put into trying to forget about Samantha Chan's Four Elements. Any magician worth their salt can perform a half-decent Four Elements. But never in a lifetime of studying magic have I seen a Four Elements performed quite like that.

With talent like that, Sam's way too good to just be someone's second, even if that someone is Lysander Rook himself. I know respected magicians on the dueling circuit—all of them with major wins in the arena—who would kill to be able to pull off a Four Elements sequence so smooth, so precise, yet so casually powerful.

Samantha Chan should be a duelist. So why is she content to play second fiddle to Rook?

I tell myself it doesn't matter. I tell myself that I need to quit thinking about Rook's second and think about the opponent right in front of me.

I'm not the one dueling you in a matter of weeks.

Sam said it herself. She was, in fact, very pointedly, politely unfriendly when she said it, so she probably wants nothing to do with me at all, if she can help it. That shouldn't hurt. That shouldn't matter to me in the least. Who is she to me, except my opponent's second?

Nobody. Nobody at all—except, apparently, for a damn good magician.

Besides, Samantha Chan clearly wants me to forget what I saw. And given that she's been gracious enough to forget—or at least pretend to forget—my father's plans to rig the betting odds on this duel, the least I can do is erase her from my mind.

So I distract myself productively: by studying tape on her champion instead. I'm definitely doing it in order to better understand my opponent's strengths and weaknesses. I am definitely not watching these videos to search for some sign of what makes Rook special enough for a girl like Samantha Chan to forsake her own opportunities in the magicians' arena. And I'm absolutely not watching grainy old footage of his duels for a glimpse of his second, slouching in the corner, slinking around at the edges of the camera shots, just barely out of focus.

Rook's incredible, obviously. His style of magic is relentlessly aggressive, a dynamic display of power that implements curses so nasty and so complex that I can barely follow what's happening in some of his duels. The way he chains spell to spell to spell, from hex to curse, as arcane energy bends and twists with his body, it's like watching the principal dancer of a ballet. He's beautiful, the way he performs in the arena. He's pure art in motion. He devastates his opponent, destroys them, and he makes it look beautiful. He makes you want to cheer him on as he tears another human being limb from limb.

But he's not Sam.

It's infuriating. I watch my opponent string together an ingenious series of curses—each more intimidating than the last, some of which I've never even seen magicians pull off in the dueling arena before—yet my mind keeps wandering back to the Four Elements. The fundamental Spells of Water, Air, and Earth are simple, almost laughably so, compared to what Rook does to the magicians who cross him.

Yet it's Samantha Chan's magic, not Lysander Rook's, that's enchanted my mind. This is a problem.

Time starts to trot by: hours, days, and then, eventually, a full week. The night of the duel draws closer and closer. But the problem doesn't go away. I try to solve it with long hours in the hotel gym or the training arenas. I definitely don't hope for another glimpse of Sam every time I go.

Dad schedules me for a press event opposite Rook. It's supposed to be this big thing for our fans, a chance to see us meeting face-to-face in advance of the duel. A hype builder, through and through.

I'm dreading the damn thing.

I actually kind of like doing press, most of the time—interviews and podcast appearances and even full-blown press conferences are a great opportunity to say my piece about magic with an audience that might actually care about my opinions—but I cannot think of anything I am less excited for than being set up as an obstacle to Lysander Rook's meteoric rise to the top.

I get why we have to do it this way. You need a good narrative to sell a duel. "Two magicians of roughly equal experience and talent fight each other in an arena to find out who's better that day" is not a narrative—or at least, not a narrative that the average Joe will pay to watch live in a sold-out New York City arena. On the other hand, "Reclusive teen heartthrob who conveniently happens to be an undefeated up-and-coming genius duelist looks to destroy spoiled nepo kid" is A) a narrative, and as such, B) sells tickets—and news subscriptions—like hotcakes.

Which means that the esteemed members of the press are going to do everything legally in their power to push the narrative. And I can't blame them for it. I'd do the same in their shoes.

Pushing the narrative, you see, benefits us all—the two magicians, the sponsors, the reporters, literally everyone who has any kind of financial stake in this whole dog and pony show. But the thing is—and maybe this is juvenile of me—I really don't like playing a minor villain. I don't like being framed as an obstacle, or a supporting antagonist, or an inconvenience to the hero, even if it does get me paid. And that's what I am, in their story.

Never mind that I'm favored to win by the betting odds. Never mind how hard I've worked to get where I am. So far as everyone else is concerned, the most interesting things about me are my father's surname—and the fact that I'm currently standing in Lysander Rook's way.

The actual night of the duel is still a couple weeks away, which means that I need to endure a couple more weeks of listening to my father—not to mention seemingly every magical world news outlet known to man—go on and on about how brilliant and dangerous and special Rook is.

It puts me in a foul mood the night before the press event. I try to ignore it as I drag myself down to the hotel gym for my evening workout. I've buried myself in an oversized hoodie and slung my headphones on over my ears: modern-day armor. As suspected, no one else is at the gym at nine p.m. on a Friday. Even Dad doesn't bother following me to gym sessions this late at night.

At last, blissful solitude. I pick an assault bike and settle my weight down. Less than three weeks out from a duel, I'm probably not going to make truly significant gains in either strength or cardio levels for the arena, but I want to keep myself moving. I need to move, to sweat, to feel my heart pounding its familiar rhythm of protest against my rib cage. It's a delicate balance to strike: stay warm, stay mobile, stay hungry, but don't overtrain. Don't tire yourself out beyond repair before showtime.

I lose myself in the music as my lungs start heating up. It's nothing special, just a randomized playlist, but all the songs I picked have the right beat, a nice up-tempo rhythm that keeps my legs pumping. It's a moving meditation for me, this kind of late-night steady-state cardio. And it's probably the first time in days that I've truly felt at peace.

So naturally, that's when the door slams open to admit another gym rat.

I don't bother looking up at first. It doesn't matter to me who else needs to drown their sorrows and insecurities in sweat and exhaustion, so long as they don't hog the equipment. I'm in the zone right now. I don't want to risk any distractions.

Too bad I'd also be the first one to tell you that we don't always get what we want.

The intruder has the nerve to come right up to my assault bike. I still don't look up, so all I see are a pair of bright white designer sneakers. Great. I'm probably about to have my workout interrupted by a status symbol chaser with a closet full of overpriced athleisure outfits that they never actually wear to the gym.

"Excuse me." The intruder's voice is slightly muffled over the music blasting from my headphones but, unfortunately for me, still audible.

I pause the bike with a sigh. "What?" I jerk my headphones down off my ears so they can rest on my neck. "What's so important that it can't wait until I—"

"So it is you."

I finally look up. I regret it almost immediately. Lysander Rook stares back at me. He's wearing a shit-eating grin and twisting one of the drawstrings of his plain black hoodie around one finger. Aside from the too-nice shoes, he's shockingly modestly dressed. No sponsor logos, no ostentatious designer names printed all over him, human-billboard style. Past nine p.m. on a weekend night at the gym, Lysander Rook apparently dresses just like any other gym goer at our ritzy all-expenses-paid hotel.

"I'm sorry for interrupting cardio day," continues Rook, who doesn't sound particularly apologetic. "I just couldn't resist the opportunity to meet Tamsin Blackwood in the flesh."

I roll my eyes. "I'm sure her autograph isn't worth as much as Lysander Rook's," I tell him dryly. "Seriously, man. You couldn't wait until the presser tomorrow?"

"Where's the fun in that?" He waggles his eyebrows at me in this way that should be cheesy, but for Rook, it somehow works. I hate this for us both. "No one's ever their real self at a presser."

"But they definitely are after nine p.m. at a bougie hotel gym."

Rook cants his head from side to side. It makes him look like a particularly handsome bird. "Realer than they are at a presser. Especially . . ." He trails off, lips twitching as he looks me up and down.

I let him look, unembarrassed. I'm aware of my own attributes and how to spin my own narrative with the assets that I have. I'm not the hottest chick in the magical world, but I've been gifted with reasonably symmetrical features, and I know I can look striking when I'm styled the right way—and for some, striking might as well be the same thing as beautiful.

I didn't exactly dress myself to the nines for a late-night solo session at the gym—but I've had the public eye on me long enough to master the art of not looking like a schlub, even if I'm not expecting to be seen.

"Especially when they work as hard as you," says Rook as he finishes his once-over. "Which you obviously do." He smirks.

"I was working harder before you interrupted me."

"Oh, come on, Tam—"

"It's Tamsin."

"Is that what my second called you?"

I pause. I shouldn't be surprised. Of course Samantha Chan would tell her champion about our meeting. Presumably, he's the entire reason she agreed to meet with me in the first place. "When we met each other for literally the first ever time in real life over lunch in a strange city? Yes, she called me by my given name."

"I shouldn't be surprised." Rook sighs, looking fondly disappointed. "Sammy's a great magician but such a square sometimes. Won't even let me smoke. Claims it's bad for my cardio. As if I've ever needed cardio to win a duel."

My eyebrows climb. In fairness, Rook has forced pretty much every magician he's ever faced to yield within the first three minutes of a duel—hardly marathon material. But I rarely hear that kind of confidence, bordering on arrogance, spoken aloud. I suppose the pretty white boy darlings of the world really do live differently.

"I, for one, would love for you to smoke," I venture in arch tones. "As much as you'd like, in fact. Want to scrap this silly little duel between us and hire me as your second instead?"

I earn an appreciative laugh for that one. "Tempting. But no."

There's a brief pause between us—not quite an awkward one, but I'm always one to nip tension in the bud where possible. I clear my throat, jerking my head toward the rest of the empty gym. "You going to get your workout on?"

Lysander Rook, the nerve of him, just shrugs. "I considered it. But mostly, I wanted to be alone without Sammy fussing over me for once. I figured I'd have a good shot at it here." He flashes a sideways smile at me. "My mistake, obviously."

Well, that's one thing we have in common. "Does Samantha fuss a lot?"

"Sammy? Are you kidding? That girl has exactly two settings: mother hen and natural killer. She's one in the arena and the other one outside of it. Guess which is which."

"Is that why you chose her as a second?"

"What, you think I enjoy being mother-henned?"

"I think a natural killer recognizes a natural killer."

Rook quits smiling. Instead, he gives me a long, measured look. "You've seen Sammy perform magic, huh?"

"Not on purpose." Not at first, anyway. "I went over to the training arena next door to get some practice reps in on the dummies there, but I ran into Samantha instead." I hesitate. "You two have very . . . different magical styles."

Rook snorts. "That's a diplomatic way of putting it."

"How do you mean?"

"Oh please, you don't have to play nice with me. Not me, of all people." Rook rolls his eyes. "You know exactly 'how I mean.'" He makes air quotes as he mimics my voice.

"I really, really don't." I truly don't. But the charm-to-annoyance ratio that Rook's inflicting on me is tilting steadily toward annoyance.

"Which spells did you watch Sammy cast? Let me guess. The Hex of Mirrors? The Curse of Arrows? Oh wait, don't tell me, the Four Elements?" He smirks at the look he sees on my face. "Ah, I knew it! The Four Elements. Of course it had to be the Four Elements. She's obsessed with all the basic shit, but that damn sequence is a fixation. You'd think she never learned a spell that was invented after the 1950s."

I don't know why I bristle. "Basics are what foundations are built on. They have staying power."

"Yeah, but basics are basics for a reason. They're easy. Boring. No one gets excited about basics." Rook's tone is frustratingly dismissive. "You wouldn't catch me casting a Hex of Mirrors or Spell of Earth in a high-profile duel. It's not what the fans want to see. They pay to be entertained. That means giving them something they don't already see every day in the same elementary magic classes for day-one beginners."

"Sam could get people to pay to watch her cast the Four Elements," I insist. "Based on what I saw. Anyone can reproduce fancy new school for flair, if that's all they want to focus on, but it takes real mastery to elevate foundational magic at a high level. That's what your second does."

Something shifts in Rook's face, hardening his expression. The devil-may-care good humor is gone. My mouth goes dry. For a moment, I see what so many reporters and promoters and opponents probably saw when they saw Lysander Rook standing in a dueling arena: the beautiful boy monster.

The boy monster purses his mouth, then asks, in a voice that sends shivers down my spine, "So what exactly are you trying to tell me?" He takes a step closer to my assault bike. "Are you saying that Sammy can do something I can't?"

Yes. "No."

"You are." Rook's blue eyes are somehow unusually bright beneath the scant illumination of the half-lit gym. "That's exactly what you're telling me. And hey, hey, look at me—it's okay." He closes his eyes, takes a deep breath, and lets it out slowly. "That's all . . . perfectly okay."

My chest tightens. I get the impression that it's very much not at all okay.

Opening his eyes again, Rook fixes me with a dazzling smile, wide and white. I wonder how many girls he's convinced into his bed with that smile. I've heard all the rumors about the appetites of the magical world's favorite reclusive heartthrob, but I've always wondered how much truth there is behind them. I suspect it must be awfully logistically difficult to be both a recluse and a stealth ladies' man.

Maybe he doesn't sleep with the girls. Maybe he just kills them in back alleys while whispering sweet nothings and flashing that smile at them.

"My second's very good at what she does," continues Rook. "She wouldn't be my second otherwise. But there's a reason why she's just that—a magician's second—while I'm the champion."

"Yeah?" I don't let my voice tremble. I won't give him that satisfaction. But I've given up on getting a longer sweat on the assault bike by now, so I dismount. Then I draw my spine straight, so I can look my opponent in the eye. "Enlighten me."

Rook's not much taller than I am. He is, in fact, surprisingly slightly built for such a fearsome duelist. But he looks and sounds exactly like the monster he is when he ducks his head to rest his chin on my shoulder and whispers against the shell of my ear, in a voice of pure venom, "Allow me to let you in on a secret, Tam. Sammy's a real mean little piece of work, but between her and me? I'm the only one who has the balls to put another magician's head on a stick." His breath ghosts against the sensitive skin of my neck as he chuckles. "And that's exactly where yours will be by the time I'm through with you. You're not special, Blackwood. You're just in my way."

My heartbeat stutters, practically a spasm against my ribs.

When Rook draws back, he's all pleasantries again, the monster gone, tucked safely behind the beautiful boy with the casual swagger and easygoing smile. "Enjoy your workout, Tamsin. I look forward to seeing you at the presser tomorrow." He winks at me. "I'm sure the whole thing will be nothing short of a goddamn delight."

10

SAM

ONE HOUR BEFORE SHOWTIME with the press, and Rook's in the foulest mood I've seen him contend with in weeks.

"Tamsin Blackwood's a bitch," he tells me for probably the fifteenth time in the last thirty minutes. I try not to sigh aloud. "You never warned me that she was a bitch."

"Well, she hasn't been a bitch to me," I tell him blandly. "Or to anyone besides, apparently, you. So I'm not sure how I was supposed to know."

"You're my second!" seethes Rook. "It's your job to know these things! You've watched all that tape on her, and you never figured it out yourself?"

I close my eyes for a few precious seconds. *I will not murder my own champion. I will not murder my own champion. I will not murder my own champion.* If I repeat the mantra enough times, maybe I'll successfully manifest it. I haven't killed Rook yet, so hopefully it's working.

"Aw, princess." When I open my eyes, I address my champion with a smile and a poisonously honeyed voice. "Watching all that tape, as you put it, taught me exactly as much as I need to know about Tamsin Blackwood—which is that you can beat her. Everything else is irrelevant."

I see him open his mouth to protest and raise my own voice, talking over him before he can get going. "I don't care if Tamsin Blackwood is actually a bitch or if you just pissed her off by being yourself. All I care about is making sure that you don't make the news cycle for the wrong reasons after we finish up press today."

The truth is, I'd like nothing better than for Lysander Rook to savage Blackwood's daughter in front of the entire press corps. A girl like Tamsin—a nepo kid well-versed on the art of social media and public appearances—is going to be way more sensitive than she lets on. Rook, at his most ruthless, can give her confidence a good shake. It might not be enough to guarantee his victory on the night of the duel, but it'll be enough to get her stuck in her own head when she faces him in the arena.

The less present she is in that moment—the less capable she is of defending herself—the better for Rook. The better for me.

Rook won't tear into Tamsin just because I want him to do it, though. As in all things, Rook needs to be carefully managed, especially when it comes to public behavior. He'll listen to me—to a point, if it concerns the craft of magic directly. But when it comes to all the other component pieces of his star-making vehicle—social media clout, etiquette, and maybe most notoriously of all, the do's and don'ts of talking to reporters—he chomps at the bit. The harder I nag at him to be sweet and sportsmanlike, the less he'll want to do it.

Good.

"Pressers are almost as important as actual duels, if you want to make a living on magic," I tell Rook in the most condescending tone I can muster. I channel my inner pedant. I pull out all the stops. "You should know that by now. Which means some things are going to be taboo." I tick them off on my finger, one by one: "Don't insult Tamsin ad hominem. It makes you look petty. Don't goad her, you should save that for the duel." I hide a smile as I deliver the coup de grace: "And, for the love of God, don't bring up her father. It's obviously going to be a sore subject."

I watch my champion's eyes narrow at that last order. It's all I can do to keep from patting myself on the back. With those words, I've all but ensured that Rook is going to label Tamsin Blackwood a useless daddy's little girl in front of the entire magical community. And Tamsin, bless her heart, will fall to pieces when it happens.

"So, tell me, princess, so I can hear it for myself." I tip my champion's chin toward my face with one finger. "Are you going to behave yourself in front of the esteemed members of the magical world press corps?"

Rook gives an exaggerated roll of those big blue eyes but doesn't pull his face free from my hand. If anything, he leans into my touch a little as he pouts up at me. "Is that what we're calling petty vultures now?"

"It is if you want to keep your reputation intact."

"I don't care about my reputation."

"Yeah, you and Joan Jett both. Too bad." I let go of his face to tap my own chest. "I care." Then I say the magic words: "So let's remind all those reporters what a good boy Lysander Rook can be."

Rook looks like he wants to claw his own eyes out. I suppress a grin. This is going to be a bloodbath.

For what it's worth, Rook does wait until the halfway point in the presser to really lay into Tamsin. By the time it happens, I'm almost relieved.

The whole thing was going far too smoothly in the first half hour. Both magicians arrived on time and offered reasonably genuine-sounding pleasantries to the press corps. You'd never guess what a tantrum Rook had been throwing just minutes before he was due in front of the cameras. They're oddly lovely together, Rook and Tamsin, which surprises me a little because the two of them look nothing alike. Rook is all sharp angles and cool colors, bright blue eyes and blue-black hair, his white skin nearly translucent under the blinding flash of the cameras. He rarely smiles in front of the press, but when he does, he looks like a wolf showing his teeth to its prey, which thankfully for me just feeds into his brand as the magical world's mysterious yet highly dangerous bad (but not too bad!) boy duelist.

Tamsin's a lot softer-looking, her features more rounded and inviting. The hint of red in her thick curls is more obvious under this lighting, and it brings out the warmth in her rosy, freckled cheeks. She smiles more than Rook does, and it looks exactly like the one she gave me when I intercepted her at Agatha's: genuine, friendly, and well, happy.

Blackwood's daughter is either a happier person than Rook by default or very good at faking it until she makes it.

But at the halfway mark, the mood shifts.

It all starts with Jensen Sykes. The guy's a notorious contrarian, even among reporters, known for deliberately provoking interview subjects. Everyone knows he only does it to get a good story out of the inevitable outburst, but people somehow still fall for it almost every time. When Sykes raises his hand to ask a question, my heart leaps.

"My question is for Lysander Rook." Sykes has this great dulcet voice, projecting to be heard easily, even over the disgruntled murmurs of his fellow reporters. "You've made a mockery of every magician who's ever entered the arena with you—to the point where established adult magicians are reportedly afraid of facing an eighteen-year-old."

The disgruntled murmurs grow louder and, well, more disgruntled. My heartbeat hammers against my rib cage. Something's about to happen. We can all feel the tension in the air. The question is what.

Sykes eyes my champion over the frames of his designer glasses. "So my question is this: How do you feel about being considered an underdog, for the first time in your career, against Master Mateus Blackwood's daughter?"

It's a question that cuts to the quick. Everything about it is calculated, from the veiled implication that the oddsmakers have erred to the fact that Sykes doesn't even bother using Tamsin's name.

I spare a quick glance for my champion's opponent. Sykes has done half of Rook's work for him. The habitual smile on Tamsin Blackwood's face freezes as she blinks rapidly, lashes fluttering. Her mouth parts for a moment. I wonder if she'll defend herself or chastise Sykes.

But the question was directed at Tamsin's opponent, not at Tamsin. She seems to remember that at the last second. She shuts her mouth again, pressing her lips into a thin line as she looks away from the press corps. She blinks again, several times, very quickly, as she takes a deep breath. There's no smile on her face now.

Rook, meanwhile, stares right at Sykes. At first, my champion says nothing. For a moment, I wonder if my needling has backfired—if my champion, for once in his life, is actually going to play the good boy for the press.

He doesn't, of course.

Rook leans back in his seat and rests his head on his hands. He smirks at Sykes. "I was a little insulted by the oddsmakers at first," he drawls. "But giving credit where credit's due, there's something special about Tamsin Blackwood. Something that none of my other opponents have going for them."

The previously disgruntled murmurs take a turn for the curious. The other reporters smell blood. Rook's got them eating out of his hand. Much like his magical style, when it comes to certain sorts of conversation, my champion's got a great sense of timing and setup.

Sykes leans forward in his seat. He's practically salivating. If he weren't playing so perfectly into my plans, I'd want to wring his neck. "Oh? Care to enlighten us, Mr. Rook?"

"Sure." Without so much as glancing at the still-frozen Tamsin, Rook tells the entire press corps, "You see, unlike every other magician I've ever beaten, Tam here has the remarkable distinction of being one of the greatest duelists of her generation. The veteran of over fifty duels, the owner of one of the longest careers since— Wait, wait, wait." Rook's bright blue eyes go wide as he feigns embarrassment. "Oh, whoops, I misspoke. Silly me! That would be her father I'm talking about. But does that really matter? I mean, the way the reporters in this room talk about her, Tamsin Blackwood is the closest the magical world can come to having Mateus Blackwood back in the arena in the flesh."

My champion's gaze is flinty as a young god's as he surveys us from behind the microphone. "Here's the question that you should really be asking, Mr. Sykes: Who exactly is Tamsin Blackwood without old man Mateus?" Rook smiles. "We all know the answer, I think. But I'll say the quiet part aloud, for everyone's benefit: without Mateus Blackwood, his daughter is . . . well, nothing at all, really, is she?"

The words hit me like a gut punch. I'm not the only one. The collective intake of breath from everyone in the press room is audible. There's smack talk between duelists. And then there's blatant cruelty.

This time, I can't quite bring myself to look at Tamsin.

My champion rises and sketches a mocking bow to the press corps. "I look forward to dueling Old Man Mateus's cute little clone in a couple weeks. Truly, I anticipate an experience like none other."

I keep telling myself my guilt is misplaced, but I can't really bring myself to believe it.

Maybe I've gotten so good at misdirecting the truth that I can't tell when I'm lying to myself anymore. It doesn't seem to matter how I justify what Rook did—really, what I did—to myself. I can reason with myself, offering logic and excuses and tough love self-talk.

I needed to rattle Tamsin. I needed to shake her confidence. I needed to give Rook the mental edge ahead of their duel. I accomplished all of those things. I owe Blackwood's daughter nothing. Less than nothing.

Yet I still feel absolutely rotten.

It gets worse when I hear someone crying down in the training arena by the fitness center. I freeze as soon as the sound of it hits my ears. All I want is to take my mind off my own guilt by practicing my spells. I was hoping to find the arena empty. No such luck.

Naturally, I panic immediately. I'm terrible with crying people. I always have been. Jamie—who, naturally, was excellent with crying people—used to tell me that dealing with crying people is just a matter of offering a shoulder, an ear, and when possible, a pack of tissues. In my own personal experience, crying people do not generally seek out any of these things from me.

The door on the training arena room—the one with the lock that won't close properly—sits ajar. Inside, I discover Tamsin Blackwood trying to muffle her sobs against the sleeve of her hoodie.

Oh, hell.

For a moment, I simply stand on the threshold like an idiot. A garden-variety crying person is bad enough. A crying person who's probably crying because of what I did to them is considerably worse.

This is what you wanted, whispers a traitorous voice from the bowels of my mind. *You wanted to break her, physically, mentally, emotionally. You wanted to ensure Rook's destruction of her. Making her cry should be the least of what you do to her.*

It's true, every word.

I just didn't expect it to feel like this.

I didn't expect to have to witness the wreckage left behind by my own handiwork.

I should just leave. I'm going to leave. I can go back to the suite I share with Rook and quarrel harmlessly with him until I feel better, and then I can forget I ever saw this. I'll never have to think about a swollen-eyed, red-nosed Tamsin Blackwood bawling her heart out ever again.

I turn away. And bang my knee directly into the still-ajar door. "Shit!"

Tamsin looks up immediately. "Who's there?" She sniffs. "Sorry, I'll be out in a minute."

Like we're in a high school bathroom and she's hogging one of the stalls to have a self-pitying bawl over getting dumped by a prom date.

I step out from behind the door. I've raised my hands in front of me, which is ridiculous—what do I think I'm doing, turning myself over to a cop? Still, I keep them raised. It looks stupid, but looking stupid feels better than looking threatening. I don't want Tamsin to think I'm going to hurt her.

Well. I don't want her to think I'm going to hurt her any more than I already have.

"It's just me," I say. "I didn't mean to intrude. I, um, I'm just going to head back up to my room—"

"Oh no, don't!" Tamsin blurts out. "You were going to train, right? If you need the practice space—"

"I really don't."

"I wasn't using it, really—"

"It looked like you were." The words are out of my mouth before I can stop them. I swallow, then say, "Crying is a totally respectable use of a magicians' training arena." I try to smile. "Ask me how I know."

Tamsin's eyebrows climb, but at least she's not sobbing anymore. "You've cried in a training arena?"

"Are you kidding me?" I fix her with an expression of pure disbelief. "I've probably cried more in training arenas than I've cried anywhere else in my life." I count the locations off on my fingers. "In bed, at the movies, in bathroom stalls—"

"You don't seem like the crying type."

I stop talking. Tamsin's watching me with an unreadable look on her face. Even tear-streaked, she's remarkably pretty. Her makeup is still largely intact, which means she probably uses waterproof mascara. Which, in turn, tells me that she knows a thing or two about crying while remaining presentable.

"You don't seem like the sort of person that anyone could just . . . crack like that," she elaborates. If I didn't know better, I'd say she sounds jealous of me. "I bet you don't let anyone get under your skin."

Ah, sweet, naive little Blackwood girl. If only you knew.

"You'd be surprised," I tell her. "Besides, I'm pretty sure every magician who spends enough time on the dueling circuit is the crying type. How could we not be? It's too much, all of this." I gesture vaguely around us. "The arena. The public eye. The magic, god, the magic most of all."

Tamsin offers me a tiny, red-eyed smile. "But the magic's the best part, right?"

I can't help but smile back despite myself. "Yeah. I guess it kind of is."

"So why aren't you a duelist?"

The question catches me off guard. "What do you mean?"

"You're really good." Tamsin speaks with a bluntness that's more like Rook—or even me—than herself. She's not buttering me up, just stating a fact. "You could do well in a dueling arena in your own right. So why settle for being Lysander Rook's second? You can't tell me a guy like that is worth it."

"Aw, come on, you're just mad at him for all that smack talk at the press event. You can't deny he's a brilliant magician, or you wouldn't want to duel him yourself, would you? But, um, about what happened with the presser." I bite my lip. "I . . . look. I'm sorry. I shouldn't have let him tear into you that hard. He crossed a line."

Maybe we both did.

Tamsin shrugs. "Not like he said anything that wasn't what everyone else was already thinking. I should thank him, really. At least now we're not dancing around the elephant in the room." There's no bitterness in her voice, just gentle resignation.

It should make me happy. I should take it as a sign that my gambit's working. That I'm slowly but surely breaking Blackwood's daughter down, mentally and emotionally.

It doesn't make me happy, though. It doesn't make me happy at all.

"Hey," I say impulsively. "You know what I think might cheer you up?"

She throws me a suspicious glance. "If it has anything to do with talking to Rook, forget it. He doesn't owe me any apologies or—"

I snort. "Don't worry, you won't get one from him. He's got to maintain his reputation as a brilliant jerk, right? It's all about the branding. No, I've got something better than half-baked contrition from my champion."

"In that case, I'm all ears."

I grin at her with more sincerity than I care to admit. "Arcane New York."

"What about it?"

"You wanted to explore it." I offer her my hand. "So screw it. Let's explore."

Tamsin eyes my hand dubiously. "I don't know—"

"Look, I promise that if you hate it, at the very least, I will scout out an appropriate place there where you can continue crying to your heart's content."

That finally gets a watery laugh out of Tamsin. "Well, when you put up an offer like that, how can a girl resist?" She hesitates for a few more seconds then gingerly puts her hand in mine. It's just as warm as it was that day we shook on her promise at Agatha's.

"Okay then, Samantha Chan." She matches my smile, her eyes fierce. "Let's take on Arcane New York together."

11

TAMSIN

LYSANDER ROOK DESERVES A round of applause for what a fool he's made of me.

I should have had a zinger ready to lob back in Rook's stupid face. Something all those hungry-eyed, eager-faced reporters could churn out in hyperlinks for their requisite clickbait on the next magical world news cycle. Something that would have at least made me look witty and thick-skinned, and not like a sensitive little girl who doesn't know how to play verbal hardball with Lysander Rook, let alone stand across from him in a magicians' dueling arena.

Instead, I did what I'd been trying to avoid doing for weeks. I looked out across the sea of reporters, searching for the spot where I knew Samantha Chan would be standing on the periphery. And sure enough, I found her face amid the lights: stark, strong bones, plain black ponytail and careworn hoodie, her mouth a tiny little O of dismay.

I couldn't help but wonder, right then, if she was the one behind Lysander Rook's poisonous words. If she told her champion to say the things he said. If that's what Sam really thinks of me—that I'm nothing without Dad.

"What are you thinking about?"

I start and glance over at Sam. She doesn't look so different from how she did at the presser. She's still in what seems to be her uniform: oversized hoodie, ponytail, and sneakers. She's not smiling, but her eyes are kind.

I'm not sure I can trust that kindness. I give her a wry look. "You want the polite, inoffensive answer or the awkward, honest one?" I ask.

Even as I speak the words, a weird mix of guilt and suspicion stirs my gut. I don't know if I've ever met anyone who sends out as many mixed signals as Samantha Chan. One day, she's full of graciousness, taking my hand as she earnestly tells me that all she wants of me is a good duel with her champion. The next, she's put up all her walls, cold-eyed and calculating, looking like she'd rather do anything in the world besides talk to me. I never know which version of Sam I'm going to get, which makes me skittish about trying to pick up anything she puts down.

Sam huffs a laugh. "Well, if awkward and honest is on offer, I'll take it."

"I'm thinking about your champion," I admit. I glance sidelong at Rook's second. "I'm thinking about what he said at the presser. And about how he'd feel about his second cozying up to, what was it again? Oh right, the nepo kid who's nothing without her father." I exhale hard, and tear my eyes away from Sam's face, which has settled back into that familiar, guardedly neutral expression. "I can't imagine he'd approve of the company you're keeping."

"Let me worry about that." Sam's fingers slip into the crook of my elbow, unobtrusive and gentle. I'm pretty sure that if I shake her off right now, she'll let me and pretend it never happened.

I don't. The fingers remain.

"I've been handling Rook for nearly three years now. I've dealt with a temper tantrum or two in my time. I can manage him. Trust." Sam's voice is light, but there's an undercurrent of bitterness lacing the words. "Rook wouldn't be Rook if he weren't also a diva. Forget him for a bit. Let's just try to have fun. Be teenagers instead of serious magicians, for once."

I laugh. "Okay, fine, fair enough. We'll . . . be teenagers." We keep walking toward Arcane New York in companionable silence.

It's surreal to think about being a teenager without thinking about being a magician first. Still, Sam's doing a good job of pulling off the vibe. With her hand resting on my elbow, we could be any two girls hanging out on a cool weekend evening in the city. We might even look like best friends. Or maybe we're not familiar enough for that. Maybe we're still getting to know each other, a couple of kids on a date in the Big Apple. Carefree teenagers in the first throes of a budding puppy love that might yet be.

We aren't any of these things, though. The only reason I have the luxury of pretending is probably because Sam's feeling bad about Rook's behavior.

I still haven't decided whether or not to trust her. But I can't deny that I want to.

It doesn't take us long to descend upon the section of the city dubbed Arcane New York. It's funny to think that this little piece of New York City—so steeped now in mysticism—was originally named by economic-minded magicians to drum up business for our industry: just an easy-to-remember, tourist-friendly name for a collection of streets off the beaten path where you can find a bunch of fun, sparkly magic shops.

Beneath the fashionable veneer of arcane history and lore, the shops in Arcane New York mostly sell supplies for magicians active on the dueling circuit: everything from special recovery creams for spells gone awry to instructional tomes on the most effective dueling strategies.

"I think this counts as having fun," Sam decides, staring at one of the shop fronts. "We're being very good teenagers, I'd say. Isn't this what other kids our age do to hang out with each other? Go shopping?"

"I can't actually tell if you're being sarcastic or not."

Sam finally smiles at me. She's got a surprisingly goofy grin. "People tell me that's part of my charm," she deadpans.

"I don't know if it counts as shopping if neither of us buys anything."

"Don't say that." Sam's gaze drifts across several other shop fronts. "That's too much temptation in one sentence."

I follow her gaze. I see immediately what she means. The store window displays on this street are a honey trap for magic enthusiasts everywhere. One shop front boasts the latest in magicians' fashions. Mannequins have been outfitted in dueling robes in a glorious array of colors, from a lustrous midnight blue to a shade of pink so delicate, it looks stolen right off the petals of the palest cherry blossoms. Sweat-wicking compression gear is advertised in the next window: sleek bodysuits worn like a second skin beneath the robes, some in classic monochrome neutrals like black or white, others boasting patterns and artwork in a burst of color.

I catch myself eyeing one of the bodysuits, a pretty lilac number with a subtle crisscross pattern of shimmering gold over the V-neck bust, and immediately jerk my gaze away only to have it caught by the next shop front, which is running a sale on rare instructional tomes. I drift that way, almost unconsciously, scanning titles for familiar names: Maurice Ibrahim, who's considered the foremost authority on using defensive shielding to create offensive openings; Robin Suzuki-Carlisle, one of the most prolific writers in the magical community, who's credited as the father of modern dueling rulesets for today's magicians; and of course, Anna Maria Kim, who wrote the book—literally—on magical enhancements to physical hand-to-hand sequences in a duel. Some of their earlier books are out of print, but perhaps—

Sam clears her throat behind me—very loudly. "Are you feeling sufficiently distracted from that presser?"

I tear my eyes away from the shop fronts. "Is that what this was about? Cheering me up?"

That's almost, well, sweet.

"No," she tells me mulishly. "It's about having fun." I don't miss the way her own gaze flicks back toward the shop front—nor do I miss the faint look of longing behind her eyes. Even Samatha Chan isn't immune to the capitalistic charms of Arcane New York, it seems. "I think it counts as having fun, even if we're just window shopping. Girls at school do it all the time."

I laugh. "You talk about girls at school like they're exotic alien creatures."

"They might as well be." There's no heat or defensiveness in how Sam says it. She's still staring at the bookstore display. "We're the same age. Same demographics. But we live completely different lives. Aside from like, three hours in the day where we share the same physics lab and maybe a couple study hall periods, what do we have in common?"

From anyone else, a statement like that might have sounded lofty or dismissive. Another cringey, self-important I'm not like other girls–style speech. But that's not what it sounds like coming from Sam, though. Coming from Sam, it sounds like yearning.

I know because I've felt it, too. Yearning born from too many hours studying magic with Dad, born from missed slumber parties and rejected birthday party invitations. Magic always came first. I stare at the mannequin display, trying to remember the last time I had another girl my age to go shopping with. Another girl who knew me well enough to want to.

"I don't know," I tell Sam at last. "Do you know how to have a conversation with other girls about anything other than magic?"

"Nope." It's bluntly said, without regret, but she offers me a curiously sad smile. "I wish I did."

Damn. I bite my lip. I'm pretty sure I just put my foot in my mouth, but if I apologize—it's so hard to curb the constant instinct to apologize—I'll just draw even more attention to my faux pas. I glance back at the bookstore display to escape Sam's gaze, but I'm not really taking in any of the titles. "Let's check some of these out," I offer, hoping I still sound sufficiently chipper. "I want to see if they've got any of the other Maurice Ibrahim titles. Who knows? If they've got some of his earlier stuff, it might actually be worth splurging on."

"Can't argue with that. Lead on, Tamsin Blackwood."

I do. I love bookstores, magical or otherwise. I make a beeline for the display I saw. I'm rewarded when I discover three other Ibrahim books buried beneath the first tome. My eyebrows climb when I notice a discount sticker on one of them. Temptation, indeed. The last thing

I need right now is to be spending money I don't have—but surely, buying a Maurice Ibrahim book would count as an investment in the future of my career.

I look around for Sam and find her poring over what looks like a coffee table book—a huge, luxuriously well-crafted tome of black-and-white photographs.

"What is that?" I snag the discounted Maurice Ibrahim title before I can chicken out—or before another customer can snap it up first—and wander over to where Sam's flipping through the glossy photo collection.

"I think it's a photographer's account on the history of underground dueling." She glances up at me over the book. There's a flat, unreadable look in her eyes that puts me oddly on edge. "Weird to think the heyday wasn't that long ago, isn't it?"

"I guess it depends on what you mean by long ago." I examine the book warily. "Magicians' duels were legalized before we were born."

"Sure, but that was what, less than a generation ago?" Her voice is hard. "And it's not like legalizing dueling made the underground just, like, suddenly go away, you know."

I do know. All too well.

My stomach churns uncomfortably. I've never known the exact nasty details of Dad's involvement in the underground scene, but I know he did a whole lot more than just dabbling. It's not unusual to find an old-school magician who maybe had a passing flirtation with illegal dueling, back before they had legitimate means to practice their craft. It's not even that unusual to find a few who soured on the mainstream circuit for one reason or another and dipped their toes in the underground in defiance.

What Dad's done is a whole lot more than toe dipping, though. I'm pretty sure he operated at least one full-blown underground dueling club, but there were probably more that he never told me about.

"There's whole section in here on illegal duels that went badly wrong," says Sam. She shivers. "Can you imagine?"

"I don't think I'd want to. That's pretty gnarly."

"How many of these dueling clubs still exist, you think?" Sam turns a page slowly, careful not to wrinkle or tear anything. "The illegal ones, I mean. There's got to be a few underground clubs still in operation, right? The scene's probably never going to totally die. Too many people out there hungry for a taste of something illicit."

"There definitely are," I say, maybe a bit more sharply than I should. "Why does it matter?"

Sam looks up from the book, startled. "What's up with you?"

"Sorry." I backpedal so hard, it's embarrassing. "I just . . . The underground scene is a pretty nasty business. The way it exploits magicians who don't have anywhere else to go, the way it plays fast and loose with legitimate dueling rules and, like, romanticizes the idea of using really dangerous spells. I don't like thinking about it." I shake my head. "I don't even know why anyone would willingly put themselves through it, knowing what it is."

Sam looks, for a minute, like she wants to say something. Then she goes quiet as she flips another page in the book. Her brow furrows.

"Sam?" I slide a few inches closer to her, my movements cautious. "Look, again, I'm sorry. I don't mean to sound like I've got a stick up my ass."

No answer. Sam's just staring at the photograph spread across the center of the page. I follow her gaze.

A young man lies prone in the center of a magicians' arena. Blood has been spattered from his body like paint on canvas, soaking into the stark white floor of the arena. He's contorted at an angle so extreme, it looks posed on purpose, and it's more horrifying because we all know it wasn't.

A few feet away, his opponent kneels with one knee up, one dipped in a puddle of the young man's blood. The opponent's face is bent toward his victim, caught in shadow, the expression hidden.

It's a gorgeous piece of photography. It's also the most horrifying piece of art I've seen in a long time.

"He looks just like my brother," Sam says dully. "That man, lying there in his own blood. There were all these pictures people took of the night Jamie died, and they all looked just like this one."

Her words pull my gaze off the book, toward her. She's gone gray as she stares unblinking at the photograph. Her fingers tremble as she moves to turn to the next photograph. Her pinkie nicks the side of the page. A drop of bright red blood spatters onto the edge of the book.

I catch Sam's bleeding hand and slam the book shut. Sam barely reacts. Her hand sits cold and clammy in mine as she continues looking dully at the book. "I should pay for that," she says. "I've stained it."

"It's nothing," I say roughly. "Come on, let's get some air."

I tug Sam back toward the shop exit. She offers hardly any resistance at all, stumbling after me, her fingers limp. I pause to return the Maurice Ibrahim book to its shelf with a mental apology. *I'll come back for you*, I promise silently.

Then I push Sam out into the open air of the street outside.

12

SAM

THE SKY'S GROWN DARK. Night embraces us as Tamsin drags me down the block. She finds a bench near one of the boutiques on the next corner and plops me right down on the edge, as if I weigh nothing at all.

The world tilts around me. All I see is the camera footage all those Internet denizens shared of my brother's disastrous, final night in an arcane arena. The blood, the broken limbs, the way he barely even looked like himself anymore. Jamie's ghost might as well be screaming in my ear.

The daughter of my brother's murderer kneels beside me, her hand on the small of my back. "Hey. You okay?"

What an absurd question.

"You're going to be okay," says Tamsin Blackwood. Her fingers rub my back, warm to the touch. "You're going to be just fine."

And strangely, horribly, in that moment, I believe her, just a little. I hate that I believe her. I hate how soothing her touch feels on my body. But I don't hate either of those things enough to pull away from Tamsin.

We stay like that as minutes crawl by: me shaking like a leaf in the wind while Tamsin Blackwood rubs my back.

"Thanks," I finally croak.

Tamsin frowns, leaning a little closer. "What was that?"

I lift my head. "I said thanks." I wince at how rough my own voice sounds. "I— You didn't have to do that for me."

"Of course I did." Tamsin sounds a little aghast. "You think I'd just leave you in there with that book?"

"It's just a book, Tamsin." I laugh harshly. "It can't hurt me."

"But it did, didn't it? Or that one photo did, anyway." Tamsin gnaws at her lower lip, sucking on it through her teeth. I'm briefly mesmerized. "We don't need to talk about it, if you don't want to." She hesitates. "But if you want to, I don't mind." She peers at me with eyes full of caution. It would be kind of cute, under different circumstances. "You said something about . . . about your brother?"

I close my eyes. This is dangerous territory. I never planned to breathe a word about Jamie to Tamsin Blackwood. What would be the point? Tamsin was never the Blackwood I intended to punish. As long as her father got his just desserts, what his daughter did or didn't know about my brother wouldn't matter.

And then I saw the photograph in that book, and all my neatly laid plans came crashing down around me in a roar of awful, blood-soaked memory.

"Jamie," I say at last. "His name was Jamie."

"And your brother, Jamie, he—"

"He got mixed up in the illegal dueling business, and that same business got him killed." I get the words out quickly, spitting them out like bile.

"I'm sorry."

I rub at my eyes with the heels of my palms, breathing out slowly. *Come on, Chan. Get a hold of yourself.* With a grunt, I force myself back to my feet. To my relief, the world around me remains in focus this time. "Walk with me."

"Where?"

"I don't care. But let's walk. I can't stand looking like I'm sulking. At least let me disguise it a little." I glance down the block. Eenie, meenie, miney, mo. I pick a random storefront. "How about this? Let's window shop, as girls like us do, and I'll tell you all about my tragic dead brother."

Tamsin looks hilariously horrified at my word choice. She really is adorable, for a Blackwood. "You don't have to—"

"But I want to." I hesitate. Maybe I'm playing the painful truths angle too hard. "Unless this is all too much. We can head back to the hotel, and—"

"No!" Tamsin grabs my hand again, so hard that it actually startles me this time. "I told you I wanted to listen, if you wanted to talk. I still do."

I feel the side of my mouth quirk upward despite my best efforts. "Okay, okay, twist my arm. Window shopping it is, then."

Tamsin follows obediently in my wake. As luck would have it, I've picked a good shop to peruse for eye candy. The interior décor is gorgeous: dramatically dark wooden finishes on everything from the walls to the furniture that lend an era of mystique to the whole place. Silks and velvets in rich jewel tones ranging from ruby red to amethyst purple are draped across display counters and hung up as curtains in the windows, while crystal chandeliers overhead cast everything indoors into simulated twilight on an autumn evening. It's like something out of the fabled old world of magicians, the wild, dangerous place that existed before magic was confined within the walls of magicians' arenas for the safe and largely sanitized entertainment of the world at large. It's one of those all-purpose magical boutiques that seems to stock a little bit of everything—and this one, with its spot on one of the most prominent streets in magical New York, is definitely higher end.

There's one section for sartorial needs: robes designed for both active dueling in an arena and for the rigors of daily training, plus the accompanying bodysuits to protect the magician's skin. There's a miniature book display featuring most of the same titles we saw in the window of its neighboring bookshop, minus the discount markers. There's even an apothecary's section full of potions and tonics to use as supplements—all guaranteed to be competition legal under the latest dueling ruleset regulations. I know some magicians who budget in the hundreds for a veritable medicine cabinet full of those potions, to aid recovery, to enhance strength gain, to improve the conversion efficiency of a body's physical energy into usable magic.

It's the kind of thing my brother would have gone nuts for when he was alive.

"Magic was the only thing Jamie and I really had in common," I say aloud. I've practically forgotten that Tamsin is still standing there, she's so quiet. I might as well be talking to myself. Still, it feels weirdly good, to talk about Jamie. I don't remember the last time I talked about my brother, even to empty air. "But it meant everything to us. Having a brother like Jamie can be . . . Well, he was wonderful, but he could be a lot."

"Like a diva?" asks Tamsin.

"Nah, that would have made things easier." I chuckle. "He had every right to be an arrogant dick. Handsome, smart, charismatic, and of course, good at magic. When I was younger, I wanted to hate him, but he was just so *nice*. You can't hate someone that nice, even if they are your brother and better than you at everything, on top of it all."

"You were jealous of him."

"Not quite." I do actually have to stop and think about that idea. "I mean, I don't think I wanted to *be* Jamie. I wouldn't know what to do with all the attention and adoration he got. I think I'd find it overwhelming. But he did make me feel . . . wistful, I guess. Having to constantly stand beside him. Constantly being treated as a pair. There was Jamie, who was that talented, that good-looking, that extroverted, and just so effortlessly *easy* with people. And then there was me." I offer Tamsin a wry look and hold out my palms, partly covered by the cuffs of my careworn hoodie. "Who was just me."

Tamsin chuckles. "Fair."

"Jamie sometimes felt like the sun itself. So full of warmth and life. So bright and comforting. So easy to love. But hard to look at directly, sometimes. And when you got him in a shitty mood, god, it was like standing in direct sunlight on the most sweltering summer of the year. Exhausting. Miserable. Genuinely painful, sometimes."

"He sounds like Lysander Rook," observes Tamsin.

Her words hit me right in the gut. I stiffen without meaning to. "Not really."

Before Tamsin can apologize again, I recover—enough to smile at her, hoping that I look at least a little reassuring. "I get why you'd think so," I allow. "Both pretty boys who know they're pretty boys—and both peacocks as a result, if in different ways. Both more talented in magic than seemed totally fair to the rest of us. Both capable of totally taking over a room full of people without even trying."

"But?" ventures Tamsin, sounding cautious.

"But Jamie was . . . well, happy, in his default setting." I speak slowly, trying to choose the right words. The right words are always so important. "Don't get me wrong: He got mad and sad and pissy just like anyone else. But I know, at baseline, my brother was happy with his life. Content. Stable."

"And Rook's not?"

I almost laugh, and I can't quite tamp down the hint of cruelty in my voice when I snap, "You just shared a press event with him. Does my champion strike you as an especially happy person?"

To her credit, Tamsin only looks cowed for a moment before she retorts, "You say Jamie was happier than Rook. But Sam, in my experience, happy people don't get involved with underground dueling."

There's that gut punch again. The truth behind Tamsin's words only makes them hurt more. "You're right," I admit because what's the point in denying it? "They don't. That's what you're asking, right? How a guy like my brother—the golden boy I've described—could possibly debase himself in an underground dueling club?"

Tamsin flinches. "That's not what I—"

"No, no, a lot of his friends wondered the same thing." I'm pretty sure I'm dissociating. As I speak, the past envelops me, more wholly than it has in years. "The truth is, the night he died in that club, he wasn't there for himself. He was there for one of them. His friends." I chuckle bitterly. "His many, many idiot friends."

"What happened?"

"Do you remember the worst of the clubs?" I ask Tamsin. "The ones that let underage kids duel?"

She should. Her father used them to finance her entire arcane career. And judging from the look on her face, she's not completely naive to that. Good. I'll feel better about destroying her, this way. Maybe telling her about Jamie isn't such a bad idea. Maybe my family's sob story will get under her skin. Make it easier for Rook to break her.

"It was a headliner," I continue. "The kid who was supposed to enter the duel was just a few years younger than we are now. Franklin Park. Less than half as experienced as you, with probably less than half the skill, obviously, but not bad for an average high schooler picking up magic as a hobby. One of Jamie's buddies, always hanging out with my brother, practically worshipping the ground he walked on. Not the brightest bulb, but a sweet kid. Always nice to me even though he didn't have to be. But Franklin always had this super romanticized idea of dueling, so when the underground promoters went after him, he didn't even hesitate to sign on the dotted line.

"Franklin's opponent was some knuckle-dragging brute of a magician way past his prime. It was terrible matchmaking, obviously. They designed the whole show for pure spectacle, more than any actual showcase of magical skill and showmanship. Franklin had delusions of grandeur like every other fifteen-year-old who's not you or Rook, and the old brute was a petty criminal paid to rough up newcomers to the arena for shock value and the cheers of a bloodthirsty crowd. The whole thing was gross.

"When Jamie found out what Franklin got himself mixed up in, I've never seen him so mad. He talked Franklin out of the duel at the last minute, but the promoter needed a replacement. They would have gone after Franklin and his family if he couldn't find one."

I make sure I look Tamsin Blackwood right in the eyes when I tell her, "You can probably guess what happened next."

"Tell me," whispers Tamsin, looking sick at heart. She wants to hear it from me. Even if she already knows how this story ends. There must be more than a little masochism in this girl.

I'm more than happy to indulge it.

"Jamie stepped up. He was a good magician, even at just eighteen. Did pretty well for himself on local—and, might I add, legal—magicians' dueling circuits. But he wasn't ready for the brutality of an illegal show, at an underground location, in front of this awful, ravenous audience calling for his blood. And he wasn't ready for his opponent's brute strength, or the scumbag's refusal to honor, you know, what would have been civilized rules in a sanctioned magicians' duel."

My voice has gone thick—it always does, when I talk about this part—but I force myself to keep going. "I wasn't there. But what I heard was that in the end, the duel that took place that night was barely a duel at all. And by the time the brute was done with him, what was left of my brother in that arena was barely recognizable."

Tamsin's face goes grayer and grayer with every word that comes out of my mouth. "Did anyone ever catch the guy who did it?"

I shake my head. "They tried, but nothing stuck. Too much gray area in all the legalities. Jamie was technically no longer a minor, and he did sign a contract." I bark a humorless laugh. "Nothing anyone could do about a consenting adult signing away life and limb to yet another grisly occult ritual, you know?"

"God, I'm so sorry."

I'm sure she is. Not that it makes a difference. I made up my mind about Tamsin Blackwood's fate a long time ago. "Nothing anyone can do about it now."

"Do you at least know who your brother's scumbag opponent was?"

"Oh, that? Yeah. Not like it matters, though." I fix Blackwood's daughter with a flinty-eyed gaze. Tamsin's not stupid. She obviously knows her father isn't all sunshine and rainbows. But now, I find myself wondering just how deep her knowledge of his evil goes.

Maybe she deserves to know what her father did to my brother. If I can drive a real rift between the Blackwoods before Tamsin even enters the arena, Rook will barely have to touch her to make her crumble. And what kind of second would I be, if I didn't do everything possible to make my champion's job easier?

"Alexei Adamovich apparently died in another dueling accident a few years later," I say. I emphasize the syllables of the offending name carefully and smile at Tamsin, all hard edges. "So I guess what goes around comes around, right?"

Tamsin's features go slack for a few seconds before she recovers, blinking rapidly. "Right," she agrees, her voice shaky. "I'm . . . glad he got what was coming to him."

It's an admirable recovery, all things considered. But I'm better at reading people than most realize. And my gut knows, immediately, right in that moment: Tamsin recognizes Alexei's name.

Which means that Blackwood's daughter has just discovered that her father's a murderer.

The next few hours blur together in the frenzy of Tamsin's aggressive attempts to impose good cheer on me. Or maybe she's projecting. I can't imagine it feels great to have the worst possible rumors about your own father confirmed. Ironic, in any case, that a night which began with my own clumsy attempts to boost her spirits would end with this kind of role reversal. You could read it as a kind of comedy, I suppose: two rival magicians falling all over each other to be the nicer one, the more gallant, the more gracious.

Arcane New York rises to the occasion. Tamsin's hand may be the one tugging me down those winding streets, but the soft-lit storefronts enchant me as surely as they enchant my companion. We're both magicians, after all.

For a while, we're both content to pivot from dark family secrets to small talk and *ooh*ing and *aah*ing over fancy displays of dueling robes and grimoires. Or so it seems to me. I'm genuinely surprised when Tamsin rounds on me and blurts out, "Do you ever worry about turning into your parents when you get older?"

I blink quizzically at her. We've parked ourselves on the outer porch of a shop selling magical antiques. Neither of us can come close to affording anything in there. The porch is nice, though. I like the comfy hammock-style seats they've set up outside the doorway, where Tamsin and I swing side by side, talking about nothing of consequence.

Until now, I guess. I lick my lips awkwardly. "I've never really thought about it," I say carefully. It's an honest response—a truly honest response, for once. "My parents and I aren't super close. That's not necessarily a bad thing," I add hastily as pity threatens to invade Tamsin's expression. "I know they love me, but love isn't the same thing as *getting* each other, as people. Mom and Dad, they never really approved *or* disapproved of having magicians for kids. I don't think they had an opinion on magic, period, as long as it made me and Jamie happy. I guess it helped that we were good at it." I shrug. "My parents aren't bad at being parents. They take care of me. They want good things for me. They'll try their best to listen if I want to talk to them."

"But you don't want to talk to them."

"More like I don't have much to say." I offer Tamsin a crooked smile. "I love my parents. And my parents love me. But it's love of duty, not preference. We don't speak the same language. And that's okay."

The only person in my family who spoke the same language as me was Jamie.

I shake my head and the unwanted memories with it. "Anyway, to answer your actual question, no, I don't worry about turning into my parents. I don't think I could even if I tried."

Tamsin pulls her knees into her chest as she rocks a little harder on her hammock. She's frowning, but not at me. "I think maybe my dad and I have the opposite problem. We're too much alike—care too much about the same things. Maybe that's why I worry about turning out like him."

I watch Blackwood's daughter carefully. It's not lost on me that this particular crisis of identity has reared its head on the heels of Tamsin's discovery of what her father did to my brother. "You think you're going to turn out like your dad because you're both magicians?"

"That's a bit of an oversimplification, isn't it?" Tamsin huffs a frustrated sigh, but I don't think it's directed at me. "It's not just that we're both magicians. It's how hungry we both are. How ambitious." She shivers as she hugs her knees tighter. "I've seen what Dad's willing to do to get what he wants. What if the only reason I haven't done the same, or worse, is because I haven't been pushed? Because he does the dirty work for me?"

"That's bullshit." The immediacy of my own response surprises me. "I've met your dad. You're nothing like him."

Truth, and more truth. What's gotten into me lately?

Tamsin glances at me sidelong. Her pretty cheeks have gone pink. I can't quite read her face, but if I were the betting type, I'd call her expression hopeful. Something flutters in my belly. "You're a good friend, Sam. You know that?"

I swallow hard. Now it's my turn to feel my cheeks go warm. "Not really. I don't have many friends. Well, unless you count Rook."

Tamsin laughs. It seems to unlock something inside her. Her posture finally loosens up a little as she lets that white-knuckled grip on her knees go. Her long legs dangle off the edge of hammock, mesmerizing me. "You poor thing."

"Hey! He's not that bad!"

Tamsin keeps chuckling for a few seconds before growing somber again. She doesn't pull her knees back into her chest, though. Instead, her legs continue to dangle as she looks at me thoughtfully, head tilted to one side. "It's hard, isn't it?"

"What, being Rook's second? You have no idea."

"Making friends." She kicks my ankle lightly. "It's hard for me, too. You said earlier that you don't know how to talk to other girls our age about anything but magic. I feel that, too." She shrugs. "I tell myself all the time, that's the cost of living the way we do. It's not like we have time to go out for movies, or play normal sports, or god forbid, go to parties. We're too busy. Always chasing another victory in the arena. Always trying to prove to the world how good we are. Trying to be our best." She bites her lip. "Being the best is lonely."

I snort. "Master Silverstein—our arcane master—used to tell me and Rook that magic is a jealous mistress. If you're going to master her, she won't tolerate time spent on much else."

"It's true," groans Tamsin. She rubs her eyes with the heels of her hands. "God, I hate how true that is. We're going to die alone, Sam."

"Hey." Impulsively, I scoot sideways on my hammock seat so I can knock my knee against hers. "Not quite alone. We've got each other now, don't we?"

Tamsin looks up at me, eyes wide with surprise. Then, all at once, her face breaks into the biggest smile I've ever seen. It practically stops my heart in my chest, right then and there. God, forget Blythe Davison and her perfect lipstick. When Tamsin Blackwood smiles, she's prettier than any girl has any right to be. "We do, don't we?"

Without warning, Tamsin grabs the crook of my elbow and drags me off my hammock. I yelp as she begins marching me toward the entrance of the antique shop. "Well, come on, then. If we're going to fill each other's sad teen quota for actual friends, we've got to spend at least thirty minutes looking at a bunch of pretty things we can't afford to buy. It's like, teen girl friendship rules, or so I hear."

Who am I to deny the rules of teen girl friendship? With an artfully exaggerated groan, I let Tamsin drag me into the shop.

It's past midnight and dark as sin by the time I get back to the hotel suite I'm sharing with Rook.

I've had alcohol once, maybe twice, in my entire life. A few sips of wine at my parents' dinner table when I was younger. A very light beer that Jamie snuck me once, at some party I insisted on following him to when I was fifteen, after which he watched me like a hawk all night long.

I've spent a few hours in the company of Tamsin Blackwood, and I feel drunker than I ever have in my life. Yet I haven't had a drop to drink.

I need to get ahold of myself. Blackwood's daughter is a means to an end. That's all. I can't afford to make this personal, not when I'm so close to everything I want.

Even if I still feel the ghost of Tamsin's hand rubbing my back, as I saw Jamie die in my mind's eye, over and over again. Even if the image of her face, open and guileless and utterly sympathetic, is imprinted on my memory. Even if I can still see the horror dawning on her face as she silently realized what her father must have done to my brother.

Before I met Tamsin, I thought she'd be more like her father. But she's not. She's nothing like Mateus Blackwood at all.

And I hate that for us both.

With a frustrated groan, I fling myself onto the hotel bed. Immediately, I bury my face against one of those fresh, fluffy pillows. I'm warm everywhere, and my heart rate must be through the roof.

Blackwood is the reason my brother is dead. Alexei Adamovich, the big dumb brute, may have been the one to strike the killing blow against my brother, but Alexei was simply a weapon. Tamsin Blackwood's father was the hand that wielded him. I will never forgive Mateus Blackwood for that. I won't let myself betray Jamie that way.

But tonight, Tamsin has come dangerously close to making me second-guess myself. If there were a world where I could destroy Mateus while sparing Tamsin, maybe I'd choose that one. That beautiful, perfect fantasy world.

But I live in reality.

So why does the thought of Rook destroying her in that arena—and he will destroy her there, I've done everything possible to ensure that—make my heart freeze in my chest?

I don't have time for this. I scroll through my phone, hunting for a productive distraction. There's the mess from the press event that needs to be smoothed over, of course. Rook accomplished my intended task of shaking Tamsin up, all right, but it won't do for his fans to turn on him. The last thing I need is for Tamsin to be painted as some poor, sympathetic damsel in distress. It's a delicate balance to strike, letting Rook ruin her without making her a martyr.

I draft a few pithy little social media statements to post from Rook's accounts that will likely mollify some of the less virulent haters, the ones who can still be reasoned with. Social media and online conversation has always come easier to me than person-to-person interaction. I like having the distance of a screen between myself and the rest of the world. I like having the time and space to choose my words carefully and the safety of curation in a world where the look on my face won't give me away.

I wonder if Mateus Blackwood ever does this for Tamsin. Lies around in bed trying to clean up her image from behind a phone screen. Probably not. For one thing, Blackwood doesn't really seem the type, and for another, I doubt there's much to clean up. His daughter is so stupidly, infectiously charming. It's a charm that stems from either a genuine desire to listen to people talk about whatever they want or a very impressive talent for faking interest. Either way, it works wonders for her.

It even, apparently, works on me, despite my best efforts.

I deal with the problem the way I think most people deal with problems they can't solve at nearly two in the morning: I go to bed in hopes that my brain will somehow invent a solution by the time I wake up.

I've changed into pajamas, and I'm about to close my eyes when I hear the scream.

My heart stops. I'd recognize that voice anywhere. And it's not the first time I've heard that sound.

I'm out of bed before I realize it and sprinting toward the bedroom in the other half of the suite. I swear loudly, when I stub a toe rounding the corner, but even that doesn't slow me down. I bang a fist on the bedroom door. "Hello?" I demand. "Hey, are you awake?"

All I get in response is a second cry of distress. Then the muffled sounds of sobbing.

Screw this. I fling the bedroom door open. Rook's twisted up in his sheets, bare chest heaving, dark hair plastered to his forehead.

I'm at his side before I even notice my own feet crossing the floor. "Rook. Hey, it's okay, princess, it's okay, wake up."

Rook continues to twist around, whimpering, eyes squeezed shut. I reach cautiously for him. I need to wake him. I need to put an end to the night terror he's stuck in.

"No!" Rook cries out on his sleep. Magic threads its way through his fingers.

I barely summon a shield in time as Rook's power roars over me. My spell is flimsier than it would normally be, though. One piece of the shield breaks off. A crackle of magical energy bursts through, grazing my cheek.

I hiss in pain, clapping one hand to my face as our collective magic simmers down.

"Sammy?" Rook's voice is still panicked, but he sounds awake now, if still groggy from the nightmare. "Sam, is that you?"

"I'm here." I dab gingerly at my cheek. No blood, though the spell will probably leave a mark. Still half-blind, I fumble for the bedside lamp and flick it on. "Are you all right?"

I realize it's a stupid question as soon as I look up at Rook in full lighting. He's staring back at me with wild blue eyes. His already dark hair is tousled and further darkened with sweat, sticking out in every direction. He's sickly pale with deep purple shadows under his eyes. He looks like he's been through a duel already and taken his first loss.

He's very obviously not all right.

His fingers close over the hand I've pressed to my cheek. "You're hurt." Then, in a different voice, "I hurt you."

I shake my head. "You didn't know what you were doing."

"But I hurt you."

"You were literally asleep, Rook."

He peers up at me through a dark, sweat-soaked fringe of hair. "Are you mad?"

"About what?"

"Jensen Sykes," he clarifies. The side of Rook's mouth twists as he shakes his head. "How many times has that guy written about me? You'd think I'd be smart enough not to take his bait by now. But I'm not. Now I look like an asshole."

I open my mouth and close it again, trying to figure out how best to weigh my words. What can I possibly say when Rook did, in fact, exactly what I wanted? "What's done is done," I settle on at last. "You wouldn't be the first magician Sykes has provoked. He's always had that weird sixth sense for what buttons to push to get a reaction on any given day, you know? And most of the magicians he gets a rise out of are years more experienced than you."

Rook snuffs a bitter little laugh. "*Every* magician on this dueling circuit is years more experienced than me. It's only because I'm young, you know."

"What's that supposed to mean?"

Rook looks me in the eye. He seems more himself now, but there's always been a sort of haunted quality to him whether he sleeps or wakes. It's usually overshadowed by other things: swagger, or cheek, or that same obsessive dedication to magic that we share. But right now, he just looks haunted. Haunted and tired.

"Half my appeal is my age," says Rook. "As long as the press get to print clickbait about the teen phenom who can beat up adult magicians, they know they can go viral and make their advertisers happy. But what happens when I turn twenty? What about twenty-five? Thirty? Forty? What then?"

"You won't be forty when you duel Tamsin Blackwood."

"Sure. But I will be, twenty-two years from now—if I'm still alive, anyway. And what then?" Rook spreads his hands over the comforter and offers me a wan smile. "How long do I get to stay a child prodigy? No one's a child forever."

Unwanted guilt claws at my heart. I've never thought about what Rook's career would look like past age eighteen. At eighteen, he'd be my weapon in my private war against Mateus Blackwood. At eighteen, he'd fulfill the purpose for which I'd forged him.

I never really thought about what would happen after that final battle. To either of us. It never really occurred to me to care, I guess.

Jamie would have cared.

I recoil from the thought. I'm not my brother, and I never will be. No one will be Jamie ever again, not even close.

"Twenty-two years is an awfully long time," I tell Rook, which is a coward's answer, but I don't have anything better for him. "I don't think it's super productive to spend all your time at age eighteen brooding over what your life's gonna look like a couple decades from now, you know? For one thing, we have no clue what the world's even going to be like twenty years from now. Maybe hot fortysomething-year-old magicians will be all the rage. Silver foxes making their comeback, or something."

Rook doesn't smile. "I just want to know how long I'll be relevant for. At least then I'd be ready."

"Ready for what?"

He shrugs. "I don't know. To be abandoned, I guess. It hurts less if you know it's going to happen."

I sigh and straighten the blankets around him. "Is that what you were dreaming about? Being abandoned?"

"I dreamed about you."

My hands pause on the blankets. "Me?"

He doesn't make eye contact with me, but there's a telltale vacant look in his gaze. Rook gets like this sometimes, the same way he gets petulant or arrogant or insecure. Sometimes, he's none of those things. Sometimes, the lights are on with him, but no one's really home—or someone is, but someone determined to keep their door shut, speaking only through walls and shuttered windows.

"I dreamed that you'd vanished one night," Rook tells me. "So I looked for you." He finally raises his eyes toward me, bright and blue and haunted. "I kept looking and looking, but you were gone. I just knew, after a certain point, that you were gone and never coming back."

I take his hands and squeeze them tight between mine. I pray that it's enough to remind him he's awake. That I'm right here with him. "And then you woke up?"

"And then I woke up." A harsh chuckle escapes him. His hands are clammy and cold between mine, but he doesn't try to tug them free of my warmth. "And here you were. Thank you, by the way."

I bow my head. "I'm your second." I don't know what else to say but that.

He sighs. "And so you are." Dryly, he adds, "Cuddling me after my night terrors probably goes beyond even that call of duty, though."

"I'm an overachiever," I deadpan. Encouraged by the wan smile that earns me, I barrel on, "You're not going to lose me, you know."

And I find that in this moment, our fingers curled together, I mean it. I don't want to let Rook go. I've spent so much of our time together making him mine. My monster of a boy. My weapon. And, against all odds, maybe, just maybe, my friend.

Rook looks down at our entwined fingers. "You know there are rumors about us, right? You and me."

"There have always been rumors about us." I roll my eyes. "That's what happens when a girl and a boy of roughly the same age spend all their time in close quarters. It's never bothered you before."

"Who says I'm bothered?"

I do drop his hands at that. "Why bring it up, otherwise?"

"Just to remind you that I'm not the only one that people have eyes on." Rook's blue eyes practically glow in the dark at me, his expression deceptively neutral. "Do you really think a second is so invisible?"

I don't know where this is going, but I don't like it. "You're the one they're interested in. I'm only interesting by association."

"Not if you keep hanging out with my opponent."

I balk. "Rook—"

"You were with her out past midnight, Sammy." The words don't sound like a rebuke. Rook speaks softly—unusually softly, for him. He blinks those thick-lashed blue eyes at me. "You're smart enough to know how nuts the Internet will go over me starting beef with Tamsin Blackwood over some stupid question from Jensen Sykes. You're right, that can't be helped at this point. But what exactly do you think the Internet will do if enough people cotton on to you cozying up with the same girl I'm supposed to destroy in the arena?"

"And what exactly do you want me to do about that?" I retort. "Ignore her completely? The second's job is to study their champion's opponent. To make sure you're ready for anything she throws at you." I'm reaching, and I know it, but there's something hot and heavy in my chest spurring me on. "I need to make sure you win."

"Why?" Rook sounds genuinely curious. "I know why I need to win. But why does it matter so much to you?"

"It always matters to me. I'm your second, you're my champion, your wins are my victories, too."

"You don't sound like you're excited for me to win," my champion says. "You sound like you're afraid that I'll lose."

I try to retort, but I'm out of words. The stink of truth hangs in the air between us.

"I'm right, aren't I?" Rook wags a finger at me, wry faced. "I knew I was right. You've never been like this before a duel before."

"I always study your opponents."

"Not the way you study the Blackwood girl." Rook leans forward slightly. "What exactly is she to you?"

What, indeed.

"The way you look at her," Rook continues slowly, "I don't know if you hate her or if you're in love with her. Wouldn't that be a story for the Internet?"

"Bullshit," I insist.

"Bullshit that you hate her? Or bullshit you've fallen for her?"

"Neither! She's nothing. You said it yourself."

Rook shrugs. "Okay."

"I'm telling the truth."

"And when has the truth mattered to people on the Internet?" Rook's gaze bores into me. "If it really matters that much to you, though, it wouldn't take much to make a different rumor about you come true. Distract the gossip hounds with a more palatable story than whatever's going on between you and sweet little Tamsin. After all, I'm all yours—my time, my energy, my victories. You said it yourself. And I'm right here." He stares up at me through those stupidly thick black lashes. "You must have thought about it, at least a couple times. Everyone else has, you know. Those rumors about us didn't come from nowhere—and it's not just about being the same age. We're good together, Sam."

"At magic. We're good at magic, together."

He grins. "Precisely. We'd be the power couple of the magical world. No one would be surprised if you and I turned out to be a little more than a duelist and his second. Hell, the press probably expects us to announce we're dating any day now."

My mouth goes dry. I hate myself a little for that. The same way I hate myself for the way my gaze automatically drifts from Rook's fine-boned face down to his bare, moon-pale torso. He could be a classical statue, carefully honed, well-earned muscles popping out in stark relief beneath white skin still sheened in sweat. How many girls back at school would kill to be where I am right now, sitting on a bed with a half-naked Lysander Rook baring his body toward me in the dark? How many girls have thought about this exact view: Rook, beautiful and vulnerable, staring blue-eyed through long black lashes at them?

Everyone wants a piece of Rook. And now I'm the one who gets to have him—if I want him, that is. And why wouldn't I want him? Rook's objectively one of the hottest people I've ever met in real life—and I've collected enough unwanted phone numbers from lovelorn girls at school to prove that I'm not the only one who thinks so. Getting to be Lysander Rook's girl is the offer of a lifetime.

So why don't I want to say yes?

"If we got together," muses Rook, "you'd probably have to quit spending so much time around Tamsin Blackwood. I hear I'm the jealous type. At least according to all the gossips on social media."

I snap out of my reverie. "Is that what this is?" I demand. "Some weird honeypot ploy to get me to stop hanging out with Tamsin?"

"Would that be so bad?" Rook hasn't denied the accusation. He looks utterly unashamed, in fact, meeting my gaze directly, unblinking. "I'm your champion, Sam. Don't I matter more to you than whatever fascination you've got with the Blackwood girl?"

I stand up and, with an effort, jerk my gaze away from his body. "This is a ridiculous conversation, and you're a ridiculous person," I inform my champion. "I'm going back to bed before you propose some sort of unhinged arranged marriage."

"You know I'd ask Master Silverstein for your dowry, too." Despite his physical beauty, now that the immediate aftermath of the night terror has passed, Rook mostly just looks like what he is: exhausted, probably mildly overtrained, and terribly young. He grins up at me, defiant blue eyes hauntingly bright over the purple shadows underscoring them. He's challenging me, even now.

"Don't be stupid, princess," I tell my champion. "You'd obviously be the one paying the dowry, not me."

I turn on my heel and leave before he can steal the final word from me.

That night, I have dreams of my own.

I'm training with Rook in a simulated duel that's taken us into close quarters. I'm backed into a corner of the training arena, trying to stay in the pocket while I throw sloppy discs of magic toward him, but my energy wanes rapidly.

Air explodes from my lungs as my back hits the ground. Rook's not even touching me, but I'm pinned in place, both shoulders flat on the floor. In Rook's hands, my magic has been multiplied a hundredfold.

Almost casually, he ambles toward me to inspect his handiwork. "Yield?" he asks.

I shake my head, refusing to quit. I'm not ready to give up, not yet. Rook's suddenly nose to nose with me. I'm still pinned flat, and my champion is everywhere, overwhelming my senses, the hard planes of his body ghosting over mine, the scent of aftershave and sweat filling my nose.

I don't know who initiates what happens next. One moment, he's still hovering above me as I try to assess my options in our simulated duel. The next, our mouths are pressed together, sudden and inevitable and desperate.

But when he pulls his head back from the kiss, it's not Rook's familiar blue eyes that I'm looking into.

Tamsin Blackwood smiles down at me with that warm dark gaze, freckles stark against the blush misting her golden cheeks. "I've been waiting for you to finally do that," she breathes against my mouth.

Her lips brush over mine gently, then more insistent. I close my eyes. I lean into the kiss. And for a moment, I lose myself in it.

When I wake, my room is dark, and I'm alone in my bed. I've never felt more lost.

Master Silverstein makes me meet him for coffee the next morning.

I mumble an expletive at the text message on the screen. Noah Silverstein isn't one to give a ton away in his messages, but I've known our arcane master long enough to have a good guess at what this is about. When I stride into the coffeeshop whose address he sent me, the expression on his face all but confirms my suspicions. Silverstein's bushy brows are furrowed hard over a steaming mug of black coffee, and he doesn't smile when I sit down across from him.

"You were out late last night," he tells me without preamble.

I bury my automatic groan into my hands, which I rake through my unbrushed hair. I didn't even bother slicking it back into a ponytail before I left the hotel. "Which snitches are about to get stitches?"

"Come on, Samantha." Silverstein puts his coffee down and settles back into his seat. He looks like a detective interrogating a suspect, and I hate that the visual automatically makes me squirm. I can't be guilty if he hasn't accused me of anything. Yet.

"Was it Rook?" I ask from between my fingers.

"It was my own damn ears, if you must know." Silverstein fixes me with a thoroughly unimpressed stare. Judgment practically radiates from him. "You're not as quiet sneaking back into that suite as you think you are. And, as I've reminded you before, I'm right down the hall from the two of you."

"And I hate that for us both."

"Be serious, Chan." My master instructor leans forward, still unsmiling. "You've been off since we arrived in New York. And now you're sneaking around on your own in the city?"

I contain an involuntary little sigh of relief. So he doesn't know I was with Tamsin Blackwood. That's something, at least. One less thing I'll have to make up a lie or a half-truth to explain away.

"I'm sorry." I am, kind of. My respect for Silverstein is genuine, and I like him. But right now, all his mother-hen behavior is getting in my way. I can't afford to piss him off, so I can't say that, obviously. But I do need to convince him to back off.

"I just needed to clear my head" is what I settle on, at last. "I've told you before. Being here, for a duel of this magnitude, it's all just a lot, okay? I went for a walk through Arcane New York to get my head back on straight. I'm sorry it got late. I lost track of time. It won't happen again, okay?"

Silverstein keeps eyeing me like he wants to say more. I meet his gaze head-on. I don't want to give him any reason to think I've got something to hide. "How's Rook?" he asks at last.

"He still gets nightmares." I bite my lip then add, with what I hope is breezy confidence, "You know Rook, though. It's a natural response to being in the limelight. He'll still perform just fine on the big day."

"And in the meantime?"

My tone shifts. "I'll take care of him." I don't have to fake the steel in my voice. "You know I will. I always have."

Silverstein makes a noncommittal noise, but he doesn't look away, and he doesn't question my promise. For a moment, he looks like he might keep pushing the issue. Instead, he just grunts. "You been practicing much magic yourself?"

I'm surprised by the question. "A little when I need to blow off steam. Not really important right now, though, is it?"

"Come on, Samantha, don't keep kidding yourself." The old master gives me a wry look. "You need magic like you need to breathe. It's not just about the arena for you. It's not even just about winning. You love this shit. You love *magic*. You always have, long before you came to my training center. I could tell from the first day I met you."

Unbidden, my mind drifts toward the Four Elements. The flow of the sequence, every time I cast it, and how for just a few minutes, the act of magic sets me free. As free as I've ever felt, even when Jamie was still alive.

And, of course, how Tamsin Blackwood interrupted my last attempt to finish it.

I shut down the memory like a lock clicking into place. "Love is overrated. I'm here to make sure my champion brings his next victory home. That's what you sent me to New York for in the first place, right?" My jaw works. "I won't let you down. Either of you."

Silverstein looks, for just a moment, like he wants to argue with me. Then he sighs, obviously too weary to argue whatever point he was trying to make. "See that you don't stay out so late again," he orders instead. "It's game time. But remember that I don't just need you to take care of Rook. I need you to take care of yourself, too, you hear?"

"Loud and clear."

"I mean it, Samantha." Silverstein leans forward on his elbows. "You do anything that convinces me that either of you are endangering yourselves, I'll take you both straight home like a pair of schoolchildren, duel or no. I'm not scared to call the commissioner and cancel this whole deal. I don't care how hard you worked on negotiating it. I'll throw the whole thing out the window the second I believe that either of you can't handle it. Understand?"

That does, in fact, get my attention. I swallow hard. "Understood."

Noah Silverstein isn't a man in the habit of making threats lightly. I'm not sure what he knows—or what he thinks he knows. But I am sure of this: I'm going to have to tread carefully around him. I can't afford to get Rook pulled out of this duel. Not when I'm this close to everything I've wanted for the past four years.

I sit back in my seat and smile at Silverstein. "You won't have to make any calls to the commissioner. We'll be just fine. And this duel is going to be the magic show of the century." I lean forward. "Now that that's settled, let's talk duel strategy. I should update you on how Rook's practices are going."

13
TAMSIN

ONCE UPON A TIME, Alexei Adamovich was my father's favorite magic student.

It's all I can think about after Sam and I part ways. That I knew her brother's killer—knew his killer for years, in fact. Worse yet, I liked the guy. Because here's the thing: Alexei was always kind to me.

Isn't it awful to remember a villain that way? Alexei can't be anything other than a villain if what Sam told me is true. But I don't remember a villain. I remember Alexei the man. We didn't interact much when he was alive, but he always had a smile for me, kind words and easy praise, where Dad only offered criticism.

It might not sound like much. But when I was a kid, it was everything. All I wanted was for someone to tell me I was doing something right. And Alexei—big, brutish-looking, incongruously sweet-natured Alexei—never failed me.

But I also remember the last night Alexei ever spoke directly to me. And I hate how much of it makes sense now.

Dad had been running me through my usual drills at the training arena when Alexei stopped by. "I need to talk to you," Alexei said without preamble. He didn't look like himself. His face had gone gray. It made him look like a gargoyle: a hulking, nervous-eyed creature hovering over the mat where I'd been summoning the same streak of crackling magical power over and over again, left and right, ten times on each side, on the ninth rep on the right side, and already bored out of my mind.

"Hi, Alexei!" I piped up. I immediately dropped the ninth rep of the spell, pleased for the excuse to stop practicing that godforsaken drill.

Alexei hadn't been addressing me, though. He'd been addressing Dad, who greeted him with open arms. "Good old Adamovich," crowed Dad. "Come now, what's the matter?"

"You didn't say it was a kid."

"Didn't a replacement step up?"

The big man's gaze darted from side to side. He looked, if anything, even more nervous. "Yeah, another kid. God damn it, Mateus!"

Dad clapped Alexei on the back like this giant gargoyle of a man was a child. "Not in front of young Tamsin here. Let's discuss the matter out back." He glanced over his shoulder at me. "Tamsin, another ten reps on each side, please, then move into the Diving Lotus sequence."

For once, I didn't obey right away. I didn't even move, absorbed in this strange, heated exchange between the adults in my life. I'd never once heard Alexei swear at my father before. I'd never heard Alexei play anything other than the obedient student. The perfect magician, loyal to Master Mateus Blackwood, like so many other fawning disciples.

Like me.

Alexei didn't leave immediately, either. Instead, he looked past my father's shoulder, right into my eyes. He tried to smile, but even to my fourteen-year-old eyes, the smile didn't look all that convincing. "Listen to your dad, Tamsin," he said. "You'll be grateful to have a decent command of the Diving Lotus once you're a duelist yourself, even if you think it's boring right now."

"I never said it was boring," I insisted. I couldn't help pulling a face, though.

Alexei laughed. That, at least, sounded real. "Well, I'll help you practice once I clear up business with your dad. So make sure you're ready. I'm going to test you!"

He and my father disappeared after that. And, obedient as ever, I practiced the Diving Lotus sequence. I wanted to impress Alexei, which at least was a realistic goal. I'd already mostly given up on ever impressing Dad.

Alexei never tested me on the Diving Lotus sequence, though. Alexei never spoke to me again.

The remainder of that night still feels like a fractured memory. A bunch of guys from one of the clubs Dad wouldn't let me visit—one where he told me he sometimes did side hustle work—came by and kept talking to Dad in hushed voices. He'd sent them all away, impatient, but I overheard enough to know bits and pieces of what happened.

A boy had died. A teenager, barely old enough to be considered a legal adult. More specifically, a boy had died in an illegal duel at Dad's club.

In the weeks that followed, news of some anonymous teen magician's inglorious, back-alley death started appearing in all the magician forums and minor news sites. And coincidentally, Alexei stopped coming by the training arena.

For whatever it's worth, I did see Alexei Adamovich one last time before he died. Or, more accurately, I caught a few glimpses of Alexei in the aftermath of the death at the club—all the little puzzle fragments of which probably should have added up to a more substantial "one last time" in the real sense of the phrase.

Fate isn't that kind, though.

By then, big gentle Alexei was a hollow-faced, haunted creature dogging my father's steps. A ghost of what he'd been. My father was avoiding him—Alexei may not have been looking at jail time, but he'd have been a persona non grata after killing Jamie Chan.

In the end, Dad must have gotten sick of ducking Alexei and making up new excuses. Alexei never seemed to get the message that he wasn't welcome anymore, so Dad had to spell it out with starker messaging. He finally took a meeting with Alexei—really took a meeting, without hemming or hawing or pretending to be indisposed—one night after I'd wrapped up running hex-casting drills with the regular students.

I never saw Alexei again after that night. No one ever did. People assumed he packed up and left the city. Or maybe that all his petty crimes finally caught up to him and got him gunned down or jumped by the wrong guys in the wrong corner of town.

I had another theory. But I've never had reason to test it until now.

Dad's still awake when I get back to the hotel. That's normal for him. I don't know if Dad ever actually sleeps. He told me once that he's suffered from insomnia since he was my age. I'm never sure when Dad's embellishing, but I do actually believe him about the insomnia. Shadows the color of bad bruises always seem to linger under his eyes.

He tells me he's used to it. He tells me he's gotten used to a lot of unpleasant things. Sometimes, he winks when he says it.

I've never wanted to know the specifics. I wonder if that makes me a coward. I wonder if that makes me complicit.

Some part of me still doesn't want to know, not really, but *want* isn't as important as *need*. And I need to know. After seeing the look on Samantha Chan's face when she named Alexei as her brother's killer, I need to know what really happened that night.

Dad, of course, can tell I've got something on my mind as soon as I show up. He's on the couch, flipping through old footage of magicians' duels, but his eyes cut directly toward mine when I enter the room. "Tam." He doesn't set the remote aside, but he stops flipping through footage and hits the pause button. His brow furrows, which somehow deepens the tint of those permanent shadows under his eyes. "What's the matter?"

My face goes warm as heat pricks my eyes, traitorous. I've learned to hate moments like these. Moments where Dad seems to actually care about his daughter and not just his champion. They never last, and it always makes what comes after feel worse.

"Do you remember Alexei?"

The furrow between Dad's brows deepens further. "Alexei? Alexei who?"

"Adamovich." I twist my fingers together. "He used to be one of your magic students. A duelist who made extra cash by competing . . . off the books."

"Alexei." Dad rolls the old brute's name around with a reluctant click of his tongue, like he's savoring something distasteful. Wine that's gone off, which he refuses to spit out for appearances' sake. "Yes, I do remember a Mr. Alexei Adamovich. An unfortunate soul, really."

"I thought he was one of your favorites."

Dad chuckles. "All my students think they're my favorite. That's part of being a successful master. Mr. Adamovich was no exception."

"What made him so unfortunate, then?"

Dad goes quiet for so long, I'm briefly convinced that he might drop the subject entirely and send me on my way.

Then he says, in startlingly harsh tones, "You know I'm not a good man, right, Tamsin?"

I blink at him. My father likes to gloat sometimes—in a self-aware yet gleefully ostentatious sort of way—about the brutality that's ruled his personality and reputation alike. He makes no secret of having been a brutal man during his days in the arena and remaining a brutal man in the days that followed.

This, though, feels different.

"I'm not a good man," Dad continues. He heaves a great sigh and drags the heel of his hand down his face, massaging slowly, as if he might erase his own features. "Guys like Alexei know it. And that's why they come to see me. Because here's the thing: they're not good guys, either."

"Alexei was always kind to me," I say.

"Alexei always *behaved* kindly to the only daughter of his master. There's a difference." Dad offers me a long, considering stare. "Like is always drawn to like. And we recognize our own kind. You'll do well to remember that in the magical world and beyond, Tamsin."

"Well, I'm your student, too." I raise my chin. "So what about me? Am I . . . good?"

Dad looks surprised by the question. "You're my daughter."

"That's not an answer."

Dad shrugs. "Does it matter?"

"It does to me." I take a step closer. My heart rate climbs, but I persist. "What really happened to Alexei, Dad? He used to come to the training arena all the time, and one day he just disappeared. We never saw him again." I swallow. "Why?"

Dad chuckles. There's an odd, dark quality to the sound. When he speaks again, he sounds almost wistful. As though mirth, black-humored though it might be, might prevent him from reckoning with a different feeling.

"Mr. Adamovich got in over his head," says Dad. "Magicians like him often do. There was only so much I could do for him, after that. You won't be seeing him duel again, if that's what you're wondering. He's long dead. Tragic, really."

"What do you mean, 'duel again'?" I shuffle closer still. "What happened during Alexei's last duel? Before . . . before he passed?"

"Oh, spare your old man the ingenue act, Tamsin. I'm not a member of the press corps." Dad gives me an exasperated, knowing look. "You know exactly what Alexei did to expel himself from my good graces."

I fold my arms. My heart's pounding so hard, I think it might explode right out of my chest cavity. "Refresh my memory, Dad."

"That big fool of a brute killed a kid," Dad spits. "At the club I ran. My damn club! In a duel I arranged, no less."

"It didn't exactly seem like he wanted to duel in the first place."

"Oh, really?" Dad's dark eyes go flat. "And what, pray tell, gives you that impression, my girl?"

I draw my spine straight and square my shoulders, trying not to look as anxious as I feel. Heart palpitations or no, I need to know the truth. I deserve the truth. Sam and I both do. "I remember the day of the duel. The last time Alexei ever really spoke to us—or at least to me. He was upset. He kept trying to talk to you. Saying something about how he didn't want to duel a kid."

I look my father in eye. "'You never told me it was a kid,'" I recite. "Isn't that what he said to you?"

Dad scoffs. "Yet he went right ahead and took the duel anyway."

"Did he want to?" I refuse to break eye contact. "Or did you make him do it, Dad? Did you give him a choice?"

"Everyone has a choice, my girl. I taught you that much." Dad doesn't even blink. "I never forced Alexei to do anything. I simply explained that his livelihood was on the line."

My stomach sours. "That's coercion."

"That's business." Dad shrugs. "I may not be a good man, Tamsin. But I've always done what was necessary to thrive in a world that's unkind to most. I do no more and no less than that much. That means doing what I'm good at. I'm a good magician. And I'm a good matchmaker. If promoters want to cut me a check or two to send duelists their way to drum up ticket sales—I'm not going to turn away free money. And the promoters at my club offered an awful lot of free money."

The sour feeling inside me intensifies. "So you sent Alexei their way to beat up a kid."

"Hey, I didn't tell the kid to take the duel either. He did that himself." Dad doesn't even look sorry. "And as for Alexei, he was always more brawns than brain. Needed someone to do his thinking for him. So I took the job." He spreads his hands. "What's so wrong with that?

Everyone got what they wanted in the end. My club's promoters got their duel. Alexei got his money. Even the kid got his shot at glory. It's not my fault he squandered it. If that fool Alexei hadn't panicked and killed the idiot boy in the arena, the whole night would have been a celebratory one."

I close my eyes. It's one thing to suspect the truth. It's another to hear it confirmed aloud. "Do you even remember the kid's name?"

"How should I know? Some pretty boy, Asian, if I recall correctly. Jason or James or something."

"Jamie," I blurt out. "His name was Jamie Chan."

My father blinks at me, looking surprised. "You have a good memory." His eyes go distant. "Yes, Jamie Chan, you're right. That was it. A pity. If he'd lived, we could have made a lot more profit off a kid that good-looking and that talented." Dad shrugs. "What can you do, though? The world's a mean place, my girl. And the magical world is even meaner."

"Dad." I take a deep breath and will my voice not to shake. "What really happened to Alexei after he met with you? After Jamie died?"

"I told you already, Tamsin; Alexei died, too." Dad sounds impatient. "Many magicians who fall on hard times do. It was an accident, nothing more."

I meet Dad's eyes again. "Was it really? An accident?"

My father falls silent, eyebrows climbing.

"Tell me the truth, Dad. Please." I press my advantage. "What killed Alexei?"

Slowly, Dad smiles at me. He chuckles softly before he speaks again. "Nothing he didn't to himself, Tamsin. Nothing at all." He pauses then adds delicately, "So far as anyone can prove, at least."

Oxygen flees the room. My chest tightens. "You could go to prison," I whisper.

"On what charges, exactly?" My father's dark eyes flash dangerously at me. "The crime of having a suspicious teenage daughter? I wasn't aware that was a felony."

I balk. "Dad. I never said—"

"You implied," Dad snaps. "You insinuated. That's as good as an accusation."

"I didn't mean to."

"And Alexei didn't mean to kill poor Jamie Chan." Dad finally tosses the remote aside and stands up. I back away instinctively. "I'm not a good man, Tamsin. But don't make the mistake of thinking you're so virtuous, either. You asked me earlier if you were *good*. As if human beings are so easily divided into good and evil, like characters in a fairy tale." Dad gives a bark of laughter. "Tell me, Tamsin. Are you good if you live under my roof and eat my food—all of it paid for by the profits I earned off the backs of petty criminal goons like Alexei? Like the obviously less-than-legal promoters at that club?" His voice rises. "You tell me, my girl. You tell me!"

"I'm sorry!" I blurt out. I'm humiliatingly close to tears. "I'm sorry, I shouldn't have asked about any of this."

"Oh, Tamsin." Dad's face softens, full of pity. "Where would you be without me?" His voice is gentle again but still laced with venom. "Ask yourself that instead. Where will you go without my money? Without the work I've done, that you apparently disdain so much?"

"I don't disdain you," I whisper.

Dad snorts. "I'm relieved to hear it."

"Dad." I force myself to look him in the eye again. My stomach churns. "If I upset you. If I screwed up. Would I . . . would I meet Alexei's fate?" I blink back the prick of heat behind my eyes. With an effort, I keep the tremor out of my voice when I ask, "Whatever happened to him, would it happen to me, too?"

I can't read the look on Dad's face. But he doesn't blink at me, and he doesn't speak for some time. I want to throw up. I want to cry. I do neither while I wait for my father's answer.

He closes his eyes and sighs, all the tension going out of his body. His shoulders slump. In this moment, my father is transformed. He looks so frail, ancient and withered, exhausted by the burden of life. Every line etched onto his face stands in stark relief behind the glow of the TV screen, the hollows beneath his eyes practically painted black.

When he opens his eyes, they're wet. He doesn't smile. He doesn't shout. He just stares at me for a long moment with those wet eyes.

"Don't be ridiculous, Tamsin," he says at last, his voice rough. "I told you already. You're my daughter." He turns away from me. "It's late. Go to bed."

If I were actually a good person, I'd be looking up how to turn my father in to the authorities. I'm sure there's a hotline I could call, a website I could find, an emergency number I could dial. Even without hard evidence against him, Dad could at least face the threat of real consequences.

I should want that for my father. He's right. He's not a good man. He never has been. Maybe Alexei killed Sam's brother, but Dad's the reason they were together in that godforsaken arena at all. The duel never should have happened in the first place. Dad's just as guilty as

Alexei—maybe even guiltier. Dad and his eternal need for profit and power.

Dad, who as good as admitted to killing Alexei, too, just to tie up loose ends.

If I don't beat Rook in our duel, I'll be tied to a murderer forever. And I'll spend the rest of my life surviving off his blood money.

Unless, of course, someone puts Dad away for everything he's done.

I eye my phone where it sits plugged in on the nightstand, the blank black screen somehow accusatory. Could I make it happen? I'm his daughter and his student; I'm the favored disciple to a great man. People would listen, at least. The shadow of a doubt would be cast if I were the one to cast it. And that shadow maybe—just maybe—could be enough to open up a real investigation that would force Dad to answer for all the blood he's spilled, the families he's broken, the hurt he's wrought.

But where would that leave me?

The thought hits me like a bucket of cold water. Dad's right. If he goes down, I go down with him. Without Dad, I have no one. I have nothing.

I close my eyes. At the end of the day, I'm not such a good person after all. At least I know it. At least it shames me.

But shame doesn't solve the problem at hand. I'm back at square one: where Lysander Rook remains my only way out. A boy who wants to tear me limb from limb. A boy who probably will if I make the smallest of mistakes in this duel.

So in the end, I don't call anyone. I tell nobody about my conversation with my father. Instead, I sleep fitfully that night, waking from half-remembered dreams over and over again.

The next day is hilariously unproductive. I zombie-walk my way through my usual strength and conditioning routine at the gym, my mobility exercises, even my favorite hex and curse sequences. Mustering focus is impossible. Instead, I keep staring at my phone, scrolling aimlessly through social media and old texts, refreshing email with no specific purpose.

I still don't call the authorities.

I do finally use my phone for something other than doom scrolling, though. I can't stomach the idea of talking to a police officer or even a magicians' dueling commissioner. I need someone familiar. Someone who knows how to listen.

I thumb through my phone until I find the contact I want. I send the text before I can think better of it. And then I simply wait.

"Is everything okay?"

What a loaded question. I look up as Samantha Chan enters the training arena. Concern colors her face when she speaks. For once, she's not in her signature oversized hoodie. Instead, she's wearing a plain white tee, unisex fit, which hangs loosely on her broad shoulders, a messy bun on her head. She usually looks dressed for the training arena; today, she looks dressed for a grocery run. Who knows? Maybe I interrupted one when I texted her.

I struggle over my answer to her question. "Everything is . . ." I trail off then begin again. Who am I kidding? "No, I guess everything's not okay."

"I kind of figured." She takes a seat beside me in the middle of the arena. I've commandeered one of the target dummies to use as a makeshift bench of sorts. She plops down on its head while I sit on its belly. "You didn't really sound like yourself in your text."

"Oh?" That gets a weak laugh out of me, but it's a laugh, all the same. "And how do I normally sound?"

"Happy." Sam's response arrives without hesitation. "You sound—you always seem—happy." She pauses, and adds, a little wryly, "Lots of emojis and exclamation points. When you texted asking to meet here, you didn't use any. You even, god forbid, ended a sentence with an actual period."

"The true mortal sin," I acknowledge. "Thanks for meeting me anyway."

"Of course. So cut to the chase. What's the matter?"

I look at Sam, my throat tight. Here's the moment of truth. I can come clean. I'm sitting face-to-face with the girl whose brother died because of what my family did to hers. She deserves to know the truth. If someone's going to drag all the ugly Blackwood skeletons out of our closet, it should be Samantha Chan. It's what we owe her.

I stare at those inquisitive dark eyes of hers. I will myself to speak. I don't understand why it's so hard. Sam has always been so very easy to talk to. The first person in eighteen years that I've really, truly been able to talk to without fear or restraint, words falling from my lips, as natural as the air expelled from my lungs.

"Tamsin?" Sam whispers. "Hey. What's the matter? You can tell me."

I can't.

My mouth slams into hers before I can stop myself. It's a messy kiss, our teeth knocking together, as one of my hands flails out for balance on the target dummy. Sam inhales sharply against my lips.

I pull away, mortified. Sam stares at me, one hand against her swollen mouth, her eyes huge.

"I'm sorry," I gasp. This is it. I've ruined things between us. I've ruined everything. "I'm sorry, I don't know what I was thinking, I didn't mean to—"

With a frustrated grunt, Sam grabs me by the wrist and yanks me toward her. I yelp as her mouth catches mine again. This kiss is smoother than our first, less hasty and awkward, but it feels no less hungry.

In the tiny, liminal space of that kiss, everything else stops mattering. I don't think about blood spilled or debts owed. I don't think about guilt. I don't worry about Dad, or Rook, or even Sam's poor dead brother. And I don't give a damn about whether I'm a good person or not.

All I care about when Sam's lips touch mine is how badly I want to stay like this with her forever. How badly I want to keep kissing her with no thought for cost or consequence.

"I'm sorry," I gasp again as we come up for air. "I'm sorry, I don't—well, I'm sorry." I don't even know what I'm supposed to be sorry for anymore, but I can't stop saying it.

Sam groans, resting her forehead against mine. "Haven't I told you already?" she whispers. Her breath gusts against my lips. "You should stop apologizing so much."

Her hand cups the back of my neck, digging into the hair that's fallen loose from my ponytail. My eyes flutter closed. Obediently, I shut up.

And for another blissful stretch of time, I think of nothing at all except Samantha Chan, here in my arms.

I'm not sure how long we keep kissing for, but Sam's the one who finally breaks it off. "Shit," she mutters and presses the heels of her hands against her eyelids. "I shouldn't have done that."

"Done what?" My heart races as I straighten out my clothing.

"Kissed you, obviously." She groans into her hands. "Shit," she repeats.

"Technically, I kissed you," I point out helpfully.

"I shouldn't have kissed you back."

"I didn't mind very much." Why can't I stop staring at Sam's mouth? "I didn't mind at all, in fact."

"I know."

My throat tightens again. "Did you?"

Sam snorts. "Obviously not. That's the problem." She finally looks at me, an utterly miserably expression on her face. "You and Lysander Rook are less than two weeks out from the biggest magicians' duel of the year. Your performance in the arena on that night could make or break your career." She spreads her hands. "And I'm your opponent's second. It's a conflict of interest, Tam. A huge one."

I feel my chin jut out stubbornly. "I won't tell anyone if you won't."

"It's not a matter of telling or not telling." Sam stands up, straightening out her T-shirt and joggers as she flicks imaginary dust off her skin. "It's what . . . continuing to carry on like this with you will do to you. What it'll do to me. What it'll do to Rook, maybe worst of all. Honestly, you and me being together like this, it's not good for either of you—you or him." She closes her eyes. "It's not even good for me."

"Sam." I hate the pleading note that's entered my voice. "Don't do this."

"I have to." She makes for the door. "There's no version of this story that doesn't end badly for all three of us."

"You felt it," I insist. "You feel what I feel."

Sam pauses as she reaches the arena exit. Carefully, she looks over her shoulder at me. “Maybe,” she begins, swallows, and begins again. “Maybe after the duel,” she manages. “Whatever happens in the New York Magicians’ Arena, let it happen. And after, you can decide what you want with me.”

She flees the training arena before I can give her an answer.

14

SAM

TAMSIN BLACKWOOD HAUNTS ME for days.

Not the girl herself, obviously. If anything, I'd say she's taking obvious steps to avoid me. Whenever I see her around the training arenas or in common spaces on hotel grounds, she always avoids eye contact and mysteriously finds a pressing reason to head in the opposite direction. She hasn't texted me since the day we kissed. I don't know if she'll ever speak to me again.

This is a good thing. I keep telling myself this is a good thing.

But I can't stop thinking about her. It's the thought of her—the ghost of the Tamsin that lurks in the back of my mind—that's become a problem. She distracts me from training with Rook, from planning his dueling strategies, from everything that's actually important to me.

Rook picks up on it. Or at least I think he does. His own performance keeps stuttering. My champion is normally a force of nature, even in training. The best I can do is slow him down or prolong the inevitable—I know I can't stop him, not when he's at the height of his power. A magician like Rook, when he's in the arena, isn't a person so much as he's a young, angry god.

He hasn't become a bad magician overnight. I don't know if he could do that, even if he tried. But he's been made mortal lately. I land blows on him that I shouldn't. My hexes sneak past his defenses. His curses—still beautiful, terrifying constructions—miss me entirely when he casts them.

His heart's not in the game. For the first time in our life together, Lysander Rook has fallen out of love with magic, and I don't know why or how to fix it.

"God damn it!" he yells one day in training. The curse he'd cast—an intricately woven serpentine dragon constructed from pure, blue-white arcane energy—shatters like glass against the basic shield I cast his way.

Rook's fist slams into the floor of the training arena. "What the hell is wrong with me?" he rages.

"Nothing's wrong." I dismiss my shielding spell and go to my champion where he's hunched over on the ground, surrounded by dying sparks of arcane energy from his latest effort. "Your magic is as brilliant as ever. It hasn't changed. You just keep doing too much of it too quickly. I've always told you you neglect the fundamentals."

Stormy blue eyes snap toward me. I back up a step without meaning to. Even crouched below me like a wounded animal, Rook looks poised to strike. Sometimes, wounded animals are the most dangerous. "This has nothing to do with the fundamentals," he spits. "I'm not going to beat Tamsin goddamn Blackwood with, what, that basic shielding spell of yours?"

"It worked on you, didn't it?" I stare my champion down. I can't let him think I'm afraid of him. Not right now. Not with so much on the line and Rook already hanging by a thread. "Don't overcomplicate this."

Rook shakes his head. It makes him look like a prize racehorse that's been spooked and is now refusing to move farther along the track. "I'm not overcomplicating anything. I'm trying to do my magic, my way, and something's off."

I dig in my heels, ready to argue the point further, when someone knocks at the training arena door. For one brief, oddly hopeful moment, I wonder if it's Tamsin Blackwood. "Come in!"

The door creaks open to admit one Master Noah Silverstein. "Samantha." He nods to me then Rook. "Lysander."

"Master Silverstein." My heart plummets into my belly as I remember my last encounter with our master instructor—and the threats he made. "What can we do for you?"

"I'd like to speak to you, Samantha." He glances pointedly over my shoulder. "Alone."

Rook chuckles under his breath. "More secret meetings between my second and my venerated master of the arcane arts. Dope."

"Ignore him; he's in a mood," I tell Silverstein, whose bushy brows shoot immediately toward his salt-and-pepper hairline. "Come on, the training room next door is free."

The old arcane master follows me in silence to the next room over, but he rounds on me as soon as the door shuts behind him. "All right. I've made my decision. You need to pull Lysander out of this duel."

I force myself not to panic. I knew this was a possibility. I've known it ever since that coffeeshop conversation the morning after my disastrous, intoxicating night in Arcane New York with Tamsin.

That doesn't make it less terrifying.

I fix Silverstein with the best look of indignity I can muster. "We are talking about the same duel, right? The one with boatloads of money on the line? The one where Rook stands to make a fortune and solidify his reputation as the most gifted magician of our generation?"

Master Silverstein closes his eyes. "He's not well. Rook, I mean." He runs a hand over his face. "I had my reservations about letting this duel go forward at all, but I overruled them. Rook's always had his fits and tempers, but I thought he'd get over it. But he hasn't. Not this time. If anything, he's getting worse."

"That's bullshit," I insist. "I told you before. He's just . . . I don't know, in a rut right now. I'll get him out of it. I always do."

"Samantha." Silverstein sighs, shaking his head. He starts to pace the room, which is a surefire sign that this whole conversation is one he doesn't want to be having. Which, of course, means he'll be more determined than ever to see it through. You don't get to be a master of the arcane arts of Silverstein's ilk by shirking what makes you uncomfortable.

"How much have you been paying attention to Lysander's condition?" he asks the opposite wall as he paces. "Because I've been tracking it for some time."

"I pay plenty of attention," I say, stung. "Again, we talked about this. I've taken care of Rook for years."

"You've taken care of his ability to perform magic," says Silverstein. "You've taken care of Lysander's finest weapons: You ensure his knowledge of the latest hexes and curses best suited to his magical style, maintain the strength and mobility of his body, help devise the strategy he employs against each individual challenger he faces." The old master rounds the corner and looks back at me from the other side of the room. Something like pity sits behind his gaze. "You've ensured, in a nutshell, that he performs at the peak of his abilities in the arena. I can't fault you for that. It's the task I charged you with, after all. But listen, kid, just because Rook the magician is well doesn't mean that Rook the human being is. And sooner or later, if Rook the human being isn't well, Rook the magician will falter, too."

"He's fine," I insist once more, but it's harder to summon the same kind of confidence. I think about the way Rook screams during his night terrors. The look in those blue eyes when I wake him. The purple shadows that stain the hollows under his eyes for days afterward, and how, during those days, his magic is always just slightly, slightly off.

"Is he?" Nothing accusatory laces Master Silverstein's voice, but I feel the rebuke in my bones all the same. He's completed his lap around the arena at last, and arrived to face me, eye to eye, where I can't escape his gaze. "Remember, Sam. I knew Lysander Rook for a long time before I permitted you to enter his life. I know that boy better than most." He shakes his head again. "Hell below. I may be the only person on the planet who actually knows him better than you do."

"I'm his second."

"Because I made you his second," snaps Silverstein. "I made you his second because he needed someone like you. Someone who would push him. Someone who could see through his theatrics, his monstrous talent, his mood swings, and recognize the magician beneath. He needed someone who could shape that raw material into the best duelist he could be." His eyes are oddly sad when they find mine. "He needed someone who wouldn't be afraid of him."

"I'm not," I whisper.

"I know." Silverstein smiles, but it's small, and that odd sense of sadness hasn't left his eyes. "No warrior is afraid of their weapon. But a good warrior also knows when to sheathe the sword. Let him rest, Sam. Rook's not in a fighting state right now. Accept that."

"Rook will go ballistic—more ballistic than he already has—if I try to pull him out of the duel now. He's killed himself preparing for this! It'll ruin him if he gives up at the finish line."

"Lysander Rook is eighteen years old. He's got a long career ahead of him. Forfeiting one duel won't break him, but putting him in that arena right now might."

"Forfeit?" I repeat faintly. Of course Silverstein meant for me to make Rook forfeit when he said to withdraw Rook from the duel—what else could it mean?—but the idea of a formal forfeit hasn't fully registered until now. "No, no, we can reschedule, maybe, but no forfeit. Anything but that."

"Sam." Master Silverstein frowns. "Believe me, there's no shame in a forfeit. It's better to lose a battle and live to fight the war than to—"

"Oh, save it for Tamsin Blackwood!" I shout.

Silence rings in my ears. I've never raised my voice like that to Master Silverstein before. I force myself to continue before I can chicken out. "If anyone should be forfeiting, it should be Tamsin."

"What are you talking about?" Silverstein's eyes narrow at me. "What do you know that you haven't shared with me, Sam?"

The world spins around me. Several decisions need to be made right now. Mateus Blackwood schemed with his daughter to throw the duel against Rook. I told Tamsin I'd keep her secret, but that was before Rook started screwing up basic curse work, before Silverstein threatened to pull my champion from competition entirely.

If I rat Tamsin out now, I won't just get Tamsin disqualified, though—I'll sacrifice my chance to see Mateus Blackwood's legacy destroyed in the arena. A simple disqualification is nothing compared to that. A disqualification is something the Blackwoods can bounce back from. I don't know if I'll ever have a chance like this again: a chance to destroy their family completely and utterly, the same way Jamie's death destroyed mine.

But if Silverstein forces Rook to resign, Tamsin will emerge the victor. She and her father will have everything they want. And my champion and I will be left with nothing. Less than nothing.

I can't stomach that.

"Mateus Blackwood told his daughter to throw the match against Rook in order to rig the betting odds," I choke out. "Tamsin told me herself."

"Samantha." Silverstein utters my name under his breath like an expletive. "How long have you known?"

I close my eyes. "Since we arrived in New York, pretty much."

"God damn it!" I hear Silverstein's fist slam into the wall. "Why the hell would you keep something like that from me? That's a major breach in dueling regulations."

"Because she promised me she wouldn't do it!" I cry. "I made Tamsin promise she'd give us a real duel. But if it's between her and Rook, it's Tamsin who should be forced to forfeit, don't you see? She was the one who was going to break the rules!"

"And why on earth," Silverstein says slowly, "would she tell you, her opponent's second, about a breach like that?"

"She didn't mean to." I squirm. "I mean, she didn't know who I was when she told me. We were just talking."

"You were just talking," repeats Silverstein. His voice is flat and sardonic in a way I hate. "A completely benign conversation on your part, I'm sure."

"It was just opposition research!"

"Was it, kid?" Silverstein's gaze pins me to the spot. "Or was it because you blame the Blackwoods for what happened to Jamie?"

I freeze. "What?"

Silverstein hasn't spoken of Jamie since the day my brother died. He quit uttering Jamie's name, the same way he quit calling me Kid Sister. I always assumed it was his own curious form of grief: a way to erase Jamie's memory from daily life, where it couldn't hurt anyone, least of all the half-petrified hearts of cranky old-timer magicians.

"You blame them, don't you?" Silverstein shakes his head. "I'm no fool, Samantha. I know what kind of business Mateus Blackwood got up to before his daughter became a star. You blame the Blackwoods for putting on the duel that killed Jamie."

He practically chokes on my brother's name, like it's an unfamiliar taste on his tongue. Which I suppose it has been ever since we put Jamie in the ground. The world slows down as the bottom of my belly drops out from under me. So this is it. I've been found out. The panic spikes then, oddly, evens out. If this is how things are, I might as well lean in and ride it out. With an effort, I lift my chin. I refuse to back down now, even as my heartbeat ricochets against my ribs.

"Jamie was the same age I am now," I say. "And Mateus Blackwood let him die to turn a profit. You can't blame me for anything I've done."

"Samantha," says Silverstein again, but in a different voice this time. "I am sorry for your loss. Believe me, I'm old enough to know how hard it can be to stomach a tragedy like that, especially if you feel that someone else is at fault—"

"Blackwood is at fault!"

"But is his daughter?" the old master asks quietly. "Tell me, Sam, what role did Tamsin Blackwood play in your brother's death? Which strings did she pull? What knife did she leave bloody?"

I shake my head against the now familiar tidal wave of guilt that washes over me. "It doesn't matter what Tamsin did or didn't have to do with Jamie dying," I snap. "She can be a saint reborn for all I care. She's still Mateus Blackwood's only family. The only way I can make him understand what he did to my family is by making her pay."

I take a deep breath. Silverstein will see things my way. He has to. "If you really don't think Rook can beat her—if you think he's really in as bad shape as you say—then go to the dueling commissioner and the promoters and tell them what their beloved Master Mateus Blackwood put his daughter up to. Let the Blackwoods eat the punishment they deserve. Not us. Not Lysander."

Silverstein pinches the bridge of his nose. "We need to tell your champion about this. Rook deserves to know that your judgment as his second has been . . . compromised."

"It hasn't!" I insist. "His goals are still my goals: beating the Blackwoods. All you need to tell him is that they're cheats. Expose them for what they are." I clench my fists. "It won't be as good as giving him the chance to beat Tamsin fair and square, but it's better than running away from her with our tails tucked and letting her family get away with an . . . an unjust reward."

Besides, getting Tamsin disqualified at least gives me time to make a new plan. One that will destroy the Blackwoods once and for all.

"An unjust reward, huh?" Silverstein drops his hand from his face and looks at me with an expression I've never seen on him before. "You really do think Tamsin Blackwood deserves to be the whipping girl for what her father did."

There was a time when I would have said yes without hesitation. Before I got to know Blackwood's daughter as an actual human being. Before she kissed me. Before I kissed her back. Now I'm not so sure.

I open my mouth to say yes anyway, but the word gets stuck in my throat. It tastes too much like a lie. And my old master has always been far too good at seeing through lies.

Master Silverstein's expression settles into a knowing sort of sorrow. "You don't, do you? You know that you're being cruel and unfair."

"Maybe she doesn't deserve to suffer the way her father does," I say softly. "But that's never mattered to me." The words are ugly, but I force myself to say them anyway. I force myself to tell the truth. It's a relief, in some ways. "Mateus Blackwood wrecked my family the night he killed my brother. And I hate him for that. I hate him even more than I—more than I care for his daughter. If she'd been born anyone else's kid, maybe things could have been different between us." I blink back sudden heat behind my eyes. "But she wasn't."

"Is that really true?"

I stop breathing as a new voice—quivering, full of hurt and disbelief—hits my ears. No. No, no, no. This can't be happening.

"Miss Blackwood," says Master Silverstein. Surprise colors his voice. "What are you doing down here?"

"I came to train. My plans took an . . . unexpected turn when I heard raised voices in here." Tamsin Blackwood steps into view as the arena door creaks open to admit her. "The door to this training room doesn't lock correctly," she tells him in clipped tones. Her expression is alarmingly blank. Utterly unreadable. "Miss Chan should have remembered, from the first time we met down here."

"How long have you been standing there?" I demand. "How much did you hear?"

Tamsin's gaze slides toward me. "You never answered my question, Sam." I've never heard her speak in a voice so cold. Every hair on my body feels like it's standing on end. "Everything you just said. About what my father deserves. About . . . about how you hate him more than you care about me. Is it all true?"

I can't speak. I'm frozen to the spot. "Tamsin," I whisper.

Disgust creeps over her pretty features. "You can't even bring yourself to lie to my face, can you? You'll plot god knows what behind my back, but when you have to face me with the truth out in the open, well." She chuckles bleakly. "Turns out you're just another goddamn coward, Samantha Chan."

She turns on her heel and leaves without another word.

"Tamsin, wait!" I shout. "Tamsin!"

All that greets me is silence.

15

TAMSIN

SAMANTHA CHAN IS CHASING me down.

I run, which is absurd. We're not in an action movie or a romantic comedy, for that matter. But the last thing in the world that I want right now is a conversation with Rook's second.

Rook's second, who's been playing me for a fool this entire time.

So I run from her. We must look like idiots, sprinting out of the training arena and through the fitness center like we're testing our cardio for everything it's worth. Other exercisers exclaim in surprise as we shove past them. I'm a half-decent runner, but Sam's hot on my heels. She's in better shape than a second has any right to be.

I wait until we're out in open air, in the outdoor space between the fitness center and the hotel proper, before I finally stop and round on her. Sam's running so fast, she practically collides with me. Instinctively, I reach out to steady her.

For a moment, panting hard, Sam just stares dumbly at my hand where it's braced against her bicep. "Tamsin," she gasps. Then she utters the most cliché phrase of all time: "I can explain everything."

She definitely goddamn can't. I drop her bicep like it's a hot brand and fold my arms. "I would absolutely love to see you try."

Sam's jaw works for a moment before she tells me, "I do care about you. I like you. I've liked you since we met. I wasn't lying about that. I never have. You have no idea how hard that's been for me."

"Poor you!" I exclaim. "Wow, I'm *awfully* sorry to be so inconveniently . . . likable, I guess? Thanks for the most backhanded compliment of all time?"

"Tamsin, that's not what I—"

"Almost as sorry as I am for the crime of having been born with the surname Blackwood. You know, a thing that I obviously had total and complete control over."

"None of this was ever about you!" Sam bursts out. "It's about what your father did to my brother."

"And I was just collateral damage, is that it?" I refuse to cry. Not now. Sam doesn't deserve my tears. "I was just an extension of my dad, right? Like an extra limb: an arm or a leg that you could chop off to hurt him, never mind what it would do to me?"

"It wasn't supposed to be like this." Desperation clings to Sam's voice and colors every inch of her face. I've never seen Rook's even-keeled, calculating strategist look so utterly undone and out of her depth. Good. I should relish this. "You and I were never supposed to have a . . . friendship. A relationship. Rook was just going to beat you. It's not wrong for a second to want their champion to defeat a challenger."

"Except that's not the only thing you wanted, is it?" My voice is thick, but my tears haven't spilled yet. It's the one piece of dignity I can cling to. "You didn't just want him to beat me. No, no, that wouldn't be enough. You wanted your boy to, what was it again? Right, 'destroy' me.

You instructed your champion to leave me ruined and broken beyond repair, and he was all too happy to comply . . . up until he started getting all screwy in the head, that is."

I laugh outright at the look on Sam's face. "And yes, Samantha, before you ask, I did hear that part of the conversation. It must be nice for your champion to have a master of the arcane arts who cares more about his health and mental well-being than his own second, huh?"

"Telling Rook to break you was the only way," whispers Sam. "I wish it were anyone but you, Tamsin. Listen, I care about you—"

"Oh, you care about me, huh?" I repeat mockingly. "That's why you've been using me this whole time."

"I told you, I never meant for things to go down like that! It's not that simple."

"It is that simple!" I shout. "It is! God, just say it, Sam. You at least owe me that much. If you're going to be this big of a scumbag, you should at least be honest about the reasons why." I spread my hands. "Maybe you do really think that you care about me. Let's say, hypothetically, that you weren't just pretending to like me for the sake of your grand plan. Maybe some of that emotion was real. Maybe you could have really, truly grown to care about me the way you keep insisting that you do." I bark a sad, desperate little laugh. "But does it really matter?"

"It does!"

"No, it doesn't. Because the truth is, no matter how much you might have grown to care about me, you'd always care more about a boy who's been dead in the ground for almost half a decade."

Sam's mouth snaps shut. Her face goes sheet white. "That's not fair."

"Maybe not." I shrug. "But it's still true. It doesn't matter who you hurt—me, Rook, even yourself. Just as long as you get what you want. And what you want, more than anything else, is revenge against my father." I shake my head. "You've got to appreciate the irony. You hate him so, so much. But at the end of the day, you and Dad are exactly alike."

Sam's breath hitches like I've just knocked the wind from her lungs. Her eyes go huge. She doesn't cry, though. The look on her face is worse than crying. It makes me—at least part of me—want to walk my words back.

The bigger part of me—the enraged, betrayed part of me—relishes the sheer scale of hurt washing over her features.

"I'm going to report you to the promoters and the commissioner," whispers Sam. Her words are clipped. "You'll be disqualified for what your father's tried to pull with the betting odds."

A strange thing happens in that moment. My brain processes Sam's threat for what it is: Instead of having her boy break my body, she'll break my reputation. She'll paint me in dishonor. She'll make me eat the words I uttered so carelessly to her in that diner before I knew who she really was.

And then, a voice that sounds very much like my father's whispers in the back of my mind: *And with what proof will she back those words up?*

I laugh again. I sound hysterical even to my own ears, but I'm past the point of caring. "Go right ahead," I tell Sam. I spread my hands wide. "Report me. Report me and Dad both. I'm sure the promoters will be very interested in the recorded evidence that you obviously saved of that night we talked at Agatha's, right?"

Sam frowns. "What the hell are you talking about?"

"Wow, for someone so hell-bent on a long game of revenge, you sure are stupid." I sneer at Sam. "Did you record our conversation? Do you have a witness to my so-called confession?"

The expression dawning slowly across Sam's face tells me everything I need to know. I give her a triumphant smile, the same smile I give an opponent in the magicians' arena when I've got them backed into a corner with seconds left on the clock. "You don't, do you? Which means you have . . . well, gee, nothing at all on me!"

"They'll want to hear your side of the story," Sam says. Desperation has reentered her voice. It's music to my ears. "They'll make you swear under oath that you and your father never plotted to cheat the betting odds."

I shrug. "So I'll lie."

I feel a little cold inside as I say it. Lying has never come easy to me. It always makes me feel rotten, no matter my reasons. But in this moment, I've never been more certain of my willingness to do it.

Apparently, Sam's not the only one taking a leaf out of Dad's playbook. I've got more of his blood running through my veins than I ever realized. Maybe that's what really bonded me and Sam. Why we liked each other so readily, so easily, despite our circumstances. We were really just two sides of the same Mateus Blackwood–shaped coin. Two lonely, hungry teenage girls inadvertently painted in my father's image by the blood he's spilled over the years.

It's an ugly thought. But unlike Sam, I refuse to be frightened by ugly truths.

I take my sweet time closing the space between me and Sam. To her credit, she doesn't back away from me. Then again, maybe she can't. Maybe shame—or fear—has rooted her to the spot. "Look, Chan, I do feel a little sorry for you," I tell her. "So I'll grant you one boon. I'm going to keep my promise to you. I'm going to give your boy a real duel." I make sure to show her all my teeth as I smile. "But you'd better tell Lysander Rook to be ready for the fight of his life. Because if he's not, he'd better resign now."

I lean in close, until Sam and I are practically nose to nose. Close enough for me to plant my mouth back on hers. I can practically taste her tongue on mine.

I put my mouth up to the shell of Sam's ear, and I'm rewarded with a shudder that runs through her entire body. "Give your boy the choice, Sammy," I whisper. "You owe him a choice, at the very least. He can resign now, and I can collect my prize money and get the hell out of this town, and none of us ever have to see or speak to each other ever again."

"Or?" Sam hazards, her voice shaking.

I shrug. "Or I can be the one who leaves him destroyed and broken beyond repair in the middle of the New York Magicians' Arena. Let Rook choose his own fate. Either way, I'm getting paid."

I give Sam a mockingly friendly little shove on the shoulder to signal an end to our conversation. She stumbles back a few steps. This time, I don't bother steadying her. I don't owe her shit. And I have nothing left to say to her.

If Samantha Chan sees me as nothing more than an extension of Master Mateus Blackwood, then by hell or high water, I'm going to give her exactly what she expects. And if Lysander Rook becomes the collateral damage, so be it.

It's nothing more and nothing less than what Sam was going to make him do to me, after all.

16

SAM

ROOK'S WAITING FOR ME back at the suite when I return. He's posed with uncharacteristic expectation. Instead of his usual slouch, he's sitting up straight on the couch, one ankle crossed neatly over a knee. He looks up as soon as I enter the room. "Sammy." His tone is unreadable. "Good. You're back."

I scope out the room. "Where's Master Silverstein?"

"He just left." Rook's still speaking in that strange, flat voice. I didn't think my body could carry more tension after that conversation with Tamsin—if you can even call it a conversation.

Yet every muscle I have tightens immediately as Rook's clear blue eyes bore into mine. He's not smiling or smirking, but he's not pouting at me, either. He seems, for once, to be waiting for me to make the first move.

When I don't, he heaves a tremendous sigh. "You're not going to admit it, are you?"

"Admit what?"

"Your little scheme against the Blackwoods." My champion rolls his eyes. "How stupid do you think I am? Silverstein told me everything."

I open my mouth to tell my champion that I can explain. That Silverstein's got it wrong, that I'm being taken out of context. Or at least, that's what I intend to do. Instead, what comes out of my mouth is "After this duel against Tamsin Blackwood, I'm quitting."

Rook jerks as if I've slapped him. "What?"

"Silverstein wants you to resign from this duel. If that's what you want, that's fine and dandy. But if you go forward with it, you'll still need a second, and Silverstein doesn't have time to find you a new one before showtime rolls around. So instead, we wait until after you defeat her. Then I quit." I shrug. "That's much cleaner."

"Why the hell would you quit? And why the hell do you think I want to fire you?

"Silverstein told you, didn't he?" I shuck my jacket off. "My judgment is compromised. I care too much about screwing over the Blackwoods and not enough about your well-being. The only thing you and I have left in common is that we both want you to beat Tamsin—and I'm not even sure you want that much anymore. So this is what's best for both of us. We can make it look amicable. No scandal, no speculation, just a mutually amenable parting of ways. Your career will remain intact—hell, you'll continue to be the darling of the magical world, in all likelihood. You'll have the chance to bring a second on board that you really want in your corner. One that can actually take care of you, body and soul, instead of just turning you into her human weapon."

I tug my hoodie over my head next. "And me? I'll just have to find a way to destroy the Blackwoods myself."

"And how do you propose to do that, exactly?" Rook's voice has taken on a mean edge. It always does when he's been unexpectedly hurt. "What are you going to do, Sammy? Become a real duelist yourself? A champion? Go head-to-head with Tamsin Blackwood in the magicians' arena, all by your lonesome?" He chuckles. "Or are you going to go full psychopath and try to take on Mateus Blackwood himself?"

Ah, there's that familiar edge of louche mockery. Good. That will make this easier.

"Maybe." I hang up the jacket as I speak. "I never really gave myself the chance, did I?"

I was too fixated on shaping Rook into what I wanted. I was so convinced that Rook was the only weapon I had. I never looked inward. I never thought I'd achieve the kind of status Rook had—the kind you need to face Tamsin Blackwood in a magicians' arena. I needed a proxy.

I never thought I'd have the chance to face the Blackwoods on my own. And now I might have to.

"Sammy, are you listening to yourself?" Rook leaps off the couch. "You never gave *me* the chance."

"What are you talking about?" I demand. "Rook, I poured everything I had into you."

"No, you didn't!" An oddly wounded look crosses his face. "You never trusted me. Did you think I wouldn't help you if you'd told me what the Blackwoods really did to your brother?"

"Lysander—"

"You had to play the mastermind." The wounded look is replaced immediately with a sneer. "You had to do everything yourself. Brilliant Samantha Chan, the clever young second, the real puppeteer pulling

Lysander Rook's strings. You never once considered just talking to me. Treating me like an equal partner in your scheming."

"My revenge was never your fight."

"But you sure as hell saw it fit to turn it into my fight, didn't you?" Rook's eyes blaze at me. "You were fine with making your revenge my problem as long as I was nothing but your puppet. As long as you—and you alone—stayed in control of everything. Including me."

He gives me a bitter smile. "And you know what? That's fine. I'll duel Tamsin Blackwood, don't you worry. I'll do exactly as you please, and give her hell, just like you wanted."

"Rook, you don't have to—"

"No, I really do." The ugly smile grows. "But first, I want you to know how it feels. How it feels to be a human weapon. A spectacle."

Rook straightens his spine. He's an entirely different person all of a sudden. He can do that, shift his bearing like a chameleon. One moment, he's a wounded child. The next, he's the undefeated young champion of the modern magical world.

"Duel me," he says. "Really duel me. Right now."

"I've dueled you plenty of times in training."

"That's different, and you know it." Rook holds my gaze. The petulant child is gone. In his place is a deceptively placid young man with eyes full of danger. "You've only ever sparred me as my second. You've never really tried to hurt me. And you've always held yourself back."

"I don't."

"You do." He gives an ugly laugh. "I might not be worldly or sophisticated or any good at anything besides magic, but I *do* know magic, Sammy. I can tell when someone has another gear they haven't tapped."

Rook's blue gaze is bright and hungry on me. I've seen him cast that look on so many other magicians who he's left bruised and broken, humiliated before the jeers of an arena audience. But he's never once looked at me that way, no matter how many times I've sparred him or how hard I've thrown my magic in his face.

I scoff. "This is ridiculous."

"Is it?" He spreads his hands. "I don't think I'm asking for very much from my soon-to-be-ex second."

I sigh. "Stop trying to bait me, Rook. Duel Tamsin or don't. Either way, you'll be free of me on your own terms soon enough."

"Except that it wouldn't really be my terms, would it?" Rook closes the distance between us faster than I register. My heart stutters. "You're the one who's quitting. You're the one who's leaving me. So it's still your plan. In the end, I'm still reduced to what you want me to be. What Silverstein wants me to be. What the whole damn world wants me to be."

I flex my hands, trying not to lose what few threads of patience still cling to me. "My plan is the only one that makes sense and gives us both what we want from this arrangement."

"No." My champion plants one finger squarely in the center of my chest and taps my heart with it. "No," repeats Rook. "For once, we're not going to do what's smart, or clean, or good for me, or good for you. We're going to do what I goddamn want."

"You're not serious about this."

"I am." He winks at me, almost flirtatiously. "Watch this, and don't blink." Before I can register what's happening, I feel—rather than see—Rook's magic flare outward from his body. I barely back away in time before his spell comes speeding toward me.

I duck instead of wasting energy on summoning a shield. The spell scorches the wall behind me with an angry hiss. "Have you lost your mind?" I yell. "We're going to have to pay the hotel for that cute little warning shot."

"Oh, live a little, Sammy." He curls a spark of magic around a lazy index finger. "Just admit it. You never really wanted to be my second. You wanted to be champion." He meets my eyes. "Because you love magic. You love it more than you love me."

I refuse to dignify his accusation with a response. Instead, I push my sleeves up as we circle each other. I've taken a duelist's stance without even meaning to. Muscle memory is a hell of a drug. "This is a stupid game," I inform him. I flex my hands. "And believe me, you don't want to win a stupid prize from me."

"Maybe. Maybe not." Rook watches me with careful, calculating blue eyes. It used to thrill me, seeing that look in his eyes. It always meant the end was near. That his opponent's decimation was in sight.

It's a lot less thrilling being on the receiving end of those eyes.

The next spell Rook casts is harder to read. Rook's good at disguising his tells. I only guess them half the time because I train with him so frequently. Even then, knowing what's coming is only half the battle, and few feelings are worse than knowing what spell you're about to get hit with and remaining powerless to stop it.

Rook crooks the tips of his fingers for just a moment. It's the hint I need. I glance down, and sure enough, find tendrils of magic snaking rapidly toward my feet. I dance out of the way as they writhe and twist, snapping at my ankles. The faster I dance away, though, the more seem to appear.

"Come on, Sammy," calls Rook, crooking those fingers over and over. Tendrils hiss and multiply. "Cast something. Cast anything. What's the point of studying all those spells if you never use any of them when it matters?" He flicks another tendril toward me. "Cast, god damn it!"

"No." I leap over the tendril. "I refuse to indulge your attempts to wreck the nicest suite we've ever been assigned on tour. Not to mention get us banned from this hotel for life."

"Then make me stop."

All the tendrils vanish in the blink of an eye. I'm still waiting with knees bent, prepared to jump and evade, to do whatever I can to keep this farce from escalating. I search the floor for more tendrils I've missed, a stray piece of Rook's spell lying in wait to ensnare my ankles.

Which is why I don't see it coming, when a sizzling ball of pure power crashes directly into my solar plexus. I go down with a gasp.

Rook has landed hits on me before. It's part of my job description. But he's never hit me that hard in my life, not even on that first day when he was trying to make me quit, like all his other seconds.

I just lie there for a moment, turtled up on the floor, wheezing.

"I did tell you, Sammy." Rook's voice is soft. Through tear-blurred eyes, I see his feet padding toward me. He's wearing these absurd, emoji-face-patterned socks that I got him as a gag gift for Christmas last year. "If we're going to do this, you'll need your magic."

When his feet stop before me, I have a direct sight line to a bright red emoji wearing an exaggerated frown. Steam puffs out of its ears. I stare, fascinated by the absurdity of this moment.

I close my eyes. "You want me to use magic, huh?"

"I want you to fight," says Rook. "You've never truly fought me before. I don't think you've ever truly fought anyone before."

"You want me to fight," I repeat dully. With a groan, I drag myself up onto one knee without lifting my head. My ribs are tender. I wonder if Rook's spell bruised one or more of them. "You sure about that, princess?"

I can practically hear the smirk in his voice as he coos at me, "Surer than I've ever been about anything, Sammy."

Stupid games and stupid prizes, indeed.

When I finally lash out against my champion, I don't use magic. Not at first. Instead, my weapon is pure physical rage. I dive toward Rook's feet and yank them out from under him with both hands, throwing the power of my entire body into the movement. Rook hits the hotel room carpet with a faint gasp of surprise.

I waste no time. I pin him to the floor with one knee. When he tries to shove me off, I straddle him, scrambling high on his torso until I'm practically sitting on his chest. I don't let myself settle back comfortably, though. Instead, I move my weight forward, leaning all of it into my hands and knees to lock his straining biceps down to the floor.

"Still no magic," he gasps up at me. He tries in vain to buck me off. "You sure you're even a magician anymore?"

I don't answer him, holding the pin in place. All magicians who enter the arena are trained, to some extent or another, in physical hand-to-hand combat. We have to know the basics, at least, or we're near useless in close quarters. Casting a spell to enhance our bodies with strength or agility or dexterity doesn't do us much good if we don't know what to do with those bodies—the same way a Stradivarius would be pointless in the hands of someone who'd never studied the violin.

Rook, though, has always neglected the skill of pure physical combat. He relies too much on spells cast from a distance or from the power he generates from magically enhanced strength alone. And usually, that's enough.

But not against someone who's trained with him nearly every day for the past three years.

I sense the magic that courses through his muscles as he calls upon enhanced strength to bench-press me off of him. Predictable. I close my eyes and counter with magic of my own, slipping it into my body to make me heavier than anyone with my frame should be. It's a fraction of the power he's summoned—just enough to push back a little, force him to waste a little energy.

As he pushes me off with a grunt of triumph, I clap my hands together. Magic crackles between my palms. "You want to see me cast something, huh?"

Before he can answer me, I thrust the spell toward him. I've never cast this one against him before. I've used it on other training partners—in scrimmages, or in experimental rounds with Master Silverstein's other magicians as I learned to mimic Rook's upcoming opponents. I got good at that, too—making unfamiliar magic my own, training until I moved just like my champion's enemies, cast magic that mirrored theirs. Made myself into a tool, the perfect instrument to hone Rook into the unstoppable terror he is today.

He's right, though. I've been holding back by not letting him taste the full range of magic I can cast. So when I unleash my first true spell against him, I make sure to pick a mean one.

Before I can chicken out of casting the damn thing, my magic snares itself around Rook's body in hissing coils of crackling arcane energy. No takebacks now.

He narrows his eyes as the bonds settle into place. "What are you playing at? You've never—"

I twist my fingers and make a fist before he can finish the sentence.

Rook screams, falling to his knees. The bonds haven't moved. Rook's limbs don't break, and his skin doesn't bruise. But I have an idea of how he's feeling. Most spells that I've truly mastered, I've also endured at some point in an arena.

"I told you," I tell him quietly, "I won't damage my champion. I wouldn't risk harming you physically before a duel. So, unfortunately for us both, I have to bewitch your pain receptors alone."

I keep my tone light and conversational, but I don't release my fist—or the spell. Not even when Rook begins to whimper faintly, clawing at the hotel carpet. A part of me wants to throw up. Another part of me wants to cry.

But the biggest part of me simply wants this to be over.

The awful sounds that Rook makes begin to change. For a dizzying moment, I wonder if I've screwed up the spell somehow, if I've hurt him in some terrible, permanent way.

Before I can consider letting go of the magic, though, I realize why Rook sounds different: He's no longer whimpering. Instead, he's laughing. A harsh, crazed cackle of laughter. Swaying slightly, he rises to his feet, still laughing.

"Oh, Sammy," he manages between chuckles, "you really are a damn piece of work." Bloodshot blue eyes meet mine. "Did you really think I, of all people, would yield to pain compliance alone?"

I don't see his hands move. I don't even sense Rook's magic in the air. But in the blink of an eye, my spell is shattered. In its place, Rook's magic roars over me in a wave of pure energy, pinning me flat to the hotel room floor.

I can't speak. I can't breathe. I'm a swimmer being pulled into deep water by an ocean tide, and for a few moments, I'm utterly helpless.

"That was a pretty good move," says Rook. I see his feet padding toward me again, but his voice sounds tinny and distant, like we're talking over a poor phone connection. "You surprised me. You really did. I've got to give credit where credit's due, you know?"

Rook crouches down beside me. Perched in a deep squat with his lanky limbs, he looks like a character on some kids' cartoon. Harmless. Friendly, even. And his expression seems almost sympathetic as he finds my gaze again. "I'm not letting you out, Sam," he tells me, sounding like he actually regrets the situation and hasn't brought it on us both himself. He chews on his bottom lip for a second or two, then adds, "Not unless you yield—or unless you find a way to counter me. Which is it going to be?"

I expect to panic. I expect, at the very least, to feel furious at how thoroughly my champion has trapped me here. Instead, a bizarre sense of calm settles over me.

I've found a way to breathe around the pressure of the spell settling against my chest. I use careful little breaths, in through the nose, out through the mouth. As I breathe, I think.

I've seen Rook force at least two opponents to yield with this technique. Both successful duelists, both of whom panicked when push came to shove. Smothering spells are fairly common in the arena, and both of those unfortunate magicians had previously countered smothering spell attempts from lesser opponents. The sheer magnitude of Rook's magic, however, proved too much for them to contend with.

But I face that magnitude every day of my life. And I've never shied away from it. Not even on that brutal day when we first met, and I took the job no one else wanted.

I continue to breathe. And, in time with my inhales and exhales, I weave the counter-spell with my fingers. It's a simple little thing. All it requires is force of will.

And force of will, as it turns out, is something I have in spades.

My counter-spell is not especially dramatic when I cast it. Magical energy so frequently sparkles, or roars, or crackles, as if the arcane needs to announce itself to affect a magician's opponent.

It doesn't. And my counter-spell proves just that, as it quietly, invisibly releases me from Rook's smothering power. I stand, gasping for air.

"So you can cast after all." Satisfaction drips from Rook's words as he starts toward me again. One hand is raised, ready to cast his own spell. "Good. Maybe you'll put up a real fi—"

I don't let him finish. The spell behind my counter-spell closes around his neck, silent but sure. A skinny, near-invisible cord of arcane energy sneaking out to ensnare my champion in the wake of my escape from his assault. It's a simple little thing, barely noticeable.

Which is, perhaps, why it sneaks right past Rook's usually impeccable defenses. He's so used to grand displays and intimidation that he doesn't expect to be attacked by the mundane—by something barely visible to an arena audience's eye.

My little cord of magic would be harmless in most circumstances. It's so small, so weak, it barely even counts as a spell.

Sometimes, in a duel, it's not about the sheer power of the spell itself—or the magician. It's all about timing and placement. And right now, my almost-always-harmless little thread of power is tightening around the throat of the mighty Lysander Rook.

My champion's hands climb to his neck as those pretty blue eyes bulge. He opens his mouth, and closes it again, gasping for oxygen as my spell slowly squeezes his carotid arteries shut.

"Yield," I tell him calmly.

Those bulging eyes snap toward me. Even with his face turning purple, fury is clear as day in his expression. He shakes his head at me.

"Come on, Rook. This is stupid."

Another stubborn shake of the head. His hands scrabble frantically at his throat as he sinks to his knees.

"You're going to pass out, then, which will count as an automatic yield. If you can't speak"—I know he can't speak, if he can't even breathe—"then signal me, the way you would signal a ref during a duel. Raise your hand."

He shakes his head for a third time. He gurgles as he does it. But he doesn't raise his hand.

A strange, slow moment unfolds between us right then. I don't release the spell. Rook doesn't yield. And in that moment, a dark little thought crosses my mind: *You could kill him right now if you wanted to.*

I try to stop thinking about it. That's the thing, though; the harder you try not to think about something, the more insistently it makes itself known.

You could kill him, just as easily as Blackwood killed Jamie all those years ago. You have that power over him.

No. No, no, no.

No. I won't do it, obviously. I don't want to. I can't.

But the thought is there. I could. It would be so easy in this moment.

My hands shake. Maybe Tamsin's right. Maybe I am just like her father. Maybe I am just like the man who killed Jamie.

Master Silverstein chooses this particular moment to burst into the room. "What the hell, Chan!"

Silverstein steps between us and shoves me aside, breaking my concentration. After that, all it takes is a snap of his fingers and a tiny flare of arcane power to eviscerate the spell around Rook's neck. "What the hell were you thinking?"

"He started it," I say before I can stop myself.

Rook's heaving in great gulps of air as normal color returns to his face, but he starts laughing. It makes him cough, but he doesn't stop, sinking back down to his knees as hysterical chortles rattle his lanky frame. "She's right," he gasps at Silverstein. "I challenged her. Wouldn't let her say no."

Lysander Rook looks objectively pathetic right now, on his hands and knees before me, giggling and clutching at the hotel room carpet. Yet that blue-eyed gaze, as it meets mine, is filled with nothing short of triumph. "You see, Sammy?" he rasps. "Now you know what you're capable of."

Silverstein glances between the two of us, wary calculation running through his eyes, but he says nothing. Unlike most adults in our lives, he's smart enough to know when he's fully lost control of a situation.

"You know what you're capable of," Rook repeats in a more thoughtful tone. "I guess that means you've grown out of the second's seat. I don't think I'll need you when I duel Tamsin." He smiles, wolfish. "Because, you see, I am going to duel Tamsin. And I'm going to wreck her, just like we talked about. And I'm going to do it without you. So don't bother showing up to the arena. I don't want you there."

"Oh, she sure as hell will bother showing up to the arena, whether you want her there or not," growls Silverstein. "Won't you, Sam? After all, you're the one who orchestrated all of this."

My fists close, nails digging into my palms, but my hands feel numb. I can't stop thinking about what I've almost done. What I nearly did do.

I could have killed my champion. His life sat there, precious and breakable between my hands—and I didn't let go. My magic triumphed over his for the first time I could recall. It felt exhilarating. It felt horrifying. It felt exactly how I imagine Mateus Blackwood must feel every day.

You and Dad are exactly alike.

The memory of Tamsin's words churn like bile inside me. I force it back down. The last thing I have time for right now is an existential crisis.

"I'm glad you got what you wanted out of me," I tell Rook. "The same way I've gotten what I wanted out of you." I bow my head to him, but I keep my gaze on those blazing blue eyes the whole time. "I hope the satisfaction helps you find someone else to sit in the second's seat during your duel against Tamsin Blackwood." I offer Rook a humorless smile of my own. "I guess I'm quitting a few days early, after all. To honor your wishes, of course."

"Chan!" Silverstein's voice is laced with alarm. "You can't be serious. We're less than week away from the duel. And you're the one who wouldn't let him back out of this damn dog and pony show in the first place."

"Didn't you just hear? He doesn't want to back out of it. Refuses, in fact." I shrug. "Besides, Rook is Rook. He chased away every other second until me. I don't see why I should be any different, except that I've kidded myself for longer."

I slam my way out the hotel room door before anyone can answer me. I don't look back.

17

TAMSIN

THE ARENA LIGHTS ARE going to strike me blind. My belly's flooded with nervous energy. When I first started dueling—on small, local circuits, nothing fancy, nothing anyone who mattered cared about—I assumed that once I was more experienced, I'd stop getting jitters at all.

It probably took me about fifty more duels to realize that that jittery feeling would never entirely go away. So I learned to normalize it instead. I started anticipating that belly swoop of heart-pounding anxiety, waiting for the adrenaline spike like it was an old friend.

I couldn't eliminate fear from existence. But I could master it by making it normal. Predictable. Boring, even.

Unfortunately, it's a lot harder to normalize dueling an undefeated champion after making out with his second, who turned out to be some unhinged evil mastermind plotting the destruction of your life that entire time.

I don't think there's a precedent for that.

I'm waiting in the wings to walk out as the announcer drums up audience anticipation for the duel. At least one section of the crowd out there is chanting Rook's name at the top of their lungs, over and over again.

Again, no precedent.

Dad's at my ear, as usual, filling it with advice that I'm only half listening to. "Just remember," he tells me, "the trick is putting on a show. The audience here doesn't really care who wins or loses. They just want to be entertained. Give them what they paid for, Tam. Show off some of your flashiest magic, impress them, but yield at the correct moment. Remember, losing your own way is still a win." From the corner of my eye, I see Dad wink at me. "We'll still collect our payday—and you'll be no worse for wear. Just be sure to quit before Lysander Rook does something to you that can't be undone."

I finally turn toward my father. "What if I do something to Rook that can't be undone?"

Another second would remind me that the odds are in my favor for a reason. Another second would boost my confidence by talking about all my accomplishments, and insist that victory is within reach, that no one—not even Lysander Rook—is truly invincible.

Dad simply shrugs, his mouth thin. "Don't overreach, my girl. I'm only trying to protect you."

I close my eyes. The biggest night of my career, and I might as well be spending it alone. Then again, I guess that's something Lysander Rook and I have in common. Word is that his second has locked herself up in their suite and refuses to come out to play her usual role at his side.

Thanks, in no small part, to me and the way that I, an idiot, have allowed her to manipulate me since the very moment we met. I could have let things go after that night at Agatha's, but instead I had to go and get attached to her. To trust her, even. And all so I could fool myself into believing that, what? That a friendship with Lysander Rook's second could end in anything other than disaster for both of us? That poor dead Jamie Chan's sister would want anything other than the complete and total destruction of anyone named Blackwood?

Stop it, Tamsin. This train of thought is headed nowhere good.

So I cut it off at the root. Samantha Chan will not matter to me anymore. She can't. The only capacity in which she matters now is this: that in a matter of minutes, Rook and I will be standing across from each other in one of the biggest magicians' arenas in the world. We will duel with each other using the best of our arcane skills until one of us yields or is deemed unable to continue.

And both of us will be utterly, utterly alone when we do it—each alone, that is, except for the other.

Suddenly, facing Lysander Rook doesn't seem so insurmountable. And suddenly, Rook himself—the prodigy, the champion of champions, the undefeated teen monster of a magician—seems so completely, plainly human to me.

"Are you ready?" my father asks.

I smile even though he can't see me from this angle. Because when this duel ends, I will have what I need, finally, to be free from him.

"As ready as I'll ever be," I say and step out under the lights.

18

SAM

I'M WATCHING TV IN the hotel suite that I supposedly share with my former champion.

I say "supposedly" because for the past week, we've never really been in the same place at the same time. I've made it a point to only linger in the rooms when I know Rook's at training. Rook, for his part, has been lingering longer and longer in the training arena. And when he comes home, he goes straight to his room and slams the door behind him.

I can't blame him. I've been doing the same. And I have to believe, at the end of the day, that it's for the best. I can't serve as second to a champion I can't trust myself around. A champion I want to hurt. A champion who, it seems, wants me to hurt him.

We can't be what we were. Maybe we could have been, if only one of us was pissed off with the other. If it was just one of us, the other could have poured out apologies and mea culpas and prostrated themselves to beg forgiveness. But we're both so incandescently, magnificently angry with each other that there's no space for grace. Not for either of us. Not now, and maybe not ever.

So my former champion goes off to that beautiful New York arena I've chosen as the site where vengeance will be taken against my dead brother's killer. And I remain here, in the overpriced hotel suite we barely share anymore, watching TV. Refusing to be within ten feet of the place where Rook will hopefully, mercifully put an end to Mateus Blackwood's legacy.

With luck, by this time tomorrow, Rook will have erased Tamsin Blackwood from the ranks of up-and-coming magicians—and, God willing, my stupid brain.

I flip from one streaming service to the next. One offers up some spy thriller, starring an artfully grunged-up yet handsome white man who looks like every other handsome white man I've seen in Hollywood trailers lately. Another broadcasts a documentary miniseries about the history of magic, detailing the politics that shaped the beginnings of the modern dueling arenas. There's a period drama offered on yet another service, boasting steamy romance full of unlaced corset close-ups and almost-kisses in grand ballrooms.

Of course, there's also the option to stream the broadcast of Rook vs. Blackwood, the great duel between teen phenoms taking place tonight, the spectacle that sold out the biggest magicians' arena in the country.

For a moment, my index finger hovers over the menu page on the screen. I could see my former champion. I could see him right now.

I could see Tamsin Blackwood. Her freckles, her constantly smiling eyes, the red highlights in her magnificent curls.

My index finger moves sideways and makes a selection. I settle on the documentary miniseries.

I try gallantly to get myself absorbed in historians' arguments on who was more influential in the legalization of magical dueling as a recognized form of entertainment: Ellis Tanaka, one of the first magicians to step into the arena, or Jefferson Hewitt, the senator obsessed with all things arcane, who campaigned for the recognition of magicians as legitimate entertainers. It's actually a pretty well-made series, the kind of thing I'd find genuinely interesting if my entire life felt just a little less like it was about to crumble apart around me.

I stare at the historians being interviewed on the screen for a few more minutes, but I don't really hear anything they're saying. I try flipping the program over to the steamy romance. My eyeballs are immediately assaulted by the sight of a man with an impressive set of mutton chops eagerly groping a very well-endowed blond who's been stripped down to her petticoats.

The blond moans with exaggerated ecstasy, right as I turn the volume up.

I hastily flip the program back to the documentary.

The historians are gone. Now they're interviewing a bunch of modern magicians, active duelists competing on the current circuit. I recognize one man, currently ranked number five, as a decorated close-quarters specialist that Rook trounced in a one-sided beatdown more than a year ago. This guy is one of the lucky ones—he's still a professional duelist, and all his limbs still work the right way.

"I really thought I had him," the man tells the cameras. His name is Rufus or Rudolf or something. He's handsome and well-muscled. Still young too—barely thirty, if I remember his stats correctly. If he can survive the likes of Lysander Rook with body and mind both intact, he should still have at least half a decade of good duels left in him.

Rufus-or-Rudolf chuckles ruefully. "Pretty arrogant of me, thinking

I could out-magic the magician of magicians, isn't it? But I figured if I could just close the distance, I'd have him. He wouldn't be able to cast any of those grandiose, long-range spells he's so well known for." Rufus-or-Rudolph shrugs. "Turns out he's pretty goddamn good in close quarters, too. Good enough to keep me out of that range as he pleases. I felt like a kid trying to bum-rush his older brother and just being shoved aside with a palm to the head."

He looks directly at the camera. "Make no mistake: I'm a damn good magician. But the Rook kid is in a class of his own. And worse still?" The guy shakes his head. "I don't think he even cares how good he is. It's like he was born to do this, built specifically from birth as this vehicle for magic, whether he wants a career in the arena or not. I guess religious folks would call him God-touched or something."

Rufus-or-Rudolf points at the off-camera interviewer. "I swear I'm not exaggerating. Ask anyone who's ever shared an arena with him. Ask the best of the best. They'll all tell you the same thing." He leans forward slightly, almost desperate, like he's issuing the last warning he can to a victim in a slasher movie. "Lysander Rook is a monster."

I turn the TV off. I almost throw the remote at it before I decide I'd better quit while I'm ahead and still evading retribution from the hotel owners for the mark Rook left on the suite walls during our fight.

That's really what it was. A fight. Not a duel—a real fight. And whatever else I wanted, whatever plans I had for my then champion, in the moment of the fight, I could have killed him. It would have been easy.

Easy to do exactly what a man like Mateus Blackwood would do.

I shiver, hugging my arms, and staring at the now empty TV. The blank black screen stares back at me accusingly. I observe the faint outline of my reflection on its surface: a broken-down, hollow-eyed girl with stringy, unkempt hair. Still swallowed up by one of Rook's old hoodies.

Still dressing in my former champion's cast-offs.

Frustrated, I tug the hoodie over my head and toss it aside. I've got a sweater of my own around here somewhere. Maybe it's time to change up my look. After all, after tonight, I'll have changed up my entire life, one way or another.

While I hunt for the bargain bin cardigan I'm only half-sure I packed, I flip the TV back on. Rufus-or-Rudolf is still going on and on about being terrorized by Rook in the arena. Now they're interspersing his commentary with actual footage of the duel in question. Even now, a year later, Rook's still mesmerizing. I watch as my former champion corners Rufus-or-Rudolph on the big screen, almost lazily holding the more experienced magician at bay with little flicks of power from his fingers. Every time Rufus-or-Rudolph looks to cut an angle, close in on Rook, Rook casts a different spell, somehow perfectly timing each counterattack before Rufus-or-Rudolph even knows what's happening.

It's brutal. Merciless. Humiliating. Yet despite everything else that's happened between me and Rook, the dance between the two magicians in that arena is still so utterly beautiful to me.

Before I can help myself, I flip the TV over to tonight's duel livestream.

I'm only going to watch a little bit. That's what I tell myself. Just enough to make sure everything's still going to plan, despite my screw-up the other night. Despite the imminent demise of my career—and let's face it, the whole personality I've built—as Lysander Rook's second, part of me still doesn't know how to quit being the old me.

I have perfect timing—the duel's just about to start. Rook shakes hands with Tamsin, perfunctory and businesslike. The cameras zoom in on her face as he clasps her fingers. Seeing her close-up like that on the big hotel room screen feels like a punch to my gut.

She's beautiful. It's hard to believe that I was ever able to see her as clinically as I used to, breaking down the pieces of Tamsin Blackwood into what she'd curated for public consumption: the cute little athleisure looks, the careful taming of her hair with bright girly scrunchies, the well-angled smiles for photos on her social media feed. I could have given you an equation, if you wanted. A formula for the consumption of Tamsin Blackwood.

Two weeks ago, I saw a collection of strengths and weaknesses and strategies that my chosen champion could exploit. And now all I see is a girl I miss even more than I miss my old life itself. And that's the most damnable thing of all.

Rook and Tamsin take their places on opposite ends of the amphitheater stage. Even behind the confines of the TV screen, I feel the onlookers practically vibrating with anticipation in their seats. They want a show to remember. A night they can brag about to all their friends who missed out on the chance to see Lysander Rook and Tamsin Blackwood duke it out in a sold-out New York magicians' arena.

Rook attacks first. That part is no surprise. He moves fluidly as his hands shape the spell, all sinewy grace and deadly intent. My shoulders relax a little. This is the Rook I know. This is the Rook who takes care of business in the arena, no matter what's happening outside of it.

Rook's spell—a crackling, silvery wave of arcane energy—arcs out toward Tamsin, who looks uncertain of how to handle it. She crafts a sloppy counter and barely escapes Rook's onslaught as his spell roars over her head. She dives into a roll at the last minute to duck the spell as her counter redirects the remnants of arcane power.

A cut bleeds sluggishly over Tamsin's left eye as she staggers to her feet. My heart plummets into my belly. The referee calls for a pause to the action as he and one of the arena doctors crowd around her to make sure she can still see. I know it's probably worse than it looks—injuries that cut in that spot right over the eye bleed dramatically but rarely incur lasting or serious damage—but my heart skitters inside me all the same.

This is what I wanted. I've been working toward the destruction of Blackwood's daughter for years. This is it: the moment where Rook—the wild, brilliant monster boy I've honed into a weapon of righteous vengeance—smells blood. Where he breaks his prey for good—and her father with her. Everything is going according to plan. I should be happy.

I should be.

Tamsin shakes off the arena doctor with a smile and a thumbs-up. The crowd cheers her for her grit as she steps back onto the amphitheater stage, now sporting some Vaseline over the cut—which will no doubt start bleeding into her eye again as soon as the action restarts.

Nothing to be done about it, though. Tamsin refuses to back down, and the doctor has declared her safe to continue. So continue she will.

Rook, encouraged by his earlier success, launches his next few spells in rapid succession. He throws everything from long range: gorgeous arcs of arcane power that cover the distance between his body and his opponent's. It's a good strategy for him, one I worked on with him for pretty much the entirety of our relationship. Rook is devastating from every position, but he does his most devastating work from a distance—not simply because of his long-range magic but because of the psychological toll it takes on his opponent. There's something about pouring all your energy into trying to fend off a guy you can't even physically touch that saps your willpower. I've experienced it even in simple sparring sessions with Rook in the training arenas back home.

Rook's greatest gift as a duelist is that he makes you want to quit. And as soon as you want to quit—as soon as you're ready to give up on yourself—that's when he knows he's won.

Tamsin's not quitting, though. She watches Rook with steady, narrowed eyes. Her footwork is deft. She moves just enough to keep herself out of harm's way, but she doesn't allow him to bait her into any obvious blunders. That's more than can be said for most of Rook's opponents, even the better ones.

"Blackwood the Younger is doing some fine defensive work despite that early blow from Rook," observes the man on the commentary track, "but we all know defense alone doesn't win duels." He chuckles then adds, a bit incredulously, "Especially against the likes of Lysander Rook! Look at him go!"

"Young Tamsin's going to have a tough time keeping up this pace as she allows Rook to really settle into his preferred range," agrees the co-commentator. "She'll have to launch an attack of her own at some point—the question is, what's she waiting for?"

I'm wondering the same thing.

Rook, emboldened by Tamsin's caution, takes control of the center of the arena. Another tactic he and I have perfected over the years. He employs quick, light spells to keep her at bay, slowly forcing her to the edges of the stage. He's establishing his territory, forcing her to fight on his terms.

Tamsin doesn't look particularly worried anymore, though. The uncertainty has long since vanished from her expression. She is, in fact, suspiciously tranquil, all things considered. Almost as if—

I stop myself short at the thought.

Almost as if she's the one luring Rook into a trap.

"You clever bitch," I whisper.

As if she's somehow heard me, Tamsin chooses that moment to unleash her magic. I can't quite make out the shape of the spell at first. It's not especially showy—the spell includes no immediately visible flare or sparks, no dramatic sound effects to accompany the attack.

Then I see what she's done. I have to stare at the screen a minute or two longer to confirm it, but it's plain as day to me once I see it: the faint gathering of silvery arcane power at the corners of the stage opposite Rook. Oxygen flees my lungs.

Tamsin hasn't been countering Rook's relentless barrage of spells at all—at least, not in the traditional sense. Instead, she's been siphoning off arcane energy from each casting. She's done it so subtly that I didn't see what was really happening.

None of us did.

"The Blackwood girl's clearly got something up her sleeve," the first commentator announces excitedly. "Just take a look at that stance, folks. With that last spell Tamsin cast, she looks like she's getting in position to—oh, my goodness!"

The spell Tamsin's unleashed materializes in full. A glittering net of arcane power settles over the arena. For a moment, the crowd's shouting simmers down to hushed murmurs. The thing Tamsin has created is, simply put, beautiful. The spell looks like pure starlight—starlight woven with precise, violent accuracy.

Rook looks up at that gorgeous, deadly canopy. I see it reflected in the blue of his eyes, extraordinary even through the distance of a television screen. Those eyes widen for a moment before he narrows them and casts his counter-spell.

It's too hasty. A basic counter isn't enough for what Tamsin's cooked up in that net, woven not only from her own power but from Rook's as well. It's a brilliant move. Rook's extraordinary, devastating amount of natural power, turned against him.

The net descends upon Rook. His hasty little counter-spell barely keeps the worst of it off him. He's knocked backward to the very edge of the amphitheater stage. He shies away from Tamsin's spell, hands thrown over his head in a desperate bid to protect himself from further damage.

The net, however, doesn't simply vanish, the way so many spells do once they've found their mark. This spell, apparently, is still seeking its target.

And that target is Rook. Still Rook. The net twists and attacks him over and over again. Each time, he dodges, weaves, counters. But he's getting tired. I've never seen him sweat like this, open-mouthed, as perspiration beads every inch of his face.

"Tamsin Blackwood is giving Rook the first real run for his money I believe we've ever seen, ladies and gentlemen," crows one of the commentators. "I can hardly believe it!"

"Regardless of who wins this duel, this young lady has made history," chimes in his co-commentator. "We have officially passed the halfway mark of the duel, which is longer than any opponent has ever survived against Lysander Rook."

"Tamsin Blackwood is absolutely living up to her father's legacy—

hell, despite some early trouble in this duel, she's probably going to take that win she's been favored for after all!"

"Well, I'd say it's still too early to make that call, but she's certainly putting up quite the unprecedented fight against absolutely insane odds—"

"Look, I'll admit that Rook looked like he had the upper hand as usual in the opening minutes of the duel, but look at her now! No one can argue that Tamsin Blackwood has been dominating her opponent ever since she set up that brilliant netting spell."

"True, I have to wonder if she played so defensively on purpose, to lure in the power she needed from Rook."

"Almost certainly, I'd say. Just look at that girl go!"

"If she keeps this up, I'm not sure what Lysander Rook is going to—"

I stab the mute button on the remote, almost violently. I've lost my appetite for the commentary track. I watch as my former champion struggles in silence against the girl I've dreamed for years of tearing limb from limb.

That same girl is absolutely pummeling Rook. His normally sharp, balletic movements grow slower and sloppier. She's wearing him down, and he has no recourse. No escape from the onslaught. She's doing to him precisely what he's done to so many other magicians over the years.

What he was supposed to do to her.

One particularly nasty blow from the net knocks Rook to his knees. He tries to build back up to his feet, but the net returns, dragging him downward. An ocean current, dragging him out into the deep.

Tamsin appears, ambling toward him, her hands dancing in the air as she puppeteers her beautiful, deadly net of starlight. I've never seen her look so predatory before.

I've never seen Rook look more like prey.

His eyes are wild. He's a hunted man on the brink of defeat, and he knows it. I lean forward on the couch, elbows digging into the tops of my knees. "Yield," I whisper. "Come on, Rook." My voice breaks. "Just yield. It's okay."

And it truly is okay. I'm a little surprised at how okay I've decided it is. I will destroy Blackwood, one way or another. I'll find a way. I always do. I'll think of something. I know I will.

But first, I need my champion—my former champion—to yield. I need him to admit his loss willingly before Tamsin does something that forces it.

Something that truly can't be taken back or undone.

Rook tries to rise again. And again, Tamsin's spell forces him back to his knees. He raises one hand, and for one heart-pounding moment, I think he might finally be signaling to the referee that he's yielded.

Instead, his fingers crook. I practically flinch from the screen as Rook casts another spell.

It's useless. Tamsin's net is too cleverly made, too well constructed. She's absorbing everything in her path, and Rook's magic, powerful as it is, simply feeds her.

The net closes in around him. Rook cries out and goes belly-down on the stage. The net digs into his skin, constricting his movement. It makes the kind of picture that could go viral and fuel memes on every magic-obsessed corner of the Internet: Lysander Rook, cocooned in starlight, looking utterly helpless for the first time in his dueling career.

"Just yield," I whisper again. As if he can hear me through the screen. As if he'd listen, even if he could.

Rook looks up, glaring directly at the cameras. He's got a black eye blooming on one side of his face and a thin smear of blood trickling from one corner of his mouth. He doesn't look frightened, though. He doesn't even look especially panicked or disappointed in his own performance.

As I watch, he grins with all his teeth. Blood coats some of the whites. He looks utterly ghastly and utterly defiant. A thread of starlight slices open the skin under his good eye. He doesn't even wince. Blood trickles lazily from the new wound.

Still, he doesn't yield.

He'll never yield.

I'm moving before I realize what I'm doing. I step into untied shoes and lace them up with shaking fingers then shrug into my windbreaker. I barely remember to grab my room key before I'm racing out the hotel suite door. Thank god we were booked into accommodations directly next door to the New York Magicians' Arena.

Because I need to get to that arena right now.

Security lets me through.

I'm so relieved I could cry. Rook and I have been on such terrible terms for the past couple days, I was half convinced my name would end up on the banned visitors list.

It didn't, thankfully. And for all intents and purposes, I'm still listed in official record as Lysander Rook's designated second for this duel. What we fought about days before doesn't matter. All that matters is what the record says—and the record says that I still belong to Rook. Which means that I have free reign of the arena.

I waste no time taking advantage of it.

The New York Magicians' Arena is spectacular in its own right, but it's at its most breathtaking in moments like these: when it's filled to the brim with spectators. Before now, I'd tried, as best I could, to imagine how this place would look on the night of a sold-out magic show. I imagined this venue over and over again, replaying this night in my head, as I mapped out my plot against the Blackwoods. How loud the crowd would be. How bright the lights would be when Tamsin Blackwood's bloody body was dragged from the arena, never to duel again.

Nothing in my imagination compares to the real thing. The arena is a glittering metropolis, a city within a city, teeming with people. People who are about to watch my former champion bleed out on stage before their eyes—the exact same way my brother bled out in one of Mateus Blackwood's back-alley clubs four years ago. These audiences are always so hungry for blood, and they never seem to have enough of it.

And year after year, duel after duel, from those back-alley clubs to the grandest arena in New York City, we magicians step into arenas to sate that audience's bloodthirst. To answer their need for beautiful, terrifying entertainment.

Master Silverstein looks surprised to see me making a beeline for the second's seat at his side. "Chan?" he yells over the roar of the crowd. "What are you doing here?"

"What I should have done a lot sooner," I yell back. I slide into the second's seat like I was born to it. "Lysander!" I scream.

At the sound of his name, the hunted, feral figure curled up before me on the stage looks my way. Blood drips into his eyes, red framing the familiar blue, as his gaze meets mine. For a moment, we're the champion and the second at any other duel, thinking and moving and casting in sync. One mind split into two bodies.

I know exactly what he's thinking.

"Yield," I tell him. My voice gentles. I don't know if he can hear me over all the noise in the arena. My best hope is that he can read my lips even through the slow drip of blood off his eyelashes. "Please, just yield, Rook. It's going to be okay. I promise it's—we're going to be okay. All you have to do is yield."

He closes his eyes. He's still smiling, oddly serene, despite all the blood and bruises. Swaying slightly, he staggers to his feet.

My heart sinks. He's going to let himself die in here. His final screw you to me for all the ways I've betrayed him, and it's going to amount to his own destruction.

Then, in the flash of seconds that feel like an eternity, he raises a shaking hand.

"I yield," says Lysander Rook.

He says it to Tamsin. But he's looking right at me as he says it.

The duel is over.

19

TAMSIN

I'VE SPENT A LOT of time fantasizing about how it might feel to win a duel in one of the biggest arenas in the country. I've spent almost as much time fantasizing about how it might feel to be the first magician in history to defeat the previously undefeated Lysander Rook, the enfant terrible of the magical world. To start carving a history of my own.

Fantasy is one thing. Reality, though, is something else entirely.

Everything's kind of a haze after Rook yields. I recognize events as they happen: the referee raising my hand to make my victory official, the arena doctor helping Rook limp off the stage, the mics shoved in my face as soon as I'm deemed sufficiently cleaned-up for public consumption.

I squint at the camera flashes clicking off in my sight line and find myself vaguely concerned that some unflattering picture of me with my eyes closed is going to make it onto the front page of some magicians' news site tomorrow morning.

Am I dissociating? Maybe I'm dissociating. Maybe that's why I'm thinking about how I'm going to look in the press photos, ten minutes after making magicians' history.

After I feed the reporters a bunch of stock answers, I flee to my hotel room, where my father awaits. He's sitting at the desk chair, his hands folded in his lap. "You're back late," he observes. "Busy with your new fans, I take it?" He's not smiling, and he doesn't congratulate me on my victory.

"I'm sorry." I close the door behind me. "Did I not put on enough of a show for you?"

"You disobeyed me."

I laugh. I can't help myself. "I just made history. I beat Lysander Rook. The boy who can't be beaten."

"Anyone can be beaten."

It's a big change of tune from telling me that Rook would destroy me body and soul, but I ignore that. "I made history," I repeat. A disbelieving giggle escapes me. "And that's still not good enough for you."

"You didn't listen to me," hisses Dad. "That netting spell may be functional, but it's not audience friendly—"

"The audience sure seemed to love it, judging from where I was. Which was on stage. In front of them. More than I can say for where you've been for the past few years."

My father goes pale. "How dare you," he whispers. "You're old enough to know what I've done for you all these years—"

"Oh please," I burst out. "What you've done for me?" I laugh again. "You've done plenty for me. That's true. You bound me to contracts with promoters you owed favors to and made sure you controlled any money that came in for what I did."

"Money I used to raise you!" Dad's voice rises. "Do you know what I've sacrificed to keep you under my roof? Do you know what it costs to raise a child? You could never imagine—"

"I'm not finished," I thunder at Dad. He sinks back in the chair, faint shock etched across his weathered features. I've never spoken that way to my father in my entire life. It feels mean.

And God help me, right now, mean feels good.

"When you first told me you were going to teach me magic, I thought I was so lucky," I tell my father. "I mean, you're my *dad*. You seemed larger than life to me when I was little. And you were so, so good at making me feel special. I've got to hand it to you, Dad, you had me in the palm of your hand. Little Tam was one hundred percent convinced that you were acting out of love for me. Pure, selfless, parental love. What a joke, right?"

I shake my head, chuckling bitterly to myself. "It was perfect, really. With Mom out of the picture, it's not like I had another parent to challenge your influence. You knew I'd jump at the opportunity for your attention. And by the time I figured out that, as far as you were concerned, I was only worth whatever profits you could turn off my magic . . . well. It was too late by then, wasn't it? I was already all tangled up with your promoters, your brand, your vision for what I'd do for your precious legacy. The Blackwood name."

Slowly, I cross the room. "That all changed tonight." My father doesn't move from the chair, even as I draw closer and closer to him. He says nothing. "You didn't want me to win—didn't even think I was capable of it—but I did. On my own. Without a real second, or even a real arcane master, because let's be honest here, Dad, you haven't been a true teacher to me in years. I took Lysander Rook's crown by myself. I did that. Me."

"Don't do anything rash," Dad says. A faint note of desperation clings to his tone. I relish the sound of it. "Tam, honey, listen to me: It would be foolish to think you can strike out on your own after tonight. You need me now more than ever. To—to guide your career. To make sure you're making the best possible choices."

I cock my head. "Do I?" I tap my lip with one finger. "You know, I really don't think so. After all, I just won a boatload of prize money, didn't I? And for the first time in my life, none of it is money you can control. I'm eighteen. A legal adult. Just like Jamie Chan was when you pushed him into that duel against Alexei." I smile at my father. "Which means my money is mine, and mine alone. Nothing you can do about it, Dad."

"Tamsin, I need you to listen—"

"No, I don't think I will," I say cheerfully. "I think that it's my turn to talk, actually. And the first thing I want to tell you is this." I lean over the chair, so that I'm looking directly into my second's eyes so he can't misunderstand me.

"Thank you for your many years of service as my second, Master Blackwood," I tell him. "You're fired. Now get the hell out of my hotel room."

For what it's worth, I'm right about not needing my second anymore.

Barely an hour after my victory over Rook is announced, my phone blows the hell up. My social media channels explode. Suddenly, every promoter in the world wants to invite me onto a show—for good money, naturally, whether I win or lose, plus a bonus if I win—and every remotely magic-related brand wants to sponsor me.

Not one of them gives a damn who my second is. Come hell or high water, they all just want a piece of the girl who beat Lysander Rook. I could be a convicted murderer, for all they care. It might even help my case, at this point. Blackwood couldn't poison them against me if he tried.

I'm free.

I expected to feel overwhelmed the day I cut my father loose. Overwhelmed by joy, or fear, or even wistfulness, I wasn't sure, but I expected to feel something.

I didn't expect to simply feel empty.

All I can think about is how Rook looked in the second half of that duel. Like he'd given up already. Like he was just waiting for the whole thing to be over and didn't care if he died in the process.

Yet he wouldn't yield. Not until his second gave him her blessing.

I flinch away from that part of the memory. I don't want to think about Samantha Chan right now. If possible, I never really want to think about Samantha Chan ever again, actually, but that doesn't seem totally realistic.

Of course, now that she's entered my mind, I can't get her face out of my head. She sounded so sure of herself when she screamed for her champion to yield, but when I looked at her face, I saw something behind those steady dark eyes.

She looked hunted. The same way Rook looked hunted when he realized it wouldn't be so easy to undo my netting spell. The way he looked when he gave up and let me pummel him without complaint for nearly ten minutes.

Maybe that's why I feel so hollow. Defeating Lysander Rook should have been a challenge. A true coup. I should feel like a god right now. I should feel like a champion among champions.

Instead, I feel like a bully. I feel like Dad.

"You're free of him now," I whisper to myself. I close my eyes and say it again: "You're free, Tamsin. Be happy."

For my own sake, I have to try.

As it turns out, I'm destined to think about Samantha Chan again a lot sooner than I wanted to. Mostly because, try as I might to ignore the unfinished business between the two of us, fate has other plans.

I run into her on my way down to the gym. It's one of my late-night sessions, where—prior to my run-in with one Lysander Rook—I'd rarely ever been interrupted. My duel with Rook may be over, but the promoters will be chomping at the bit sooner rather than later to see me enter the arena once more. To ensure that my victory in the New York Magicians' Arena wasn't a fluke. Which means I need to keep body, mind, and magical ability all well-honed.

I'm pretty sure I spot Sam before she spots me. It's what I imagine a bullet through your gut probably feels like, seeing the girl who haunted my mind for weeks. The closest thing I've ever had to a real friend, before she turned out to be a lying piece of shit.

I recover faster than I expect, though. Because, of course—as I scope out my usual assault bike—my next duel is already on my mind.

And as I watch Sam slip under the squat rack, I realize exactly what I need from her.

I'm polite enough—and mindful enough of gym safety—to wait for her to finish her warm-up set before I approach her. As she re-racks the barbell with a huff, I gather the courage to call her name.

"Hey! Chan!"

She almost knocks the barbell off the rack. "Jesus Christ."

I saunter over to her. "I thought you might like to know that I just fired my second."

Sam spins around, eyes wild. "What?"

"You probably know him better as my dad," I tell her conversationally. "Master Mateus Blackwood. You know, your brother's murderer." I lean in nice and close. "The reason you lied to me for three straight weeks as you plotted to destroy my life."

Sam doesn't bother trying to rebut me this time. Instead she just sighs, leaning up against the squat rack. "What do you want, Tamsin?"

"In a couple of months, the promoters at the New York Magicians' Arena will want to see me duel again." I shrug. "They need proof, you see, that what I did to Lysander Rook wasn't just dumb luck. And for that matter, so do I."

"Why?"

"Isn't it obvious?" I roll my eyes. "Come on, Sammy, you're one of the best seconds in the country. You know all about building a brand and marketing a good magician for the dueling circuit. You of all people should know why I'd need to prove myself." I tap my chest. "When I beat your boy, I was still Mateus Blackwood's product. Still my father's daughter. I've never won a duel where I wasn't. So the next time I step into that arena, I'm going to be my own person. And I'm going to win. Not as Mateus's daughter but as Tamsin Blackwood, one of the best damn magicians in the country. I'm not just going to destroy Dad's legacy, Sam. I'm going to eclipse it. And that's where you come into play."

Sam stops leaning against the squat rack. Understanding dawns on her face. "You want a rematch with Lysander. You're going to challenge him again."

I shake my head. "You still don't get it." I chuckle. "No, Sam. I don't want to challenge the boy I literally just beat. I don't want a duel with your plaything."

I look her dead in the eyes when I finally tell her what I've wanted from that first moment I saw her cast magic. "I want to duel you. I'm going to challenge you to face me in the middle of the New York Magicians' Arena three months from now, in front of another sold-out crowd. And when you say yes—because let's face it, we both know you're eventually going to say yes—I'm going to destroy you."

"I see." Sam's eyes narrow at me. Even now, I can see the calculations spinning to life behind them. I can't help but admire her for that, however grudgingly. The girl seriously doesn't give up. "And what makes you so very sure I'm going to say yes?"

"Because I'm going to do you a solid." I smile at the surprise on Sam's face. Even before I found out about what she really wanted to do to me, Samantha Chan has always given off this vibe of being one step ahead of me. It's addictive, feeling like I finally have the upper hand for once.

"Oh yeah?" Sam folds her arms. A defensive posture. "How do you figure?"

"I can do a whole lot more besides firing Dad," I tell her. "I can give you the revenge you've always wanted against him." My smile widens at the sudden hunger in her eyes. So she still wants it, even now. That works for me. It means she's likelier to give me what I want, too.

"Once I cut ties with Dad, I'll have no reason to continue protecting his secrets," I explain. "The prize money from beating Rook in that duel leaves me financially independent. No more blood money keeping a roof over my head. No more complicity in my father's dirty little business deals. Which means I can finally expose him for what he is."

Sam exhales sharply. "You're going to turn him in to the authorities?"

I shake my head. "Even with everything I've got on him—everything I've seen over the years—I doubt I could make an actual felony stick. My father's too clever and too slippery for that. He won't do prison time. But I can do the next-best thing."

"And what's that?"

"I can destroy him myself." I watch with satisfaction as Sam's eyes widen. "I'll tell the world what he's done over the years—to me, to you, to your brother. Every respectable arcane master, dueling magician, and magic show promoter will be forced to see the great Master Mateus Blackwood in his true form: an abuser, a criminal, and a petty old man long over the hill who's willing to harm anyone he has to just to cling to a shred of relevance. I promise you by the time I'm through, no respectable arcane venue will ever work with my father again. He'll be an outcast from all places magical. Shunned by everyone who worships him now. Persona non grata, in the only world that's ever mattered to him."

Sam's mouth has parted slightly. "You'd do all that for me? After everything I did to you?"

"Don't flatter yourself. I'm not doing this for you." I lean in close and make sure to speak carefully and clearly so I'm certain that Sam understands this part. "I'm doing this for me. Do you know what it's like to live under Mateus Blackwood's roof for eighteen years? Being treated like I'm just an extension of my father—not just by him but by everyone around him?" I scoff before she can answer. "You don't. How could you? You're just like the rest of them, as it turns out. Just one more person who treats me like an object he owns. A prize that can be taken away from him, or used, or broken. Never mind what it does to me, right? It only matters what it does to him. He's the important one."

I take a deep breath. I need to stay in control here. "That ends now. I'm setting myself free. From now on, I'm no longer going to be Master Mateus Blackwood's daughter. I'm going to be Tamsin Blackwood, the girl who exposed her crook of a father for what he really is. The girl who gave justice to all the people he hurt."

I smile coldly at Sam as I wrap up my speech. "So what do you say? I'll avenge your brother—truly avenge him, just the way you always dreamed. And in exchange, you'll face me in the arena, where, of course, I'll wipe the floor with you and send you home with your tail between your legs."

Sam laughs darkly. "You're that sure you can beat me, are you?"

I laugh, too. "You're right, I guess. It's a risk. A duel is always a risk—a miscalculation you made, by the way, by pitting Rook against me. So yes, I'm giving you a chance to tear me apart yourself—if you can."

I lean in close, delighting in the hitch of her breath. "But here's the thing: if you really want to take me out, for once in your life you're going to have to get your own hands bloody." I meet her gaze and hold it so she can see that I'm serious. She's got no one and nothing to hide behind now. "No Lysander Rook to do your dirty work. No puppet to use against me. Just you and me: two magicians with unfinished business to settle."

I offer Sam a hand to shake. "What do you say, Chan? My grudge against yours, in ninety days' time?"

Samantha Chan gives me a long, appraising look. Maybe I'm kidding myself when I think I see a flash of vulnerability in her expression. But her hand is firm when her fingers close around mine. And still, as ever, she gives nothing away.

"You have yourself a deal," she tells me.

20
SAM

I CAN'T BLAME TAMSIN for wanting her own revenge against me after everything that passed between us. And what better place for a magician's vengeance than the largest arena in the country? After all, I had the same idea myself, once upon a time.

Accepting her challenge felt like self-flagellation in some ways. Maybe I've decided that Tamsin deserves her vengeance just as much as I once deserved mine.

The rest of my life, after Tamsin defeats Rook, becomes a blur for a little while. Rook and I don't speak. For a while, I make half-hearted attempts at tracking him down. I text him a few times, but they don't even get left on read—he simply doesn't bother to open them. Next, I try messaging him on one of his social media channels, only to discover that he's deleted all his accounts. When I ask Master Silverstein whether Rook has entered witness protection for some top secret crime or if he's simply trundled off to some corner of East Coast suburbia to die in obscurity, all I get is a stony look and a sigh.

"What?" I'm immediately defensive. "I'm running out of other ideas for what the hell could have happened to the guy."

I get another sigh for that particular remark. "Samantha. Lysander has built his entire life around his magical career. He's pretty much made being undefeated his whole personality. Put yourself in his shoes for a moment, would you? Imagine what it's like to have everything that defines your self-worth shredded inside of ten minutes in front of a sold-out crowd in an unfamiliar city."

Silverstein pauses then peers at me sidelong. "Adding to that, imagine that you've just had the falling out to end all fallings out with your only friend in the world. Now tell me, would you be super keen on gallivanting around for a lunch date?"

"I didn't ask for a lunch date, I just want him to answer my texts," I mutter. I chew on my lower lip, then ask, because I evidently have no self-control to speak of, "Do you really think I was Rook's only friend in the world?"

Silverstein makes a derisive sound. "I think you were the closest that poor kid was going to get, with the way he was built. No one else his age was ever going to understand him, or his priorities, or his lifestyle, not really. A boy like Lysander Rook is always going to be a magician first and a teenager—a kid—second. It's always going to hold him apart from his peer group."

"Except for me."

"You know why, right?" Silverstein's still peering at me with that oddly knowing look in his eyes. "You're more like Rook than you think, Samantha. Why do you think he took to you after chasing away all his other seconds?"

"I thought I was just crazy enough to take the punishment."

Silverstein laughs. "And you think being crazy makes you *less* like Rook? Think again, kid. The pair of you are among the most talented magicians of your age—of any age, if we're honest—but I've never seen two eighteen-year-olds worse at interacting with other eighteen-year-olds. Comedians could probably write a whole set about it. Neither of you know how to be normal kids. That's why you have each other."

"Had." I swallow hard.

A hint of sympathy trickles into Silverstein's expression. "Don't be so quick to give up on him, Sam. He needs time, is all. And I think you do, too. You'll find each other again when you're both ready. You've shared too much not to."

So I give Rook time. I give myself time, too.

Events in the broader magical world unfold almost exactly the way I'd expect. With Rook suffering a humiliating, one-sided loss at the hands of a nepo kid like Tamsin, the pecking order has shifted overnight. If Rook decided to stay in the public eye, craft statements, take interviews with the press, maybe it would be different, but he might as well be a ghost now. As far as the public is concerned, he's hiding somewhere with his tail tucked between his legs.

How quickly the world turns on you when you're a god proven mortal after all.

Meanwhile, Tamsin steps neatly into Rook's old place in the magical pecking order. She's the new teenage darling, ranked number one on the dueling circuit. The world is her oyster. Every promoter wants a piece of her. Tamsin Blackwood's face and name are everywhere, suddenly synonymous with precocious youth, success, and power: the very picture of what every budding magician aspires to be.

And I'm the one who's supposed to topple her. The idea of even trying gives me hives. But I made Tamsin a promise to show up in that arena. I won't break another promise to that girl. Not after everything I've tried to do to her.

Tried and failed.

For what it's worth, Tamsin keeps her end of our bargain: She does everything in her power to destroy Master Mateus Blackwood in the eyes of magical society. Tamsin's rise through the ranks seems to inspire the former nepo kid to give her whole life a makeover. And, true to her word, Tamsin's first act as the freshly financially independent teen queen of magical society is to expel Blackwood from her inner circle. Seemingly overnight, Daddy Dearest gets tossed out with the rest of her old life.

When asked about why she's decided to part ways with her own blood, Tamsin's too much of a class act to openly bad-mouth him, but her comparative silence—sprinkled with borderline passive-aggressive platitudes—is, if anything, even more damning.

"I'll always be grateful to my father for being so generous with his time and energy, and I'm happy to credit him with truly getting me my start as a magician," she tells eager reporters. "I wouldn't be where I am today without the foundation he provided for my career in magic. That said—"

And here, she always takes a pause, like she's truly relishing the moment.

"That said," continues Tamsin, "as I continued to grow as a magician, my ambitions grew with me. That's no fault of my dad's. Speaking frankly, however, I believe that we eventually grew in different directions. This was made abundantly clear to me by the very different visions we each expressed for the shape of my career. Ultimately, I need a second who will be capable of seeing me through some of the biggest dueling events in the world and supporting me fully."

She leans forward here, speaking very clearly: "I need someone who truly believes I can win—and knows how to help me become, and remain, a champion among champions."

The first time I watch her make that statement on some social media reel, I sit with her words for several minutes.

Tamsin was supposed to be my enemy. I couldn't stand caring about her. Caring about her meant that Mateus Blackwood was winning. Every involuntary smile I found myself offering his daughter—every secret glance toward the curve of her body or the glow of her cheeks—was like spitting on Jamie's grave.

In the four long years I spent plotting against the Blackwoods, it never once occurred to me that Mateus Blackwood's daughter and I might just be on the same side.

For weeks, I obsessively read through every Tamsin Blackwood interview I can find. I listen to all her podcast guest spots, watch all the social media reels that remix that first sound bite about her departure from the fold of her famous father.

I need someone who truly believes I can win.

Tamsin doesn't stop there. Mysterious rumors with no clear source begin to circulate with shocking fervor. People start to whisper about where Mateus Blackwood got his money after retirement. The back-alley deals. The illegal clubs. The complicity in all that blood spilled for entertainment behind closed doors, from the veins of those too young and naive to say no.

It's not long before media outlets start asking Tamsin if she knows anything about all these stories. And when they do, she's perfectly prepared.

"I never wanted it to be true," she tells one reporter, tears shining on her cheeks. "I let myself believe that it couldn't be true. He is my father. And I wanted to believe he was a good man. But the world deserves the truth. I never want Dad to hurt anyone else, ever again. I'll do anything to ensure that he doesn't."

She's the perfect repentant daughter, the martyr willing to give up her own family to protect everyone else's. The best PR experts in the world couldn't have written a better script for her if they tried.

It's not enough to put Mateus Blackwood behind bars. Just like Tamsin predicted, it's a war of reputation that she's waging now—and she wins it easily. The once famous, well-respected Master Mateus Blackwood is granted no quarter in any legitimate arena. Other magicians are polite enough to his face, but anyone who knows anything knows what's said about him behind closed doors. He's finally the pariah I've always dreamed he'd become.

And I didn't even have to destroy his daughter to do it. I just had to wait for her to speak her mind.

It should be everything I wanted.

It's not.

It's not enough for me.

I can't explain why. I should be celebrating the downfall of Mateus Blackwood. I should be ecstatic. I've gotten everything I've ever wished for since my brother died. In the four years since losing Jamie, I can't remember a single day that I haven't woken up with a hunger inside me. I've craved violence, and hurt, and destruction. It's the closest I've come to understanding audiences at magic shows, the way they scream for dueling magicians to tear each other apart.

I've avenged my brother. Yet I'm still waking up hungry.

I only know one thing that might sate it.

After a couple weeks of Internet stalking Tamsin Blackwood, I start looking into her father's current whereabouts. This takes a lot more active digging—simply scrolling through my social media feed and listening to magicians' podcasts at the gym won't cut it for this task.

I've learned patience over the years, though. After all, I've waited almost half a decade to avenge my brother's murder. If that doesn't qualify as patient, I don't know what does.

My willingness to wait and dig does eventually pay off. It takes a lot of targeted searches and pointed questions in some of the shadier corners of the magicians' Internet, but I find out where Blackwood's holed up.

As it turns out, my old enemy doesn't lurk very far from me at all. So I buy a bus ticket.

The club smells like piss.

That's all I can think about when I finally locate the address I've screenshotted on my phone. As far as my parents are concerned, I'm at a training camp. It's not so far off from the truth. The club I've tracked down is, technically speaking, a well-known magicians' hangout. It's even got a dueling arena.

What I've neglected to disclose to my parents is the legitimacy of the club. Which is to say: it doesn't have any, as far as magic and the law are concerned.

Nervous energy raises the hair on the back of my neck as I wander through the dilapidated, rusty-hinged doors. There's no actual ID check at the front, of course, so it's easy to waltz in despite being under twenty-one. That doesn't change the fact, however, that I've never actually stepped foot in one of these clubs.

I can't stop wrinkling my nose at the scent of the place. How anyone can pay attention to magic when it smells this bad in here, I have no idea.

It doesn't take me long to find what I'm looking for. All I have to do is follow the sound of heckling and applause. I push my way through the crowded bar into one of the back rooms. The good news about this is that it smells slightly less like piss in there. The bad news is that instead, the odor of human sweat intensifies significantly.

I catch the tail end of the current duel. A brown-skinned female magician with a bright purple pixie cut and a complex tattoo of vines curling down her neck controls the center of the ring. She squares off against a stout, bearded blond man who wouldn't be out of place on one of those Viking period shows.

He's advancing on her territory, throwing vicious, crackling bolts of arcane energy in a furious flurry. He looks strong and fast, and he's probably hoping to overwhelm the smaller magician with pure volume.

The woman doesn't look worried, though. She evades most of his spells without bothering to throw any counter-spells, relying on physical agility alone. A few of his blasts manage to clip her, singeing her lightly on her ribs and shoulders, but nothing that gives her pause.

Frustrated, the man draws closer and closer. This, apparently, is what the woman wants. Just as he steps within hand-to-hand combat range, she throws a vicious push kick to his torso. It's enhanced with a brutal amount of magical strength, the spell so powerful I can feel the shift in energy even here from the back row.

Her opponent flies backward from the force of it. He lands on his back, dazed. Before he can get his bearings, she's already pressing her advantage. She casts her next spell from the distance the push kick earned her. The flare of her arcane energy sears its way across his face. He cries out and goes down. When he tries to rise again, another flare of energy—once against cast across the ring—greets him. He goes back down.

"Yield!" he cries, raising his hands. "I yield, I yield the duel!"

His opponent looks as if she's considering continuing. My heart climbs into my throat. This was how Jamie died. The duel should have been stopped when he yielded, but a bloodthirsty, mismatched opponent riding high on adrenaline—combined with the nonexistent efforts of a lazy referee more interested in a hungry crowd's approval than duelist safety—ensured that my brother left a club just like this in a body bag.

Before the purple-haired woman can consider summoning more magic, however, a burly East Asian man with a pair of sleeve tattoos—apparently, the makeshift referee for this duel—enters the ring and signals a stop to the action. Gruffly, he raises the woman's hand, to a combination of cheers and jeers from the crowd. Another man enters the ring to help the blond Viking type wobble back to safety.

My heart returns to its normal spot in my chest. Both duelists are alive.

Both got luckier tonight, it seems, than Jamie did all those years ago.

"Enjoying yourself?"

I think I'm mishearing that voice at first. What I want can't possibly come this easily to me. Nothing has since Jamie died. Surely, I'd have to jump through more hoops to find my mark.

"It's a good show," the voice continues. "Nothing like some of the scraps magicians would get into in the old days, but close enough. None of this sanitized, sanctioned bullshit that's got all the kids so excited. Don't know any better, I suppose."

Slowly, I turn around. Sure enough, he's right there in the flesh: Mateus Blackwood. He hasn't shaved in a few days, his beard coming in gray and brown in sparse patches around a once clean-cut face. He's got dark circles under his eyes, stinks of beer, and is dressed in rumpled clothes. But it's Blackwood all the same. And right now, he's looking at me like he wants something.

Good. So do I.

"Jesus." He squints at me. "You're not Samantha Chan, are you?"

"Good memory." I offer him a small, flinty smile. "The very same."

Blackwood chuckles. "I thought so. I rarely ever forget a face, and to your credit, you did offer my Tamsin a good deal to duel your champion, back before . . . well, before everything that happened."

I'm careful to keep my face neutral, but I clock the instinctively possessive reference to Tamsin and the wistfulness that lingers behind those black eyes for just a moment.

Mateus Blackwood, it seems, is still Mateus Blackwood, though. He recovers quickly from the emotional slip. "What brings the great Lysander Rook's second to my humble den of iniquity?"

"Well, to start, I agree with what you were saying." I lean in a bit closer, ignoring his smell, and lower my voice into an appropriately conspiratorial tone. "These unsanctioned clubs are a lot more . . . eventful than what's on the mainstream circuit right now."

Satisfaction, along with a flicker of hope, light up his weathered features. If he weren't such a piece of shit, I might actually feel a little bad for him. "More kids should think like you," he tells me. "You thinking of taking your own shot in the ring?" He jerks his head toward the center of the room, where the poor cleaning staff is mopping up Viking Guy's blood. "I can get you on tonight's card on short notice if you'd like. I'm in charge of all the matchmaking at this club, so I can make it happen, easy as pie. I'd be happy to get you some action if you can take the heat."

"You'd do that for me?"

"I like your energy." Blackwood looks down his nose at me, all benevolent magnanimity. "Besides, the crowd here would love to see Lysander Rook's second perform."

"Really?" I tap my chin thoughtfully. "What about Jamie Chan's sister? Would they be as excited to see her?"

A wary sort of confusion unfolds across Blackwood's haggard face. "I don't follow."

"Oh, come on, you're a smart man. And you said yourself that you rarely ever forget a face." I draw still closer to him. I don't look much like Jamie, but our parents' friends used to say that we had the same eyes. Maybe mine will jog Blackwood's memory. "Jamie Chan was my brother, and he died four years ago in a ring just like that one, in a club that looked and smelled very much like this. He was a late replacement. A kid, the same age I am now, barely old enough to duel, even in a club like this, but he was good at magic, and charismatic, so he could hype up a crowd if you needed him to—and you, Mateus Blackwood, certainly did that night."

"Look, Miss Chan—"

"He fought a guy named Alexei Adamovich," I interrupt. "A real close associate of yours—and a real favorite for putting up mean fights."

Recognition flashes through Blackwood's expression. "He was the kid Alexei killed."

"Yes." I don't quite succeed at keeping the tremor out of my voice. "So before I agree to *perform* for you in that ring, I just want to know: Why did you let it happen? The night my brother died, why did you let your man kill him?"

Blackwood stares at me, incredulity slowly making its way across his expression. "Are you serious? My goodness, you are." Slowly, he shakes his head. "You poor, poor thing. Forgive me, I really didn't see this coming. You know, Samantha, there are any number of reasons I could think of that Lysander Rook's old second might have wanted to track me down. But I didn't expect any of them to involve wasting my time."

I rein in the knee-jerk flare of my temper. I need to retain control of this interaction. Otherwise, all the work I've done to get here will be for nothing. Back in New York, I let my feelings cloud my judgment. I'm not making that mistake a second time.

"Why did I let it happen?" Blackwood continues. His voice takes on a hard edge. "As if I had a true hand in any of this. Let me explain something to you, my dear. The so-called underground of the magical world is magic in its purest form. It's magic as it was meant to exist. No rules. No regulations. And every man out for himself. Your brother was one of them. He stepped up to the plate. So did Alexei. I simply facilitated what they both wanted. If it ended in a way neither of them would have preferred, well, that's the choice they both made, isn't it?"

"Jamie was just a kid." My voice cracks. I hate that it cracks.

"He was your age. And Lysander Rook's. And my own daughter's. And all three of you seem to have no trouble at all diving headfirst into the dueling circuit." No hint of remorse colors Blackwood's voice. He's not even bothering to fake it, which would maybe be the decent thing to attempt.

"We all duel with regulations and referees in place—"

"But you choose to duel, nonetheless. And you can, because you're all adults, legally speaking." Blackwood shrugs. "Your brother was an adult when he died. And he made his own decisions. That's what being an adult means, you know. You can do whatever stupid shit you want to and reap the consequences yourself." He chuckles darkly. "It's what my Tamsin's set out to do, after all."

"So to be clear, you're not sorry." My voice tightens against my will as my eyes burn. My ears ring. "You accept no responsibility for what happened."

"To be honest?" Blackwood casts a pitying look at me. "I barely remember your brother. He was nothing special, at the end of the day. That sounds harsh, but it's best that you know that. It does you no good to put him on a pedestal for the rest of your own life. Not when it could be so much more."

"Like yours, you mean?" I draw myself up, straightening my spine. If I'm going to be angry, I should at least weaponize it. Let my anger be productive. Let my anger accomplish something in this awful piss-scented hellhole. "Let's be real, Blackwood, your reputation precedes you, but it's not much of a reputation anymore, is it? You're old and washed up. The only thing keeping you relevant after retirement was your daughter's talent, and now Tamsin's gone and left you, too. You have nothing."

I see the moment of danger, when Blackwood's hands ball up into fists and the threat of violence sparks in his eyes. Before it can ignite, I smile at him again. "You and I do have one thing in common, though."

"Do we now?"

"Sure. I'm surprised you didn't bring it up sooner. We're both seconds who have been dumped by our champions." I scoff like this is a minor inconvenience and not a hideous embarrassment, and nod toward the dank, blood-stained ring a few yards away. "You say you'll offer me a chance to duel here. Your den, your rules, no pesky regulations and referees getting in the way. But you haven't offered me an opponent." I grin at Mateus Blackwood and spread my hands wide, open-chested, doing my best imitation of an easy target. "So why not take me on yourself?"

This is incredibly stupid. I should be preserving body, mind, and magical energy for the duel I've agreed to take against Tamsin. Challenging her father is the last thing I should be doing. Yet standing here, face-to-face with Mateus Blackwood, the smell of blood and piss in the air, I feel more alive than I have since the night Rook lost to Tamsin in the New York Magicians' Arena.

I catch the glint of temptation in Blackwood's eyes even as he tells me, as dismissively as he can, "I'm retired."

I shrug. "Magicians come out of retirement all the time. Don't know how to quit the game. And you're not exactly ancient and infirm. Come on, old man. Isn't that what you've really missed? A chance to return to who you were. Mateus Blackwood, the terror. Mateus Blackwood, the most bloodthirsty of duelists, win or lose."

"And what's in it for you?" Suspicion colors Blackwood's voice. "Even with the advantage of youth on your side, you'd be risking quite a lot doing this on my home turf, under rules of my choice."

"What's in it for me?" I laugh. I don't quite mean to. It just bursts out of me, a bitter little chuckle. "You know, Blackwood, all these years, I've blamed you for Jamie's death. I must have thought about destroying you in his name a hundred million times, in a hundred million different scenarios. I wanted to see you humiliated. I wanted to see your family wrecked, the same way you wrecked mine when you killed my brother.

"Then your daughter gave me exactly what I wanted. All on her own. I thought that would make me happy. I thought that would give me closure. But it just made me angrier. For years, I've replayed that night that Jamie died and wondered how he must have felt in that ring. What it was like, that moment when he realized he wouldn't be coming home. That you'd outplayed him."

I pause. "So I guess, in a way, this is my chance to find out if I can succeed where my brother failed. My one chance to know how he must have felt that night in the ring and see if I fare any better."

"And if you don't?"

I spread my hands again, nonchalant. "Then I don't. But I do want to make one thing very, very clear."

"And what's that?"

I make sure I look Blackwood dead in the eyes as I say the next part. Ever since I held a gasping Lysander Rook's life in my hands during that fateful fight in our hotel room, I've known exactly what I'm capable of. I refuse to forget it now. "You're not sorry for your part in Jamie's death. You've made it obvious that you don't blame yourself at all. That's all fine and dandy. But if I don't make you sorry before our time in the ring is done, I'm going to give you the same death that Alexei gave my brother."

"And if you can't?"

I hold my hands out, baring my chest toward him. Vulnerable. "Then you might as well execute me in that arena like an animal and laugh about it, too. I'm not above dying like my brother, either."

I'm not sure how Blackwood's going to react. I'm braced for anger or maybe a scoff of disbelief. He must recognize that accepting my challenge poses a risk. I'm a lot younger with more recent experience fighting in a magicians' arena. I'm by no means an easy mark.

But Blackwood is still an arcane master with years of experience on me. He probably still sees me as an arrogant whelp, a girl who can be put in her place with a few well-placed blows. A child that he can bloody up as an example to any others who might dare defiance against him.

At the end of the day, Mateus Blackwood is still, at his core, a vicious son of a bitch who built a career on breaking other magicians as brutally as possible. And I've goaded him here, on his turf. He won't be able to resist the opportunity to punish me.

"You're full of surprises all right, Samantha Chan," crows my brother's murderer. His eyes glitter with anticipation as they meet mine. "You've got yourself a deal."

21

TAMSIN

AFTER SHE ACCEPTED MY challenge, in my mind's eye, I tried to turn Samantha Chan into a faceless opponent. I tried to forget everything else about her. I really did.

It's not like I didn't have plenty of distractions after beating Rook. Everyone loves you when you win. It's easy to get addicted to the accolades: the praise, the attention, even the jealousy from up-and-comers or has-beens who haven't collected victories of the same prestige levels.

And this, of course, isn't just a win. This is Lysander Rook.

For weeks, I throw myself into social media and public relations and promotional obligations. My victory is one of the greatest triumphs in magical history, or so the news cycle informs me. So I lean into that. I talk about how hard I worked, how diligently I prepared to face the young terror of the magical world. I even talk about my father, and why I left him—to a point, of course.

The rest, I leave to the rumor mill. People immersed in magical society are almost as hungry for gossip as they are for bloodshed. All I have to do is plant a few seeds with the right people, and suddenly, all anyone who's anyone can talk about is what a crook Mateus Blackwood is.

I keep leaning into it. I tell my sob stories—only when prompted by the right people, and only sparingly. Sympathy is a finite resource from the public. If I spend too much time crying on livestreams about my awful father, people will stop feeling sorry for me and talking about how brave I am. They'll dub me annoying, or worse yet, opportunistic. They might even call me a liar.

I've been careful with my words, but I haven't once lied to anyone about who my father is or what he's done. I'd rather die. And I won't risk my credibility. Not after everything I've done to earn my freedom.

I do nothing but talk for a few weeks. It's fun for a little while, in a twisted sort of way. But it's also exhausting. Being the new darling of the magical world is, as it turns out, an awful lot of work. Everyone wants something. Everyone's eyes are always glued to me. Every word out of my mouth gets scrutinized, overanalyzed, studied. I think I understand a little better now why Lysander Rook could be such a jackass, if this was how he felt all the time.

I'm so tired. I'm more and more tired every day. And the more tired I become, the harder it is to focus on Samantha Chan, my opponent, and the more tempting it is to think about Samantha Chan, the girl I once kissed. The girl I might have once called my only friend in the entire world.

Pathetic, isn't it?

When I do finally break, I binge. I spend three hours one afternoon doing nothing but scouring the magical Internet for any trace of what

Sam's been up to these days. I read all her posts on the forums, mentally tracking the dates. I think about texting her.

I think a lot about texting her, actually. Or messaging her on social media. Or even calling.

I don't actually text or send a message, or god forbid, call her. I don't know what I'd say. There's a reason opponents don't typically talk much before a duel, unless it's for a press event. Just for kicks, I compose a few possible missives. None of them make it past the second sentence.

Hi, Sam, I'm looking forward to our duel. Just taking a minute to check in on—no.

Hey, Sam, how are you? Isn't it wild that in just a couple months, we'll get to try to kill each other for entertainment—no.

Sam, this is probably overdue, but I'm so sorry about—no, no, absolutely not.

So I remain silent. I don't reach out to Sam, and to her credit, she doesn't reach out to me, which I take as a sign that I'm doing the correct, mature thing by remaining silent.

Instead, I busy myself by keeping tabs on my estranged father.

In the beginning, I tell myself it's just due diligence. I want to make sure he knows his place now. Samantha Chan may be an asshole of the first degree, but she was right about one thing: my father deserves no place in magical society. I refuse to see him get another kid killed.

Dad behaves, mostly. I track him down to one of the few remaining clubs seedy enough to put on illegal duels, but most of the magicians Dad lures into the ring are over-the-hill has-beens or meat-headed men in their twenties and thirties too stupid to know better. He does, however, avoid putting children and teens in the ring.

I drop by that club from time to time, hanging back in the shadows to watch the sad little displays that my father now promotes to eke out his living. I never speak to him. Maybe he knows I'm there. Maybe not. I'm past the point of caring.

But I keep coming back, all the same. I come, I buy myself a nice nonalcoholic beverage, and I watch Dad's comeuppance in action.

I don't miss him. I don't. I just do it to ensure that he stays in line. And, for the most part, he does.

Then, one night, a familiar silhouette slips through the door. I don't need to look twice to recognize Samantha Chan's gait, that careworn hoodie, the perpetual ponytail.

I don't know what another magician from a legitimate dueling circuit would be doing in a place like this, but given that it's Sam, and given that this is Dad's haunt, I have a couple ideas. I don't like either of them very much.

I think about calling out to Sam or approaching her, drink in hand. I consider, very briefly, asking her what the hell she thinks she's up to.

Instead, I do what I've gotten so good at these past few weeks: I sit in the shadows and I watch.

Sam positions herself exactly where I'd expect her to: perched on the peripheries of the dueling ring, far enough from the action to avoid being overcrowded or unduly noticed, close enough to get a full view of the magic on display.

Then my father takes a seat beside her. Things escalate pretty quickly after that.

After a conversation that looks like it's on the brink of coming to blows, Dad and Sam vanish from view. When I see one of the gaudily-dressed club announcers climb into the currently empty ring, my heart sinks.

I know exactly what's about to happen. *God damn it, Sam. You absolute idiot.*

"Ladies and gentlemen!" bellows the announcer. "Have we got a show for you to close out the evening!"

Jeers and cheers alike fill the air. This is a crowd that's grown accustomed to mediocrity. They're rightfully skeptical, but they'll watch anyone duel as long as someone's blood gets spilled.

"Known best as the one-time second to the legendary Lysander Rook, fresh off her engagement at the New York Magicians' Arena, I am honored to present our guest and challenger: Miss Samantha Chan!"

Shocked exclamations fill the air—alongside a few skeptical murmurs. Sam silences them by emerging from the crowd, still clad in that well-worn black hoodie, and climbing into the ring. Her facial expression is utterly blank as she strips out of the hoodie, revealing a plain white tee hanging square and baggy over her modest curves. She rolls out her neck slowly and shakes out her hands. She offers neither smile nor frown to the onlookers. She could be washing the dishes for all she seems to care about the task at hand.

"And who better to face off against Miss Chan than our very own legend, the great Master Mateus Blackwood!"

My father grins at the crowd as he joins Sam in the ring. In contrast to Sam's apparent indifference, Dad bathes in the immediate adulation of the crowd. He raises his hands, begging for a crescendo as his audience cheers him on, and they're all too happy to comply. These are the outcasts from magical society, after all. The handful of die-hards who still believe in my father's legend.

The announcer beats a hasty retreat as the bell rings. Immediately, Sam springs into action. Arcane power wreathes its way around her knuckles as she closes the distance across the ring. My father throws up a shield, but Sam smashes right through it.

She's on top of him in the blink of an eye, mounted high on Dad's chest as he struggles to throw her off. The crowd barely has time for its cheers and gasps of shock before Sam's savaging Dad with all the fervor of a wild animal. Magic crackles along the length of her back, down her arms and through her fingers. With methodical viciousness, she rains magically enhanced fists and elbows down on my father's head.

Dad covers up with his arms, elbows tight, and tries to conjure another shield. A sputtering ghost of arcane power flickers briefly between his face and Sam's fists before it crumples beneath her onslaught.

"Yield," gasps my father. "I yield—"

Sam shuts him up with another fist across his mouth. "Don't you remember?" she demands, voice pitched loud enough to be heard by the rapt crowd. "This is your den. Your rules. There's no yielding here. We stop when I'm ready to stop." Magic crackles between them as she hits him again. And again. And again.

Of course. This is one of my father's clubs. No real rules, no semblance of safety regulations. Sam is going to kill my father here in this ring, the same way Alexei killed Jamie Chan four years ago. That's why she came here. That's been her plan all along.

I move like a woman possessed. I'm cutting through the crowd faster than I've ever moved outside an arena. "Stop!" I scream. "Sam, stop it!"

Sam doesn't stop.

Someone tries to hold me back when I reach the ring. A crackle of my own arcane power frees the stranger's fingers from my sleeve. I climb under the ropes into the ring and narrowly avoid slipping in a puddle of bloody sweat. "Stop!" I scream again.

Sam finally looks up. Shock paints her face white beneath the glaring overhead lights. "Tamsin?"

My father stirs at the sound of my name. "Tam," he whimpers. "My girl, you're back. I knew you'd come back."

Sam isn't even listening to him. "It's really you," she says. She sounds half dazed, like she's still convinced she's in a dream.

"It's really me, all right." I stumble over to the pair of them and grab Sam beneath the crook of her shoulder. With a grunt, I haul her off my father's bloody body. "Enough is enough," I hiss at her.

Behind me, the crowd is booing. I ignore them, too, shaking Sam by the shoulders. "What the hell are you thinking?" I demand.

Sam struggles weakly against my grip. "Let me do this, Tamsin. Let me finish. I need to finish."

"Finish what?" I shout. "Beating my father to death with magically enhanced strength?"

"It's the only way!" cries Sam. "I thought it would be enough to win the war of reputation. I thought it would be enough to see him expelled from magical society. But it's not. Nothing is ever going to be enough, except, except—"

"Except by becoming another Alexei Adamovich," I snarl. "Or worse yet, another Mateus Blackwood. Because you're well on your way to becoming exactly like my father. You really want to be an honorary Blackwood? After all that effort you put into destroying us?"

Sam looks like she's just been hit herself. She backs away from me, silent.

"My girl," moans Dad. He's still curled up in a corner of the ring.

"My Tamsin." He struggles to his feet. He spits a tooth out as he stands, blood streaming down his face. Both his eyes are blackened, but he still manages to grin at me. "I knew it," he crows. "I knew you'd see sense one day. I knew my daughter would come back to me." He stumbles toward me.

I catch my father before he can fall. For a moment, he hangs there in my arms, trapped in my embrace. I close my eyes. "Thank you," I whisper against his ear. I cling to his bloody body, and I'm not faking it when tears begin rolling down my cheeks. It's never taken much for Dad to make me cry, even when he doesn't mean to. "For what it's worth, I really am grateful to you," I continue. "For better or worse, you've made me who I am. You're always going to be a part of me."

"I know," Dad whispers back. "And you can always come home to me, Tamsin. I love you."

I cling a little harder. "I love you, too," I tell him. "I think that maybe I'll always love you, whether I want to or not. I think that might be my curse, you know, as a Blackwood—as your daughter. Loving someone I hate so much."

I finally force myself to detach from him. My father stumbles again. He's looking at me with confusion in those bruised-up eyes. "Tam?"

"I love you, Dad," I repeat, more firmly this time. "But you will never see me again."

I spit at his feet.

Then I grab Sam by the elbow and haul her out of that ring for good.

22
SAM

TAMSIN DRAGS ME OUT of her father's underground club like Orpheus pulling Eurydice forcibly from the land of the dead. Of course in most versions of that story, Eurydice never put up quite the fight that I do.

"Let go of me!" I shout as she drags me out the door past the half-snoozing bouncer. "Who the hell do you think you are!"

"Your opponent for the biggest duel of your career." Tamsin continues to drag me down the street then around a corner. We're approaching the nicer part of town, at least. "I refuse to let you get yourself thrown in jail for manslaughter by killing my father in front of a hundred witnesses, at least not before I get the chance to take your head off myself in front of thousands."

I could probably tug myself free from even Tamsin Blackwood's steely grip without too much trouble. I don't. Instead, I scowl and fuss and fume, biding my time, as I allow her to continue steering us down yet another street.

I don't have to wait long. Tamsin drags me into the empty parking lot of some anonymous diner. As I suspected, like me, she wants the convenience—and relative safety—of privacy. Knowing Tamsin, she wants that privacy for some annoyingly civilized reason, like a real heart-to-heart conversation, or the chance to yell at me without witnesses who will write about it on Reddit an hour from now, or an opportunity to grab me by the face and kiss me one last time before we return to the very important business of hating each other.

I don't want privacy for any of those reasons. And the minute she steers us into that parking lot, I snap my wrist free, jerking it toward her thumb, where the grip is weakest. I waste no time once my hands are my own again. The curse I've been preparing trickles readily down to my fingertips, a heady swirl of arcane energy hungry for the retribution Tamsin Blackwood denied me when she pulled me off her father's bloody body.

My curse arcs toward Tamsin, but she's no longer there. I blink once before my knees pinch together of their own accord and I'm flung unceremoniously to the concrete by an invisible cord of magic. I let go of my curse and break my fall in time to avoid banging my head on the wheel of someone's bright red Toyota, but I'm going to have scrapes along my elbows and thighs to clean up later.

Tamsin steps over me, looking unimpressed, and dismisses her counter-spell with a careless flick of her fingers. "Save it for the New York Magicians' Arena, Sam." She cocks her head, looking down her nose at where I sit crumpled up against the Toyota with the wind knocked out of me. What a silly sight I must make. "Like I said, it serves neither of us to delay this duel with jail time."

I can't help it. I start laughing. I don't mean to. It just bursts out of me, giddy and near hysterical. Tamsin watches me for a moment, looking incredulous. Then her mouth twitches.

"Oh, come on," I gasp between giggles. "Quit fighting it. Just laugh. It's funny. This whole mess is goddamn funny."

"It's not that funny." Of course as soon as Tamsin says it, a giggle escapes her.

"Go on, give in."

"No!"

Tamsin's laughing in earnest now, though, which only makes me laugh harder. We howl together in that parking lot, clutching our bellies, until we're both in tears.

"Come on," Tamsin finally manages to say once we can both breathe again. She offers a hand. "Let's talk."

I look warily at the hand, but she's not telegraphing any signs of casting magic, so I take it and allow her to pull me to my feet. "All right." I fold my arms. "Talk."

Tamsin doesn't beat around the bush. Carefully wiping the lingering tears from her eyes, she says without preamble, "I hope you realize by now that killing my father tonight wouldn't have brought you peace or satisfaction. And I can't imagine it would have made your brother happy."

I'm immediately on defense. "I don't know what would have made my brother happy. He's dead, and when he was alive, the thing that made him happiest in the world was magic." I sneer at Tamsin. "I'll spare you my incredibly depressing speech about the irony of magic also being the thing that killed him."

"It was also the thing that made you happiest, once upon a time," says Tamsin softly. "That's what you told me that day at the bookstore. That magic was something you and Jamie shared. Something you both loved."

"Love never avenged anyone."

"Oh, for—" Tamsin makes a frustrated sound. "Don't you get it yet, Sam? You already won. You blame my father for your brother's death? Well, consider Jamie avenged about a hundred times over. Dad is trapped in a hell of his own making, and it's a hell that smells like blood and piss and eternal mediocrity. His reputation is wrecked forever. Soon, his money will probably be gone, too. His ability to duel is a joke now—you proved that tonight, if nothing else." Tamsin closes her eyes. "And the cherry on top if it all: You did, in fact, succeed in breaking his family. The one thing you wanted more than anything else."

I falter. "Tamsin—"

"I meant what I said to him tonight," she interrupts, her voice hard. "He and I will never speak again. His daughter—the one thing he had left after he aged out of the dueling circuit—is gone forever."

"Then why don't I feel any different?" I whisper. I shake my head. "Avenging Jamie was supposed to give me closure. It was supposed to change everything. But all I've felt for weeks is just . . . empty. Even tonight, beating Mateus Blackwood's face in over and over, every time he smiled back at me through all that blood, I just thought, 'It's never going to be enough. I'm never going to feel better ever again.'"

"Then quit throwing your life away on a guy you hate!" exclaims Tamsin. "Don't live for my dad, Sam. Believe me, it's extremely not worth it. Ask me how I know."

I chuckle bitterly. "Then what, pray tell, do you suggest that I live for?"

"Hell if I know. But I think living for yourself would be a decent place to start." Tamsin gives me the first real smile I've seen all evening. I'm not prepared for how much it hurts. She hasn't smiled at me like that since we kissed in New York. "The way I understand it, once upon a time, your magic wasn't wholly consumed by hatred for my family. Once upon a time, magic—for you—just meant loving yours. Loving Jamie."

Tamsin blinks rapidly, a faraway look in her suddenly too-bright eyes as she turns away. "I know you can't bring your brother back. But maybe you can still have the next-best thing. Maybe you can learn to love magic again, the same way you both did when Jamie was alive. And maybe that, more than anything else, keeps some part of him alive."

She swallows hard and shrugs slightly too casually. "Or maybe I'm full of sentimental crap." She clears her throat. "Either way, I'll meet you in the New York Magicians' Arena a few weeks from now—assuming you haven't gotten yourself arrested or killed before then. Ball's in your court now. I won't be going out of my way to save your ass again, Samantha Chan."

Tamsin Blackwood, my one-time object of vengeance, target of all my hate and all my lust, walks away from me without so much as a goodbye. She walks aways just like she walked away from her father earlier tonight. Her step doesn't falter, and she doesn't look over her shoulder. She walks with assurance.

I don't know if I'll ever be capable of that kind of assurance.

I close my eyes for a long moment as I lean on that stranger's Toyota, breathing in and out as carefully as I can. I wait for my heart rate to slow. Then, with one last deep breath, I dig my phone out. There's a conversation I'm long overdue for.

Finding Rook is a lot harder than finding Blackwood.

For one thing, Blackwood wanted to be found—by the right people, at least. He needed to attract the right kind of broken, desperate people down to his little underworld. It was his only means of staying afloat.

Rook doesn't need or want to attract anyone to wherever he is. Maybe he's struggling to stay afloat, too, or maybe he's just fine. Knowing Rook, he wouldn't care either way. He could be up to his elbows in debt and living out of a hovel, and his pride would still never let him change his ways.

In the end, I do the old-fashioned thing: I take one last stab at reaching out to him directly. He didn't want to hear my apologies or explanations, or even my anger, after what went down in New York. But maybe, just maybe, he'll want to hear this:

> Hey, Princess. You don't have to answer this if you don't want to. And maybe you've already heard about it. But in case you haven't, I thought you should know: I'm going to duel Tamsin Blackwood at the New York Magicians' Arena a month from now.
>
> I don't know what to do.

I send it as text and then as email, too, for good measure. For several days, I get no response. And then, one day, I get a phone call from a number I don't recognize. I assume it's spam at first, but on the off chance that it's important, I pick up anyway. "Hello?"

"For the smartest person I know, you're pretty stupid, you know that?"

I close my eyes. "You know, you're the second person this month to call me the smartest person you know. Think there's something to that, princess?"

Rook huffs a laugh on the other end of the line. "I wouldn't know."

"You changed your number."

"Nah, I just have an extra phone now. I'm turning over a new leaf."

My eyes pop open. "And you need a whole new phone for that?"

"Sure doesn't hurt. But hey, we're not talking about me. We're talking about you." Rook's voice shifts slightly like he's trying a little too hard to be casual but not quite succeeding. "Is it true? You're going to duel Tamsin Blackwood?"

"Yep. She's issued a formal challenge and everything."

"And you said yes."

"Honestly? I don't think I could have brought myself to say no."

"Why?" Rook sounds hunted. "You feel like you need to avenge my loss to her or something?"

"No, actually." I blink at the shock of truth in my own words. "But I think I owe her this duel. And— Lysander, I can't explain it. But I also think that maybe I owe myself this duel, too."

Rook is silent for so long that for a precious few seconds, I think he's hung up on me. Then he says, quietly, in another voice, one I've never heard him use before, "Come see me."

I laugh, more out of surprise than anything else. "I have no idea where you live these days. You didn't answer any of my earlier messages."

"I know. I'm sorry. I needed to get . . . settled."

"And you're settled now?"

"You could say that." He pauses, then says, "I'm going to text you an address. We can meet up this weekend." Another pause. "You know, if that works for you."

"Lysander Rook, so polite all of a sudden."

"Like I said. I'm turning over a new leaf."

I shake my head slowly, even though I know he can't see me. "You know, I might actually be starting to believe you."

"Good. This weekend, then?" He actually sounds nervous.

I close my eyes again. And before I can think better of it, "Sure. This weekend. I'll come see you."

When I arrive at the address Rook texted me, I think I've made a wrong turn at first. It's a cute little walk-up in an equally cute little suburb, about ten minutes from the nearest train station into the city proper. It's the kind of place with an aesthetic I'd associate more strongly with bubbly, bright-smiled young women in sundresses than, well, Rook.

It's not a bubbly girl in a sundress who greets me at the door, though.

"Sammy." The boy who opens the door looks me slowly up and down. I do the same to him. He's still recognizably Lysander Rook, but his whole energy is different. If you told me Lysander Rook had a secret identical twin this whole time who'd murdered him and taken his place, I might actually believe you in this moment. A cleaner-cut, brighter-faced twin. A twin who, despite saying all of one word to me so far, just seems so much less haunted than the boy I once knew.

"You look good," says the Rook-shaped boy at the door. He sticks his hands in his jeans pockets.

"So do you," I tell him. It's true. Rook—or Rook's secret twin slash clone, I'm still not fully convinced it's really Rook—has gotten a different haircut, a shorter one, that makes him look more approachable. He's in a simple white tee and jeans, but there's not a smudge or stain in sight—shocking for the white tee, particularly—and most notably, he doesn't smell like cigarette smoke anymore.

He must notice me sniffing the air because he chuckles. "I quit smoking, if that's what you're wondering."

My eyebrows climb. "Damn, princess. What happened to 'the principle of the thing is bullshit'?"

He chuckles. "I never said it wasn't. But there's more important stuff to worry about than gassing out during a magicians' duel. Lung cancer, for example." He wrinkles his nose. "Also, I never really liked the smell, if I'm honest. Couldn't get it out of my laundry worth a damn."

I chew that over for a few seconds. "You really weren't kidding about turning over a new leaf."

"No, I wasn't." An awkward pause descends between us. Rook's hands fidget, like he's not sure what to do with them when they're not playing with a lighter. Or twirling a cigarette. Or planting a magically enhanced fist into an opponent's belly.

"You wanna come inside?" asks Rook.

I do.

Rook's place is quaint and modest but charming, all exposed brick and clearly recently restored appliances. He sets out steaming mugs of coffee for us both on the tiny kitchen table. I'm surprised at how good mine is when I take a sip. "Wow. Forget magic. You could turn pro at this."

He laughs. "Oh, I did, actually."

I almost drop the mug. "Excuse me?"

"Turned pro at coffee. Well, sort of." He scratches the back of his head, looking uncharacteristically bashful. "I've got a gig as a barista at a local coffeeshop in town, among other side hustles. The pay is . . . well, it's not money I'm gonna retire on, but all things considered, it's actually pretty decent when you count the tips. Definitely, like, way more generous than market value."

I stare at him. "You're . . . a barista."

Rook shrugs. "I also walk dogs."

I keep staring. Maybe there's something to my twin theory from earlier. Or my clone theory. Either or, really.

"It's a good life," says Rook, almost defensively.

I glance around the premises. It's not a McMansion, by any means, but it's nice. Nicer than I'd expect for the kind of work Rook describes. "And you afford all this by . . . making coffee and walking dogs."

"Hey, now, I'll have you know that walking dogs pays more than you'd expect! Especially rich people's dogs. Better than most magicians get paid, in fact."

I snort. "Now that I do believe."

"I've also got a couple of roommates—not that they're rich, either. One's a freelance musician slash violin teacher, the other one works for a nonprofit. We split the cost."

I try to picture Rook with roommates. For so long, I was used to being the only person in his life. "Do you like them? Like, do you guys get along?"

"Eh, I don't know if I'd call us friends, but they're good guys. Maybe louder than I'd like, but friendly, and they keep the place clean, and the rent here is low."

"And what do they think of rooming with the mighty Lysander Rook?"

"Are you kidding?" Rook laughs again, this time laced with true mirth. "Neither of them know shit about the magical world, except that it's splashy and violent and sometimes gets turned into memes on social media."

A strangely dreamy expression settles over Rook's face. "Neither of my roommates know who I am. All they know is that I used to be a magician and now I make coffee and walk dogs instead, which seems like a pretty reasonable life choice to both of them. Hell, I'm pretty sure at least one of them still thinks a dueling magician is the same thing as, like, those corny stage magicians that suburban parents hire to pull rabbits out of top hats at little kids' birthday parties."

I wince. "Ouch."

"It's nice actually. They don't know anything about the rules of dueling, or the kind of training we do, or who's who in the dueling circuit rankings. It's . . . well, I don't know what else to call it but 'nice.' Relaxing, maybe. Or chill. Something like that"

"Chill?" I echo disbelievingly. "You, Lysander Rook, are embracing chill?"

Rook sighs. "Listen, Sammy. I know this all probably seems really . . . weird to you. It was weird to me, too, at first, having a life without magic in it."

"You don't practice magic anymore?" I blurt out. A pang goes through my heart that I don't quite understand. "Magic was everything to you. You said it yourself. Magic was your whole life."

Rook sighs again. "Yeah. Magic was my whole life. Do you know how happy that life was?"

I frown. "You were the best at what you did."

"Sure, I was the best," allows Rook. "That was important to me, being the best, so I won't argue with you on that front."

He begins to pace around his little kitchen. "But do you know what being the best at magic cost me? How much time I spent obsessing over remaining the best? All the dark places my mind went whenever I thought about the possibility of losing? Let me ask you something, Sammy." He leans forward slightly across the kitchen countertop. "Did I seem . . . I don't know, content to you? Like, was I happy, really, consistently happy? Not just the ten-minute elation if I won a duel against someone impressive—like, someone who'd improve my ranking or earn me a fat purse—before I put my nose back to the grindstone?"

I don't have a good answer for that. Rook's moods have always been so mercurial, I've seen him cycle from the highest of highs to the lowest of lows—and back again—in the space of twelve hours or less. But one word I'd never use to describe him was content. He couldn't be. He was never satisfied with anything—too much of a perfectionist, and even at the pinnacle of his skill, too paranoid about having his throne toppled.

Now that his worst fear has come true, I've never seen him look better, honestly.

"Right now," I tell him, "you look happier—more *content*—than I ever saw you when I was your second." I swallow. "I'm sorry."

"Aw, Sam." Rook suddenly looks awkward and a little sad. "Don't be. Really. All that shit that went down in New York—I didn't see it this way at the time, obviously, but I think it had to all fall apart the way it did, you know? I needed to hit rock bottom before I could pick myself back up and figure my shit out. Which meant that—at least for a little while—I had to believe that I'd lost you."

"You didn't," I whisper. The back of my throat burns as my eyes go hot.

The side of his mouth quirks upward. "Clearly not."

I look at the plain brown tile on Rook's kitchen floor. "I wasn't the best second I could be to you," I confess. I hold up a hand as he begins to protest. "I know I gave you strategies and practice routines that won you duels. I helped you beat tough magicians. But I didn't think about you at all, beyond that, not the way I should have. And if it was easier for me to keep secrets from you—even if they were secrets that impacted your duels—I did. I only thought about myself. What I wanted. What my goals were." I swallow hard. "I told myself it wasn't my job to care about your happiness."

"It wasn't. That's not what a second does."

"Maybe not." I blink a few times, trying to stop the burn in my eyes. "But it's what a friend does."

I expect him to scoff lightly, or make fun of me, or even toss a predictable rhetorical question my way like, Friends, huh? Is that what we are, Sammy?

Rook doesn't do any of those things. Instead, he just smiles. I've known him for years, and I can count the number of truly genuine smiles he's given me on one hand. This is one of them.

It aches the same way Tamsin's smile the last time I saw her made me ache.

"Fair enough," Rook tells me. "Then, as a friend, do you want to talk to me about what's going on with Tamsin Blackwood and this duel of yours?"

"Oh, that." I duck my head and try to sound casual. "I'm pretty sure I'm going to lose."

My former champion's answer is quick and blunt. "Bullshit."

"Okay, wise guy." I laugh. "How do you figure me losing is bullshit?"

"One, I've never seen you take on a battle you can't win. And two? You, Samantha Chan, love magic far more than you realize." He offers me a sardonic little tilt of his mouth—not quite the true smile from moments ago, more like its blacker-humored cousin. "Honestly, you love magic more than I ever did. You just needed a real chance to express it. I never gave you that, not when I was your champion and your job revolved around making me look good. But Tamsin Blackwood? She gives you that in spades."

"You hated her."

"Of course I did." Rook rolls his eyes at me without denying my accusation. "She scared me, and she made me jealous."

"Why on earth would you be jealous of Tamsin when you're . . ." I trail off and gesticulate ineffectually. "You know, you?"

"Should I count the reasons?" Rook looks amused as he begins to tick them off on his fingers. "Her talent. Her hunger. The fact that the press actually likes her. The way she enchanted you, *god*, that was a biggie. But mostly? Tamsin Blackwood so obviously wanted to win more than I did. And that terrified me."

I turn red. "She didn't enchant me."

"Tell it to someone less gullible, Sammy. You light up around her. It's gross."

I turn even redder. "Shove it."

Rook does not, in fact, shove it. "I know it wasn't just magic, either." He smirks. "She's very pretty, you know. Don't let that distract you during the duel."

"Rook!"

He cackles—actually cackles. "That's what you came here for, isn't it? My advice."

"And to make sure you weren't dead or something," I say archly. I bite my lip. "You think I can beat her?"

"I don't think that's important. Do you want to duel her?" Rook searches my face when I don't answer immediately. "Not 'do you want to win?' Do you want to duel her? For you, I mean. Because you want to. Not because you need to prove something or because you're scared you won't be worth anything if you don't. Does the idea of dueling Tamsin Blackwood genuinely make you happy?"

I close my eyes and nod.

"Well, then you've answered your own question."

I open my eyes. "Any advice, princess? Given that you were the last magician to go head-to-head with her." I say it dryly, like I might be kidding.

I'm not really kidding, though.

"I guess you're not gonna let me just leave it at 'Go have fun out there,' are you?"

"Please don't make me hit you."

Rook laughs. "Okay. One real piece of advice for you: Tamsin's more like me than you realize."

I frown. "How do you mean?"

"She doesn't play to win—"

"You *always* played to win."

"No, I played not to lose. There's a difference." Rook looks me dead in the eyes. "And Tamsin is the exact same way. The idea of losing terrifies her—no doubt because of Daddy Dearest. It limits her range of magic, the kind of casting that she's willing to risk. You can use that against her."

"She's not beholden to Daddy Dearest anymore, haven't you heard?"

"Sure, she's not—and she'll become a better magician for it . . . eventually." He waggles a finger. "'Eventually' being the operative word there. But right now? Old habits die hard. She hasn't changed into a whole new magician over the course of two months, trust."

I bite my lip. "So what do I do?"

My old champion shrugs. "That's for you to figure out, Sammy. But I don't doubt you'll pull it off splendidly. Just remember, when push comes to shove: The choices that Tamsin Blackwood makes in the dueling arena have always been informed by caution. Her magic is spectacular, sure—but for the past eighteen years, her magic has also been ruled by fear."

Rook smiles again. Another true smile. "So on the big day, when you stand face-to-face with Tamsin Blackwood in that arena, hold on tight to this idea, and don't ever forget it: fear has no place in your magic, Sam."

23
TAMSIN

I CAN'T DECIDE ON a dueling robe to wear.

It's a ridiculous problem to get hung up on at a time like this. But it's all my brain wants to focus on. Do I want the midnight blue with the pale gold trim? Is that too plain—and would I look better and more striking in the crimson with the floral embroidery across the collar and shoulders? Oh, but then I might look like I'm trying too hard, so maybe a good third option would be an all-black classic, even though the fit of my own black dueling robe is slightly off around my hips and bust.

I know, intellectually, that Samantha Chan is the last person who'd give a damn what her opponent wears to a duel. But clothing—my outward appearance in general, to the extent that I can control it—has always been armor for me.

I settle on midnight blue.

Déjà vu settles into my bones as I run through my warm-up exercises backstage. The last time I ran through a pre-duel warm-up, I was about to take on the most famous opponent I'd ever faced. I didn't think anything could feel like a bigger deal to me than sharing a sold-out New York arena with Lysander Rook.

Yet here I am, fretting over an unranked magician and worrying that she won't think I'm pretty enough or, alternately, serious enough if I wear the wrong dueling robe.

I want to scream.

"You ready to go, Tamsin?"

I don't quite start, but I come embarrassingly close. I'm still not used to having a second in my corner who isn't also my father. I picked Rachel Ortega because she was the exact kind of plainspoken, bullish, no-nonsense magician least likely to remind me of him. She refuses to accept two positions as both second and arcane master ("That's too much for any reasonable human being to take on for one person," she insists, "and besides, I'm too damn poor—I don't run a training arena") but has been gamely helping me interview several options and set up opportunities for me to tour the training arenas they run. She's vetted them all herself to ensure that all my new candidates are well-qualified. Ortega's done a good job. All the arcane masters she's hand-picked are smart and sturdy and experienced. And most importantly, none of them currently or previously ran illegal underground dueling clubs.

My new second and I are still getting used to each other, though—as evidenced by the faint confusion on her face as I stare blankly at her.

"I'm ready," I finally manage.

"You sure?" Ortega doesn't look convinced. She's a stout, well-built woman in her late thirties who never turned pro on the dueling circuit herself but boasts some impressive amateur results, coupled with a respectable history of helping arcane masters produce a series of accomplished champions. "I can stall the ref if you need me to."

I shake my head. "I want to get this done."

Ortega sighs. "Try to sound a little more excited."

"Pardon?"

"It's your first title defense as the top-ranked magician on the circuit." She purses her lips at me in a decidedly schoolmarm manner. "You know how many people would kill to be where you are? Try to enjoy it."

"It's a lot of pressure," I point out.

"Sure. But to quote one Billie Jean King, pressure is a privilege. You know that, right? Pressure is something you've earned." She claps me on the shoulder. "So try and bask in it at least a little, champ."

Pressure is a privilege. Pressure is a privilege. Pressure is a privilege. I whisper it like a mantra in my head as I step out into the arena. I'm immediately deafened by the roar of the crowd. They're all screaming for me now. Barely months ago, it was Lysander Rook they were screaming for, and I was just some nepo kid whose surname had screwed up their betting odds.

I was so envious of him. So convinced that he must be living the dream, with his name in lights and the likes of Samantha Chan playing his second.

Now, Samantha Chan is my opponent. And for the first time, I think I actually, truly, honest-to-goodness feel bad for Rook. Not the present-day Rook who's fled the dueling circuit, but the champion among champions. The one who used to answer the audience's screams. The one expected to win it all.

I wonder if he thought pressure was a privilege, too. Or if he just wanted to bury his head and hide in the sand. I wonder if disappearing into anonymity was what he wanted, deep at heart, all along.

Another roar erupts from the crowd when my opponent steps up on to the arena stage to meet me. I blink a few times. Sam is still recognizably Sam, but there's something different about her today. She dresses for dueling the same way she dresses for everything else: plainly and without airs. She, unlike me, did opt for a plain black dueling robe and not an especially fashionable one. The plain, boxy cut suits her, the same way those oversize hoodies do.

But she's carrying herself differently. There's something about her stride or maybe the set of her shoulders that feels a world apart from the frequently forgotten second that so many of Rook's old opponents overlooked. You couldn't overlook this version of Sam if you tried—even in her plain dueling robes and simple ponytail. It's all about the aura she's projecting.

This version of Sam is nobody's second. She's the champion she always could have been. The only question that remains is whether she's willing to step up to that potential.

My job is to stop her.

I twist my head around to the corner where my new second sits. "Hey, Rachel?"

Ortega's at my side in an instant. "What is it?"

"No, no, it's nothing bad, don't worry." I smile, shaking my head. "I just . . ."

"Just what?"

"I think I get it now," I tell her. "What you said, about pressure being a privilege."

She grins at me. "Yeah? Good."

"Pressure is a privilege," I repeat. "And I want to wipe this arena clean with Samantha Chan."

"Really?" Ortega laughs. "If I didn't know better, I'd say you were in love with this girl."

Once upon a time, that insinuation might have made me blush. Now I just grin back at my second. "Maybe I am. Or maybe I'm in love with magic. Hell, maybe I'm in love with them both." I turn to face the ref as he prepares to signal the duel's official start. "And maybe that's the real point of it all."

24

SAM

TAMSIN BLACKWOOD IS ABSOLUTELY kicking my ass.

My lungs are on fire. My mind flashes back to all those times I ragged on Rook for his improbably perfect cardio—or, more accurately, all his attempts to destroy his improbably perfect cardio. I think, uncharitably, of Rook's cigarettes and lazy nutrition and every excuse under the sun to avoid strapping on a pair of running shoes.

I've never smoked in my life, train supplementary cardio at least twice a week, and track my macros. Yet here I am, gasping for air as Tamsin advances on me with magic crackling between her fingers.

Maybe I wasn't cut out to be a champion. Maybe I should have remained a second.

"Circle, Sam!" pipes up a timid voice from my corner. "R-remember your footwork. Um, don't let her drive you back that w-way!"

My own second is a kid Master Silverstein found at the last minute: a quiet and frequently terrified boy named Pierre, who puts up a surprisingly decent fight in training but develops a nervous stammer every time we actually have to talk outside of a dueling arena. It's thanks to sparring with Pierre that I have the reflexes to avoid significant damage from any of Tamsin's spells—but I do wish he had the nerve to yell at me the same way I used to yell at Rook about quitting smokes and spending more time on the assault bike or the rowing machine.

No two seconds are the same, though. And I can't blame Pierre for my shortcomings right now. I can't blame anyone except myself.

Also, nervous or not, Pierre's right about my footwork. I cut an angle on Tamsin, trying to rally. Trying to do anything, honestly, besides cower and run.

Tamsin's too smart for that, though—too smart and too quick. She intercepts me with a blast of arcane energy that knocks me on my ass. I force myself up on one knee and cast a shield before her second blast can knock me back down.

"Come on, Sam," calls Tamsin. "Is this really all you're made of?"

"Careful!" I yell from behind the shield. "You really think you should be wasting oxygen on trash talk at the midway mark of a duel?"

While I'm talking, I throw together a quick spell of my own. Praying that it finds its mark, I toss it over the edge of my shield right before it dissolves.

Whiplike, my little thread of arcane power strings itself around Tamsin's ankle.

Tamsin looks down at her foot and grins. "That's more like it."

I yank on the thread. Tamsin accepts the takedown, but even as she falls, she's already casting again. A net of magic, like woven starlight, speeds toward me.

I did wonder when she'd cast that particular trick. I'm just surprised that it took her this long. I'm ready with another shield—barely. The magic I cast buckles under the force of Tamsin's netting spell, but at least it keeps me from harm's way. For now.

I close my eyes, remembering Rook's words: *Tamsin's magic is ruled by fear. She doesn't play to win. She plays not to lose.*

Except that right now, I'm the one ruled by fear. And I'm the one playing defensively—doing everything possible to avoid losing to Tamsin Blackwood the same way Rook did.

And that's really it, isn't it? I want to prove that I'm more than Rook's second. That I can do more than stand in the shadows of a better magician.

That my magic is my own.

I open my eyes, grimacing as the net tightens around my shielding spell. I can't hold my defenses forever. Which means that I need to take a risk.

I need to do what Tamsin isn't willing to.

For a moment, it's like every spell I've ever cast—hell, every time I've ever practiced magic—flashes through the forefront of my mind. Learning from Jamie, week after week, until the night Jamie didn't come home. Training with Rook almost every day of our lives. Fighting with Rook near the end. Standing across from Tamsin in a duelists' arena, months ago, and wondering how her magic would taste.

Well, I'm finally finding out. Only to squander the experience by cowering under my shielding spell.

"To hell with that," I whisper.

My shield finally crumbles beneath the power of Tamsin's net. But as the net closes around me, I cast one last spell.

Tamsin's net is suffocating. It pins me in place, dampens my magic, my ability to cast. I have to hand it to Tamsin—she's made improvements in her spell-craft since she defeated Rook.

But I can still see the rest of the arena. I can still see Tamsin. And my little spell—that final piece of magic I cast before her net closed in around me—has found its mark.

I watch as my dainty little thread of arcane energy locks itself around her throat. For a moment, all I see is Rook's face, mottling with rage and helplessness, as I cut off the flow of blood in his carotid arteries.

Tamsin's hands go to her throat. Surprise, then genuine disbelief, colors her pretty features. She tugs at my thread, but the spell holds.

I'm exhausted. Every inch of my body hurts. It's all I can do to keep that little thread of magic intact. But I hold the spell. I hold on like my life depends on it.

Tamsin sinks to her knees, wheezing. The net weakens, flickering. Slowly but surely, its weight lightens on me. My fingers move of their own accord, then my hands. A sluggish sort of life begins to creep back into my limbs.

After what feels like an eternity, I struggle to my feet. They feel like lead. I'm almost gassed, almost past my capacity to cast magic, but so is Tamsin.

She's also almost out of oxygen. She gurgles as her face goes purple.

I shake off the remnants of Tamsin's net. I drag my leaden feet toward her as she struggles to keep my spell from strangling her.

What if she doesn't yield? What if the referee doesn't stop the duel in time?

What if I become just like Alexei that night in the underground club with Jamie?

What if I'm just like Blackwood?

I look at Tamsin as she claws at her throat.

Fear has no place in my magic.

I close my eyes and release the spell. But I don't let go of the magic keeping it alive.

Tamsin sucks in a great gasp of air. As she struggles to her feet, I cast my thread right back at her, altering its shape, improvising as I go.

I always told Rook never to cast anything in a duel that he hadn't tested in training. The day of a duel isn't the time to screw around with unfamiliar magic. Better to use what's tried and true.

But I'm not Rook. And this is my duel. If I lose, I'm losing on my terms.

I finish weaving my new spell. Lucky for me, thread is malleable, so far as arcane energy goes.

The netting I've woven from my thread isn't nearly as bright and strong as the netting spell Tamsin cast earlier. The binds that close in around a still-struggling Tamsin aren't half as potent as the ones she used to lock me in place. They might not even be as potent as the netting spell she used to defeat Rook.

What separates my netting spell from hers is what it's made from: heat roars from every inch of this net. The final sequence of the Four Elements: my brother's favorite. The one I always struggled with.

As it turns out, all I needed to do was make it my own instead of copying Jamie.

I've finally woven the Spell of Fire into a form that suits me. As magically generated heat makes contact with Tamsin's skin, she winces. It's not hot enough to scald—I've ensured that much in my casting—but it's hot enough to make her sweat, sapping energy from her as she sinks slowly back down to the arena floor. Heat envelops her. The harder she struggles, the more she sweats. Hydration—and energy—drain slowly but surely from her muscles.

Tamsin is an expert at counter-casting. She simply never expected me to use her own specialty against her.

She struggles, trying to cast something, anything, but her magic is spent. When you run out of energy, you run out of magic, and she's got no juice left in her body.

I keep walking toward her. I have next to no energy left either. I'm slower than I've ever been. But I keep up my plod, until I'm just inches from her.

She looks up at last as my shadow covers her form beneath those bright stage lights. There's a knowing sort of acceptance in her eyes.

We both understand what that means. It's what binds us as magicians—what binds everyone who steps into an arena.

She stops struggling. And her magic winks out.

I stretch out a hand. Tamsin clasps it. The smile she offers me is feral and incandescent. Her teeth are stained with blood—hers or mine, I couldn't say. She's never looked more beautiful.

"I yield," Tamsin Blackwood whispers through those bloodstained teeth. "I yield this duel to you, Samantha Chan."

25
TAMSIN

YOU'RE NOT SUPPOSED TO laugh when you lose a duel. You're not supposed to find any mirth in your own failure. You're supposed to hate yourself for a few days, then drag your sorry ass back to the training arena and figure out where you went wrong so you can do better in the next duel.

But as I yield to Samantha Chan and let her tug me to my feet, I can't seem to do anything but laugh. I laugh until tears stream down my cheeks. Maybe it's relief. Or maybe it's simple hysteria, some product of the adrenaline no doubt ricocheting its way through my veins.

The crowd's shock and adulation are a roar that surrounds us both. For a little while, Sam and I are in a world of our own, tucked behind walls made of pure noise, just her and I.

Our foreheads press together. The crowd disappears. The lights disappear.

It's just Sam. And it's just me.

"I'm sorry," she whispers into my neck. "I'm sorry, I'm sorry, I'm so, so sorry."

I don't need to ask her what for. I close my eyes. And finally, I say the words that I didn't know how to make true until tonight: "I forgive you."

Sam's breath hitches against my skin. And for once, I don't walk away. I don't let go of her.

"Congratulations," I whisper. My lips are close enough to hers to kiss. "You're every bit as spectacular as I always figured you'd be."

Sam laughs. She's crying, too. But when she answers me, she's still her same old characteristically blunt self. "Good."

"Good?"

"Yeah." She grins, scrubbing roughly at her eyes with the backs of her knuckles, heedless of the black eye blooming on one half of her face or the streaks of blood her fingers leave over the purpling skin. "I'm hoping that means you'll be open to a rematch."

I mirror her grin. I've never been more tired. I've never felt more alive. "You'd better count on it."

26

SAM

THE DOG AND PONY show of being declared victor happens in a blur. Someone raises my hand. Someone else makes an announcement on the mic. The crowd cheers, and cheers, and cheers.

Tamsin just stands there beside me, smiling that gorgeous, bloodstained smile, as we both cry silently like two idiots, sharing this moment as only two magicians at the end of a duel can.

Dazed, I search the faces in the crowd. In all my time as Rook's second, I always thought of an arena crowd as a sort of collective, anonymous entity. Some ancient god we needed to appease whose favor could make or break our fragile little lives. I never bothered seeking out individuals in an audience, instead focusing on the forest over the trees.

Now, I find my attention caught by random strangers: the shining face of a dark-eyed, dark-skinned girl cheering her lungs out; the craggy, bearded features of a tall redheaded man politely applauding my victory; an older woman with violently green hair jumping up and down in the aisle.

They're here for me. They're here for us.

They're here, ultimately, for magic.

A fourth face appears. I blink. Then I blink again, but even through tear-blurred eyes, I can't mistake those features: the bright blue eyes and dark hair, the familiar lanky frame.

Lysander Rook smiles at me, his face shining alone in that crowd of thousands. As I watch, my old champion waggles his fingers at me—in greeting or goodbye, I can't be sure.

I blink a third time.

When I open my eyes, Rook is gone. I scan the faces in the crowd, but he's nowhere to be seen. Vanished, as if he was never there at all.

Tamsin gives me a nudge. "You good?"

Slowly, I turn back toward my opponent and meet her lingering smile. "Better than I've been in a while," I tell her and offer my hand. "Come on. Let's go face the noise at the presser."

There's this moment before she takes my hand when I remember the last time we held hands like this. The night in that diner parking lot, laughing and crying in the shadow of some stranger's Toyota before Tamsin pulled me to my feet.

I think, dizzyingly, of old Mateus Blackwood's club: the suffocating press of shadows and stench of sweat and piss and fear. Tamsin's father, bleeding and laughing beneath me as I rained blows down on his unprotected skin. Tamsin's hand, stretching out toward me and pulling me out of the ring, tugging me free of the vengeance-haunted, tragedy-cloaked existence I'd swaddled myself in like a baby's blanket.

I once let Tamsin Blackwood drag me out of the nightmarish underworld her father created. I once followed her out of the land of ghosts. I followed the girl I'd wanted to destroy back into a life I might call my own. In that moment, I'd let Jamie and Blackwood and Rook all go. In that moment, all that mattered was me, and Tamsin, and the magic still waiting between us.

Now my fingers cling to hers, tighter than ever before. "Let's give them hell," Tamsin tells me.

I squeeze her hand. We will.

ACKNOWLEDGMENTS

Thanks, first and foremost, to my incredible agent, Thao Le, and my equally incredible editor, Gretchen Durning. You've not only been staunch professional advocates but wonderful creative partners and delightful co-conspirators in the telling of this very special story. Thank you for believing in me, and thank you for believing in this book.

Additional thanks to everyone at Penguin who helped make this book a reality: Abigail Powers, Natalie Melius, Rye White, Madison Penico, Theresa Evangelista, Felicity Vallence, Shannon Spann, Astrid Rojas, Christina Colangelo, Bri Lockhart, and Claire Young, among others. Special shout-out to Michael Rogers, the wildly talented illustrator behind my beautiful book cover!

For anyone who knows me as a martial artist, it's probably pretty clear to you the many ways in which *To the Death*, for all its magic and mayhem, is at its core also a love letter to modern combat sports. To that end, I owe a debt of gratitude to my coaches and teammates at District Martial Arts, including Scott Dance, Charles DiGisco, Sam Shawa, Khaldon Roukie, Eric Armakan, Grace Ibrahim DiGisco, and so many more.

Thank you, additionally, to my wonderful partner, Daniel Furlow, who's supported me through the ups and downs of writing this book from day one. From its initial conceit all the way through release day, you've been my rock. Thank you for cheering me on, for feeding me snacks and coffee during long days on deadline, and for inspiring me to be a better artist. I love you to the horizon.

And finally, thank you to my parents for remaining so fiercely proud of their weirdo daughter who spent her teen years assuming that when she grew up, she would become a lawyer, or a diplomat, or something sensible like that, and instead grew up to write about magic and martial arts for a living. You guys are the best, and I love you.